sticks and stones

Breaking the Silence

by

Paddy Eger

Sticks & Stones—Breaking the Silence

Published by Paddy Eger

ISBN 979-8-9854045-5-5

First Publishing: 2023
Printed in the United States of America

Author Photo by: Yuen Lui
www.YuenLuiStudio.com
Lynnwood, WA
425.771.3423

Cover Design by Julie Mattern
Cover Images © adobestock.com

Art Direction, Book Design and Cover Design
by Julie Mattern
© 2023. All Rights Reserved by
Paddy Eger

They say:
"Sticks and stones can break my bones
But words can never hurt me."

That's a lie.
Whoever said that didn't
go to high school and wasn't deaf.

The book is dedicated to people with special talents often mistakenly called handicaps.

Author Notes

Writing a book is a group enterprise. It involves research to build authenticity. With this in mind, I extend my special thanks to Amy Emond, my co-conspirator, her family, and her high school students for their assistance with ASL and keeping the story 'real'.

I also wish to thank two other special people. Linda Lane provided her editing skills and inciteful suggestions, as well as her friendship and laughter. My book designer, Julie Mattern, brought the story to life outside my head, setting it onto pages so I could share it with all of you. It truly takes a team to go from a seed idea to a finished book.

The majority of sights, sounds, and places around Seattle and the Pacific Northwest are true. However, Meg's family apartment, neighborhood shops, the tall building involved in the 'situation', her high school and the tournament are fictitious.

> As a special gift to my readers, a copy of the American Sign Language (ASL) alphabet and basic Morse Code alphabet signals are included after the end of the story.

"Sometimes you don't realize your own strength until you come face to face with your greatest weakness."
— Susan Gale

1

THE BORROWED TRUCK IDLED IN the loading zone with its blinkers flashing. Meg, her mom, and her Uncle Zach continued unloading. Nine-year old Toby sat on the front steps of the ancient apartment building as "the guard" during their trips up five flights of stairs.

As Meg grabbed the two suitcases filled with the total of her clothing, a red-haired teenage girl approached out of a street level doorway.

"Can I help?" the girl asked.

"Yes. Thanks," Meg said as she handed the girl both suitcases. "I'm Meg."

"I'm Kelsey, the super's daughter. Where are we taking these?"

"We're in 6C. Thanks, Kels." Meg grabbed an apple crate filled with books and started up the stairs.

Kelsey hesitated. Huh. *This Meg-person called me Kels. What's that all about? She doesn't even know me.*

Kelsey slumped forward under the weight of the cases and followed her up the stairs. "Too bad the elevator's on the blink. It always happens when someone moves in, especially into a top floor apartment. Guess you'll be going to my high school. It's only a thirty-minute walk, but I sometimes take the bus when it's rainy or snowing. How does that sound?"

She waited for a reply, but Meg appeared to ignore her. Kelsey sighed and kept climbing. *Hm-m. I thought she might be a new friend, not just some gangly, stuck-up girl. Well, her loss. I could've helped her face the cliques and catty girls who haven't changed since last year when I arrived. Probably never will.*

The door to 6C stood open. Kelsey followed her inside, set the heavy suitcases out of the way, and shook out her arms. As she turned to leave, a woman emerged from the bedroom.

"Hello! Thank you for helping us." The woman extended her hand. "I'm Della Appens. Meg and Toby's mom. I'm so glad to see a young friend for Meg. She'll appreciate help settling into school."

"Sure. No problem. I'm Kelsey, the super's daughter. We live in the basement apartment. I can help for a little longer if you'd like."

"Wonderful. It's shocking to me how much we've accumulated over the years."

Kelsey scanned the boxes and furnishings. *This is nothing compared to the last couple who moved in. How can three people fit into this tiny apartment, even with so little stuff?*

Meg stepped out of the bedroom, heading toward the apartment door, but her mother tapped her shoulder. She turned to face her mom. "Kelsey goes to your school."

"So I guessed. Hello, Kel-, Kelsey. Thanks for helping us."

Kelsey studied Meg. *She certainly talks different than my friends, and she doesn't listen very well. That's going to make fitting in hard for her. I remember how long it took for them to accept me with my limp.*

The sight of an overstuffed chair edging into the apartment made Kelsey laugh.

The cute, young Army guy she'd passed as he was going down the stairs huffed as he set down the bulky chair. "Where do you want this, sis?"

The mom laughed and pointed. "Set it near the window and come meet Kelsey, the super's daughter."

The army guy grinned and stretched out his hand. "I'm Zach, Meg's uncle. Nice to meet you. She's going to appreciate having a friend living in the apartment. Hopefully, you can show her the ropes at high school. Being deaf makes settling in much more difficult."

Kelsey's eyes widened. *Whoa! She's deaf? That explains why she said Kels and didn't reply to any conversation on the stairs.*

Meg started out the door, but Zach stopped her and signed, "Did you thank Kelsey for helping?"

"Yes, I did." She turned to Meg. "Maybe you can tell me about the high school after we finish unloading the truck."

"Sure." Kelsey smiled and followed her down the stairs and out to the street to grab more boxes.

The silent treks up and down the stairs gave Kelsey time to think about being Meg's friend. *How will being friends with a deaf person work? Will she expect me to talk for her or run interference with the girls at school? They'll probably assume she's a snob, like I did at first. Will taking on a friendship with her affect my shaky social life?*

Kelsey continued helping unload the truck, but she didn't stick around afterward for Meg or her mom to ask about the high school. *They can use their cell phones to check the school site online. If I happen to see her over the weekend, I'll share info with her. That should be enough.*

THE MOVE-IN ENDED BY BEDTIME. Mom and Zach assembled the twin beds for Toby and Meg while Meg and her brother unpacked and washed dishes, pots and pans, and other kitchen items.

Meg frowned. The almost-friendly Kelsey had disappeared once the truck was unloaded. *No surprise. Lots of people feel uncomfortable around anybody who is different from themselves. Or am I reading something into our brief time together? I'll find out sooner or later. Right now, my job is to keep Toby on track.*

So many boxes! Mom often said they had too much stuff. Maybe we do, but with only two twin-size beds, Mom has to sleep on the couch in the living area. Living area? That's a stretch. The kitchen and living area are one small space with no separation. The whole apartment is so tiny it would have fit into Gran's living room. I already miss my big upstairs bedroom at Gran's with its view of the fields and the distant Cascade Mountains. I'll miss my privacy too. Much as I love my brother, he's a busy kid and a squirrely sleeper. Mom promised this would be temporary. Once she saves enough, we'll find a roomier place. Thanks a lot, Dad.

MEG RESTED IN THE CUSHY overstuffed chair and stared out the window. Their view of Seattle consisted of tall, timeworn brick buildings. Looking down, she could see old neon signs blinking above shop windows, sections of their antiquated gas tubes no longer glowing. The upstairs probably contained apartments the same size and condition as this one; several looked abandoned. Cars passed along the two-lane street, their headlights tracing the cracked pavement. Occasionally, drivers backed into narrow parking places. A few people hurried along the sidewalk, their bodies almost ghost-like as they passed below faint streetlights. Giant neon logos, unreadable from this distance, adorned taller, more modern buildings. Towering metal cranes with lights along their sides stood beyond. Darkness dimmed the rest of the scene. *Some view! This is more like bad movie sets from silent films I watched with Gran on her black and white television.*

She let out a long sigh. She knew Mom wasn't happy about the move either, so she'd need to keep her irritation about the apartment to herself.

WHEN SHE ENTERED THE BEDROOM, Toby was hanging out of his covers with his feet dangling near the floor. She straightened him out, adjusted his covers, and headed to bed.

Minutes later, Mom came to tuck in Toby. She sat on the side of Meg's bed and signed, "Thank you for helping with the move and with Toby. I hope it won't be long before we can find a place with more space."

"It's okay, Mom. We're together. That's what matters most," she signed. "Good night. I love you."

Mom kissed her cheek, turned off the overhead light, and left the room.

Tears slid down Meg's cheeks. *What did Gran always say? Find the good in every situation? That time has arrived with this move. I miss you Gran.* She adjusted her pillow, closed her eyes, and waited for sleep to arrive.

Morning light poured in through the curtainless window beside Meg's bed. She checked her cell phone: 6:05. When she looked outside, the city view startled her. No birds roosting in trees, no smell of hay or ripening apples. Instead, she stared down at delivery trucks parked in traffic lanes. She wrinkled her nose at the noxious exhaust streaming from their tail pipes and seeping in around the old windowsills, stinging her eyes. People milled around a bus-stop sign. *How can they stand all that exhaust?* Meg shook her head. *This isn't a bad dream; this is my new home. New. Ha-ha.*

Much of the day, she continued unpacking and keeping tabs on Toby. He couldn't just run outside and play with the dogs or check on the chickens. Here, he needed to be accompanied wherever he went. Today, he needed to stay inside and help them settle in.

Meg hoped to see Kelsey, but it appeared that wasn't about to happen. Mom suggested going downstairs and asking about high school, but Meg resisted. "If she plans to help, she'd have come up. I can do this by myself."

After setting another empty box by the apartment door, Meg entered the high school address in her phone. The school was less than two miles away, a thirty-five-minute walk. No problem. After all, she played every sport available at her last school: volleyball, soccer, tennis, and her favorite, basketball. The round trip would be a great way to get in tomorrow's exercise.

2

OVER THE WEEKEND, THE APPENS family arranged and stowed the last of their belongings, leaving Meg no time to investigate the neighborhood. Early Monday morning, Mom started her new job, and Meg needed to register for school.

Mom had already dropped Toby at a local daycare, not a place he wanted to be, since he'd be there with babies. Meg promised she'd take him around the neighborhood once she returned from registering. Late the night before, Kelsey had promised to help her get to the school. Thank goodness. That would help tremendously.

Too nervous to eat anything, Meg fussed with her hair and changed clothes three times. She checked her watch, checked her hair again, and headed to Kelsey's family apartment in the basement, anxious to get registered and back home as soon as possible.

She knocked on the apartment door and waited.

No response.

She knocked again.

KELSEY HURRIED TO THE DOOR and checked the fisheye. She reached for the doorknob and stopped. *Do I want to get involved with Meg? Will helping her become a fulltime job?*

What about my friends? Will they shun both of us if I show up with her in tow? Being deaf, she'll miss out on conversations. Many of my friends will be at school this week, making welcome back posters. They'll be too busy to take the time to get to know her. Besides, I really don't know much about her.

Meg knocked again.

Kelsey tiptoed away from the door and back to her bedroom, where she sat in her furry purple beanbag chair, wondering how Meg would manage. She shook her head. *It's not my problem.*

Meg checked her watch and crossed the street to a bus stop, where a handful of adults and a few students were boarding a bus. She stepped on, paid her dollar, and sat looking at the surrounding buildings as the bus traveled toward town. She thought the school was on a hill. Maybe she'd been wrong about that.

She typed a message and handed her phone to her seat-mate, an elderly woman carrying a large briefcase and a sack lunch. **Will this bus take me to Harrison High School?**

The woman read the message, shook her head, and turned to face Meg. "You're going the wrong way. Get off and take the bus going the other direction."

"Thank you," Meg said. She reached for the cord to signal the bus to stop, hurried across the street, boarded another bus, paid another dollar, and sat down. She typed in a message to the driver, then stepped forward to show him at the next stop: **I'm deaf. Please wave to me where to get off to walk to Harrison High School.**

The driver looked at her and nodded as he opened the door for new riders to board. Hoping he'd remember to signal her, Meg sat down. She glanced at the streets she'd just passed going the other direction. The small businesses and apartment buildings looked as worn out as where she now lived.

After a few blocks, the bus started up a steep hill and began moving through a neighborhood of small, tidy homes with small tidy yards. *People here live close together. So different from the wide-open spaces around Gran's farm.*

The bus driver signaled to Meg. She thanked him as she exited. Like a flash, he drove away, leaving a foul trail of exhaust.

Meg used the mapping tool on her phone to locate the high school: up one block, turn right, then walk two blocks. She straightened, inhaled deeply, and walked quickly along the route.

THE THREE-STORY BRICK HIGH SCHOOL atop the hill faced away from her. An opening in the cyclone fence allowed her to cross a wide field rather than going all the way around the block to reach the front of the immense building. An American flag atop a tall pole in the yard indicated the main entrance. Nervous and sweaty, she hurried up the wide steps, straightened her shoulders, and entered a long hallway.

The main office appeared on her right. An arrow for the counselor offices pointed down a hallway alongside the office. She entered the hall and read the posted notice:

Sign in here for the next available counselor.
A-J - Gillis   K-Q - Slayter   R-Z - Robbins

After adding her name to a short list of people whose last names began with A through J, she collapsed on the long wooden bench to wait.

Attending a large high school with long hallways and dozens more rooms felt strange and more than a bit scary. Back in Yakima, one hallway led to wherever she wanted to go, and she could walk into the counselor's office any time of day and get her questions answered. Here it appeared she'd need patience and an appointment.

Other students arrived and sat next to her and on other benches in the waiting area. She sent her mom a text:

Waiting for counselor. Home ASAP to pick-up Toby.

One counselor door opened. A tall guy strolled out. "Next victim, I assume," she watched him mouth.

Before she could respond, he'd disappeared into the hallway. She stared after him and was startled when she noticed the counselor standing in the office doorway, looking around. "Ms. Appens, are you still here?"

"Yes." She raised her hand, stood, and entered the office. She typed a message on her cell phone, handed it to the counselor, and sat down.

Meg: **I'm Megan Appens. I'm deaf, but I read lips and sign. May we text? It's faster.**

Ms. Gillis: **Yes, for counseling, but not in classrooms during class time. I'm Ms. Gillis. Welcome to Sherman Harrison High.**

Meg: **Thank you.**

Ms. Gillis: **I've not received an official transcript. Did you bring a copy?**

Meg nodded as she pulled a folder from her backpack and handed it to the counselor. "They said they'd mail one."

Ms. Gillis scanned the unofficial transcript: **You've**

completed sophomore requirements. You're strong in math, passing other classes and scraping by in history. Is history a problem?

Meg: **I don't understand why we need to learn about what happened decades or centuries ago.**

Ms. Gillis: **To understand our world and the people around us.**

Meg resisted the urge to shrug. Sensing from Ms. Gillis' reaction she'd made a mistake being so frank, especially when the counselor pursed her lips as she looked over her transcript.

Ms. Gillis: **Do you want to wait to start school until an assistant can be assigned? Might be a couple of weeks. Or we could start making plans today if you don't want to wait.**

OVER THE NEXT TWENTY MINUTES, they laid out her tentative junior class requirements. Ms. Gillis seemed at ease, much to Meg's surprise.

Ms. Gillis: **Come back Wed. 9:00 for Math and English tests. Then we can finalize your classes. Questions?**

Meg: **Are there other deaf students?**

Ms. Gillis shook her head: **Other questions?**

Silently laughing to herself, Meg shook her head. *I have so many questions: Is the school friendly toward deaf people? Are students accepting of kids who learn and communicate differently? Will teachers understand my way of learning and help me? I'll probably need to figure most things out the hard way.*

Meg: **May I text to communicate in classes?**

Ms. Gillis: **Probably not. I'll let you know.**

Meg: **I'd like to try out for basketball.**

Ms. Gillis frowned: **Focus on academics first, sports later.**

The counselor checked the clock, gathered up pages of information about the school, slid them into a folder, and handed it to her.

Ms. Gillis: **Welcome to Sherman Harrison High. As our only deaf student, you'll face challenges as will our staff. Let me know how I can help make your transition easier.**

Meg thanked her and left.

THE FRONT HALL BUZZED WITH activity. Students carried long sheets of colored paper and were hanging them in the various side halls. Each said 'welcome' and went on to list the classroom numbers in each smaller hallway. Maybe she could find her way without Kelsey's help. Maybe.

After spending all her money on bus fare getting to school, Meg laid out a path on her cell phone and started down the hill toward their apartment. Her mind wandered back to Kelsey. *Why didn't she answer the door? I know she was home. I can feel it in my bones. I saw the reluctance in her eyes even though she suggested she'd help me. Even when I lived at Gran's house, I met hearing people who weren't comfortable if I asked them for help very often. Why should I expect people to be any different in the big city? I'll need to take care of myself.*

Knots tightened in her stomach as if someone forcefully tossed a basketball toward her, and she'd fumbled, causing a sudden thud in her gut. She'd dread the new school if she couldn't play ball. How would she survive without the chance to run and shoot?

3

MEG RE-READ THE NOTE FROM Mom as she fixed herself a peanut butter and jelly sandwich:

> *Meg,*
> *Here's the info sheet to take to the daycare. It will allow you to pick up Toby today and other days as needed.*
> *I drew you a quick map. Use your phone to locate the daycare as well. Call me when both of you are safely home.*
> *Meeting about an early evening job. Home late but ASAP.*

She scanned the form for Toby's daycare and stuffed it in her purse.

File: Toby Appens / Megan

Downtown Child Center Daycare - Seattle, WA

Information for: Toby Appens **Age:** 9 **Birthdate:** 10-2-2009

Home Address: Bel-Aire Apts #602, Colorado Street, Seattle, WA

Permissions Allowed (Contact Number on Masterfile)

Signature: _Meg Apens_   Megan Appens – Sister

The above person has permission to:

(1) drop-off, pick-up and/or transport Toby Appens.

(2) make decisions about Toby Appens health and safety.

Health Issues/Special Needs: _X_None

THE WALK TO THE DAYCARE took five minutes. Older ladies wheeled shopping carriers and strolled along the street of businesses. Shops had signs written in a variety of languages. The colorful banners hanging from the light posts read, Welcome to Seattle's International District. Asian art adorned the bottom third of each banner. Living in this area promised to be a new cultural experience.

She slowed her pace to check out the storefront windows. In addition to exotic produce, Stan's Mini Market sidewalk crates contained Red Delicious apples for a dollar sixty-nine a pound, navel oranges at eighty-nine cents for four, tired looking lettuce, two for a dollar, and locally grown cucumbers, three for a dollar.

Soo's Barber Emporium displayed an old-fashioned, rotating barber pole attached to the wall near the doorway. It turned slowly, showing off its red, white, and blue stripes. Inside, she saw two barbers working on gentlemen seated in beauty shop chairs while also talking with two men seated nearby, waiting their turns. They appeared to be laughing.

Meg peered through the dirty windows of Han's Variety Store. The hodge-podge display contained summer beach toys on sale, kitchen gadgets, assorted dusty artificial flowers priced three for a dollar, yard tools, as well as a mannequin wearing a wildly colorful beach cover-up. Toby would love spending time in there.

The Downtown Child Center Daycare building was across the next intersection. It occupied the main floor of an older brick building similar to their Bel-Aire Apartments. She saw six kids playing in a sandbox in the fenced-in side yard. Toby was nowhere in sight.

A sense of panic raced through her. *Where's Toby?*

Then she spotted him on a swing alone and apart from other kids, rocking back and forth, back and forth with his head down. When he saw her, he ran toward her, clutching the wire fence that separated them. His face glistened with tears.

Meg covered his fingers with hers, then released them long enough to sign, "What's wrong?"

"Can we go home now?"

"Soon as I check you out."

Toby nodded and ran into the building.

The outside entry door to the daycare was locked. The sign on the door read: RING THE BELL AND WAIT. *Someone loves capital letters*, she thought.

She rang the bell, then waited and waited. No one came. She pushed the bell again and again. Still, no one came. She texted the daycare she'd arrived. After another wait, a text came back: **WHO IS TEXTING and WHY?**

Meg: **I'm Megan. Here to pick-up Toby Appens.**

Daycare: **WHY DIDNT YOU ANSWER OUR INTERCOM QUESTION?**

Meg: **I'm deaf. I have permission to pick up Toby.**

Another wait.

The door opened a scant five inches. A short woman gave her a quick once over. She narrowed her eyes. "Show me your signed permission paper."

After handing the woman the information and signing in on a daily log, she was allowed entry into the main room, a large, open space with a game areas, tables and chairs, and an assortment of busy children's playing. There was no sign of Toby.

The woman's nametag said Ardis, just Ardis. She led Meg

through another door, where a dozen kids sat in a circle, playing a group game.

Toby sat away from the group. When he spied her, he ran to hug her, nearly toppling her. He signed, "Can we go now?"

After gathering his belongings, they headed out, retracing Meg's route. She entertained him by promising they'd spend time another day in Han's Variety Store. Today, they'd investigate Stan's Mini Market to play their favorite game: pretending to purchase whatever interested them, even though they didn't have money to buy anything.

Toby wandered through Stan's until he spotted what he'd pretend buy. He signed to Meg. When she walked over, he placed a strange looking red fruit on her palm. Tiny bristles sticking out all over tickled her hand. It had no smell and its name appeared on a small sign written in Chinese or Japanese or Korean with no English translation. Cost: five for one dollar.

"Can we buy this for real? Please"

Meg shook her head. "I had to spend my money on bus fare."

Toby put the fruit back just as a man approached them, stopped, and returned to the checkout counter. He followed them with his eyes as they exited the store.

Toby's shoulders drooped. He stayed five steps behind Meg until they came to a busy intersection. Once inside the apartment building, he raced up the stairs and sat in front of their door to wait for her, still wearing his pout.

"I'm sorry, Toby," she said as she unlocked the door. He continued his pout as he hurried into their bedroom. Motioning her, he tugged the stopper out of his spaceship bank and spilled all the coins onto his race car-themed quilt.

He counted his coins then grabbed them up. "I have seventy-six cents. How many strange fruits will this buy?"

She signed, "Five cost one dollar. How much is one?"

Toby thought about it. "Twenty cents. I can buy three. If you give me four cents, I can buy four. Can we go back today and get them? Please, please, please?"

"Tomorrow. We'll have a lot more time to explore. Promise."

SHE FIXED TOBY A SANDWICH to go with his leftover lunchbox snacks. He ate and rapidly signed every detail about his time at the daycare. "I don't like that place. It's noisy and no one wants to play with me. And the lady made us take a nap. I'm too old for naps. Do I have to go back?"

Meg gently rubbed his shoulder before she answered. "Only if Mom works late and I can't be home to watch you. School starts next week, so you won't go there very often."

Toby gave up his pout and put his coins in a small change purse to be ready for their next trip to Stan's Mini Market. She watched him start his version of race car tracks, where he bunched up his quilt to make mountain roads for his toy cars to drive around.

She'd just settled into the cushy chair after staring out the window at all the activity in the busy street below when Toby grabbed her hand and tugged her toward the bathroom. "I hear funny thumping coming in the window. It's too high for me to look out."

Meg stepped into the shower and peered out the high window. She turned back to Toby and laughed. "Let's go!"

They found the door to out back. Beyond the dumpster, the alley widened. Kelsey moved side to side, forward and back, shooting baskets into a hoop attached to the side of the building. When she saw them, she stopped and walked toward them, bouncing the ball to Toby.

Toby caught it and began bouncing it.

"Hey! Kid! Want to shoot hoops?"

Meg studied Kelsey as she played with Toby. She had a good eye and made several long shots as they moved around in a fun-filled game of keep away.

After a few minutes Kelsey tossed the ball to Meg. "Want to join us?"

Meg looked to Toby, then to Kelsey. "Sure!"

"Can we play horse?" Toby asked as the girls watched him dribble and shoot.

The three moved to various positions and sank or missed shots and added another letter to spell h-o-r-s-e; each added letter increased their negative score. They allowed Toby two attempts on each turn since he was more than a foot shorter than either of them.

Play continued without conversations. Meg accepted and shot the ball each time it came her direction. Swish. Swish. Swish.

Kelsey's face looked puzzled, just as Meg hoped it would. Kelsey held the ball. "You ever play on a team?"

"Yes. Youth varsity."

Kelsey bounced the ball to Meg who caught and held it. "Where were you this morning? I thought you planned to help me?"

Kelsey looked away before she spoke. "I overslept. Did you get registered?"

"Not yet. Got tests to take."

Meg tossed Kelsey the ball with a bounce so forceful it

nearly flew over her head. Kelsey reached up, grabbed it, turned, made a basket, and grabbed the rebound. She tossed the ball to Toby. "I need to go in. Keep the ball. Get it back to me later, okay?"

Toby dribbled the ball around the alley as the girls exchanged guarded glances before Kelsey disappeared inside the building.

At dusk, play stopped. Toby carried the ball inside, setting it outside Kelsey's apartment door before he headed upstairs. Meg lagged behind, deciding whether she needed to talk with Kelsey now or wait until morning—or maybe let the issue slide. Decision made, she followed Toby up the stairs.

4

AFTER DINNER, KELSEY SAT IN her near-perfect bedroom, staring at the posters on her walls. Her lies to Meg popped up like a jack-in-the-box in slow motion. *Why did I say I'd overslept? Why am I hesitating to help her? Am I afraid it will hurt my reputation, or am I afraid Meg will expect me to always be there? Maybe it's some of both.*

Kelsey had worked hard to become part of the popular group by giving them free bracelets when she charged everyone else three dollars a strand. Last year, she helped each of them with science homework questions and, in exchange, she was now part of their group. *Would befriending Meg destroy everything I worked for? Probably. They were snobs, maybe because they all had gobs of spending money, something I'll never have. To be honest, that's why I feel as though I'm constantly teetered on the verge of being cast out. Meg probably can handle everything on her own.*

She thought back to when she'd first come to school in the city. After her mom died, they'd moved to where her dad could get steady work as a semi-skilled carpenter's helper. Then they moved to this neighborhood where her dad now managed the apartment building.

Most of the time, she hated their building. It looked too

shabby to invite her group to visit. The upside was how close she lived to the city, which allowed her to wander through expensive downtown stores. Her jewelry ideas and her trendy clothes grew out of her walks through the stores. For mere pennies, she'd re-create what her group paid hefty prices to buy. Without her jewelry skills and her knack for sewing that she'd learned from her mom, she'd be where she saw Meg's future: ostracized for being less, owning less, and being different.

Kelsey hopped up and called to her dad. "I'm going upstairs for a few minutes."

MEG'S MOM ANSWERED KELSEY'S KNOCK. "Hi! Nice to see you, Kelsey. Come in. Meg's in the bedroom. Send Toby out to me."

Meg looked up when Kelsey entered the bedroom. As Toby left, she motioned to Kelsey to sit in the lone chair in the room. She crossed her arms and waited for Kelsey to speak first.

Kelsey avoided looking at her directly. Then she opened her phone and held it out to Meg: **I'm sorry about today. Give me your number.**

Meg typed it in and stared at her phone.

Kelsey: **How can I help you? Any trouble with buses?**
Meg: **Some. $$!!**
Kelsey: **I'll help you get a student pass. When are the tests?**

Meg: **Wednesday**
Kelsey: **Let me help with the buses. Payback for earlier.**
Meg: **OK**

The girls sat for long minutes in an uncomfortable silence, avoiding looking at each other.

Kelsey: **Can't promise to help every day.**

Meg: **I get it.**

Kelsey: **I can help this first week.**

Meg paused and studied Kelsey's face: **Thanks!**

Kelsey walked to the window, turned, and scanned the room before she looked back at Meg.

Kelsey: **Text when you want to leave on Wednesday.**

Meg: **OK.**

A long silence, another scan around the room, then Kelsey smiled, pointed to her phone and left.

Kelsey said good-bye to Meg's mom and Toby, then hurried down the stairs to her family apartment. *Do I feel better? Not really. Helping Wednesday will make up for ignoring her before. Then I'll be free to step away.*

Tuesday morning Meg lay in bed, thinking back to last night. *Why had Kelsey acted weird, like she didn't really want to help me? To be honest, I also acted rude. If Mom finds out, she'll be embarrassed. Gran would have given me her I'm-disappointed-in-you scowl. This move is not starting out well. I need to make this work for Mom and Toby...and for me.*

By the time she'd showered, rousted Toby, and fixed his breakfast, she'd made a plan.

Toby sat on the floor, playing with his Space Bot, watching the clock, and watching Meg. *It's 9:15. Not long now. Meg said we can go back to the market today to buy the funny-looking fruit at 10:00. Hurry up clock!*

Luckily, Meg was home all day, so he didn't need to go

back to daycare. Being the only ten-year old was no fun. Much as he tried, he felt strange playing little kid games and having them pull on him to play chase. The daycare didn't even have a TV or video games or many big kid toys. Maybe he could get Mom to let him stay alone to wait for his bus. He could take care of himself for an hour, especially since the bus came to his door to pick him up.

From the apartment to the market took less than three minutes after they crossed the busy street. Everything in Seattle was big and noisy. Toby didn't like that about the city. *Meg's lucky. She doesn't have to listen to the blasting horns and machines digging up the street. She does need to watch everything around her, especially crossing streets. Some of the cars don't stop at red lights; they turn right in front of people crossing the street. I'm glad I can help her.*

The crates outside the market were filled before they arrived. People stood pawing through them. Today they displayed foot-long green beans, funny-shaped green blobs, and a crate of icky-looking, bumpy veggies. This was nothing like the grocery store near Gran's.

Toby selected two of the red, prickly fruits while Meg picked up and sniffed various odd-looking fruits and veggies. The short, thin older man called out "Hey! You! Girl! Don't handle unless you buy!"

Toby was too far from her to let her know the man was speaking to her.

"Girl! Stop! No steal my food!"

Toby rushed to her and tugged on her sleeve. He pointed to the man hurrying their direction, but he was too late. The man was already grabbing the fruit from Meg's hand and pulling her inside the store. "I call police now!"

Meg's heart raced when the man reached for her arm. She pulled away from him, juggling the fruit as she reached out to wrap her arms. around Toby.

"Mister. Stop!" Toby called out. "She's my sister. She's deaf. She's not stealing anything!"

The man stopped and stared up at Meg then looked to Toby. "So. Tell her she not handle unless she buys."

"I'm sorry," Meg said as she released her grip on Toby. "I was curious. These are new to us."

The man puffed up and waved his arms. "She's not deaf! She talks! You are liars *and* thieves."

"No!" Toby and Meg said in unison.

"I read lips," Meg reached her hand toward the man. "We want to buy these!"

Toby held out two quarters. "Is this right?"

The man looked from Toby to Meg and back to Toby. He took the quarters and the fruit, nodded, and walked back into his store. Meg laid the other veggies she'd planned to buy back in their crates.

Meg and Toby looked at each other, uncertain about what had just happened. The man obviously thought they were thieves. But he'd not given Toby his change or the fruit. Now where would they shop close to their apartment? They turned to head home.

"Wait!" The older man was back on the sidewalk, calling to them. He had a younger man wearing an apron in tow.

Toby pulled Meg to a stop. When she turned, she saw the two men heading their way. *Now what?*

The older man held out a small plastic bag with the fruit,

two penny candies, and Toby's change. "Sorry. Come back again."

The younger man stepped forward. Toby began signing what he could understand of the man's words. "My Uncle Stan gets excited. He came here from China many years ago. His English has never gotten very good. I'm Jun. I was born here. My uncle didn't know you, and he didn't realize you're deaf. Please accept our apology. Come back anytime."

Meg nodded. The young man bowed slightly and returned to the store. The older man waved and bowed as they began walking away.

ONCE THEY GOT HOME TOBY washed the fruit and tried to bite through the prickles. "Bleck! It's tasteless. Let's cut it open."

They laid the prickly fruit on the counter and cut down the middle. Inside they found a white glob around a huge brown seed. The white glob smelled sweet. Juice ran down their faces as they bit into their halves of the glob.

Toby wiped his chin on his sleeve. "It's sweet. I like it. Let's save the other one so Mom can taste it. Can we go back tomorrow and look at more things?"

Meg nodded, but she worried about the reception they'd get if they went inside the store when the older man was working alone.

5

MEG CHECKED HER PHONE. KELSEY hadn't responded to her message sent twenty minutes ago. Maybe today would be a replay of Monday, and she'd be on her own to get to school for the placement tests. *Why do I need placement tests? I finished tenth grade. I gave them a copy of my transcript. Why don't they trust I passed all my classes?*

She checked the time on her phone again, grabbed her backpack and hurried down the stairs. As she crossed the last landing, she spotted Kelsey sitting on the bottom step.

Kelsey stood. She wore jeans and a fancy quilted jacket. The backpack she carried bore travel patches from New York, Chicago, Miami, and San Francisco. *She and her family must travel a lot. Well, I do, too, except mine are all in the Pacific Northwest. I don't need patches to remember where I've been.*

Kelsey held the door open and followed her out. She started talking as Meg turned to the right to cross the street. Kelsey tapped Meg's arm and waited for her to turn. "Let's go down the block to catch a bus. It's faster."

Meg nodded and followed her to a bus stop busy with people waiting in a ragtag line. When the bus arrived, Kelsey showed the driver her student pass; Meg dropped a dollar in the coin slot, then followed Kelsey to a seat at the back of the bus, where she immediately began texting, but not to Meg.

The bus drove away from downtown but let off most shoppers and worker bees before turning up a long hill. An uneasy feeling crept into Meg's stomach. *This neighborhood doesn't look familiar. Is Kelsey really taking me to the school, or is she pranking me?*

After a few minutes, Meg relaxed. The school came into view. They'd arrived at the front entrance of the school in record time. She grabbed her backpack and followed Kelsey toward the front steps.

Outside the wide-open door, Kelsey stopped and typed a message.

> Kelsey: **We'll get your bus pass after your tests. Text me when you finish. I'm making Back-to-School banners in the art room.**

Meg nodded and watched Kelsey hurry away down a side hallway as she headed into a classroom near the office where a testing sign was posted on a placard outside the door. She took in a deep breath and swallowed hard. *Here's goes!*

THE TESTS WERE GIVEN IN a classroom proctored by Ms. Gillis, the counselor she met Monday. Only four students sat in the room, spread to the four-corners of the space. Ms. Gillis waved to Meg and beckoned her forward. "Please sit here so you can read my lips during directions."

Meg took off her backpack, sat where Ms. Gillis pointed, and waited. At exactly 9:00, Ms. Gillis began directions: "You have two hours to complete all three tests. There's to be no talking. Hand me your cell phone as I set a test on your desk. Do your best."

Once the tests were distributed, Ms. Gillis set a timer and said, "Begin" making sure Meg saw the command and started working.

She looked through the tests before deciding where to start: Math, Reading, and Writing. Two to three pages each. Multiple choice, True-False, short answer, and one essay question. She inhaled deeply, exhaled, turned back to the first page, and began.

11:50. She used the last ten minutes to check for items she'd skipped and reread her essay, editing a few words to strengthen her ideas.

Essays always posed a concern. Writing proper sentence order caused her to stumble. Signing had built-in shortcuts, while written English contained lots of little, meaningless words and required a careful re-read. *Gr-rr. It's times like this when I wish hearing aids worked for me. Hopefully, I'll pass and not be pigeon-holed into Sophomore or Freshman English. That would be humiliating.*

When Meg texted Kelsey, true to her word, she texted back: **Meet at main office.**

Meg walked along the hallway, looking at the trophies as she waited. Debate, National Honor, Math, and Science occupied an extensive case. Sports took up two cases, leaving a smaller case for Drama and Art. It appeared SHHS had high expectations for many different things. They valued clear thinking as well as sports. She hoped she could maintain her junior status and be allowed to try out for varsity basketball.

She needed a scholarship to attend college. Even though she worked hard, she felt certain she'd never earn an academic scholarship in such a large school.

AFTER THEY PICKED UP A student bus pass, Kelsey gave her a quick tour of the school. Classrooms were organized by subject groups, except for the arts and shops situated in a separate building on the back side of the cafeteria and gym complex, near the practice field Meg crossed on her first visit to the school.

She trailed after Kelsey, trying to remember the location of each subject group.

Even with the hallway posters and a school map in hand, getting between classes in five minutes would be a challenge. Going back to her locker between morning classes? Impossible. Hopefully, she'd not end up carrying everything for every class all day!

THE BUS RIDE HOME EVEN though she sat with Kelsey, gave Meg a chance to catch her breath and think about their relationship. *She probably thinks I'm a witless junior. We need a conversation about that. I want to be independent. If she clues me in on quirky school details, I'll be fine on my own.*

Hearing people seldom realized the clues they share about how comfortable they feel dealing with deaf people. Their body language, their wandering non-eye contact, standing too close, or the way many wave their arms. I'm deaf, not blind or a slow learner.

As they walked back toward the apartment Meg turned to Kelsey and stopped.

Meg: **Can we talk away from here?**

Kelsey: **Meet me outside your door in 5 minutes. Bring a blanket.**

MEG TEXTED MOM ABOUT THE test and said she'd pick up Toby by three o'clock, leaving her lots of time to clear the air with Kelsey.

Kelsey startled her. She stood directly outside her apartment as she pulled the door open. She carried a small blanket as they headed to a doorway marked No Admittance. Using a key, she ushered Meg inside, up a flight of stairs, and through another locked door.

Once Kelsey opened the second door, the girls stood on the roof of the building. Vents and pipes covered much of the area. The edge of the rooftop had a waist high brick wall. On two sides Meg eyed nearby buildings. Turning, she gasped at the view. The harbor spread like a gigantic panorama postcard. Piers, ships, ferries, a point of land, and a range of distant mountains, as well, as downtown buildings spread in front of her.

Kelsey led her to a corner where someone had erected a small lean-to made from a canvas tarp held in place by stout poles tied to cement bricks. The back tapered down, providing protection and a backdrop. Two folding chairs with a crate as a table filled the interior of the lean-to.

Before she sat down, Meg stood at the wall and looked down onto the street in front of the apartment. A couple of delivery trucks idled as people hustled past them along the narrow sidewalks. Not much traffic this time of day. She wondered how it must feel to be up here after dark or when it rained or snowed, if it ever snowed in Seattle.

Kelsey joined her, then motioned for her to sit down. Both girls covered their legs with their blankets and took out their phones.

Kelsey: **What do you think?**

Meg: Amazing!

Kelsey: **I come up here to think and be alone.**

Meg looked out toward the view now limited to seeing just the tops of a few distant buildings, cranes, and the mountains.

Meg: **Thanks for helping today. I don't expect it every day.**

Kelsey: **???**

Meg: **I want to do things for myself as much as I can.**

Kelsey stared out across the tops of the buildings, then glanced at Meg.

Kelsey: **It was confusing for me last year when we moved here. Let me help you get started. OK?**

Meg shrugged. She watched Kelsey's eyes. She saw a change, a softening. Maybe they could be friends.

For several minutes they sat quietly with their own thoughts before Kelsey stood and reached out a hand. "Let's go shoot hoops."

BACK THROUGH THE ROOFTOP DOOR. Locked. Down the stairs to the sixth floor. Door locked. Meg hurried into her apartment for her basketball and joined Kelsey out back. They'd not really settled anything by their brief conversation on the roof, but things felt okay for now.

6

MEG TOOK THREE DOLLARS FROM the miscellaneous expenses money jar and headed to pick-up Toby. There was so much she wished Kelsey had said, like maybe she wanted to be around her or at least invite her to meet her friends. It hadn't happened. She straightened her shoulders, lifted her chin, and tightened her jaw, waiting to feel her control return. It didn't, but maybe she *looked* more confident.

Toby tugged Meg's hand as they approached Stan's Market. She nodded, handed him his coin purse, and signed, "I have a list. Mom said you can use the change to buy whatever you want."

On their arrival, they saw Stan. He stepped out to the sidewalk, waved, and bowed slightly when he saw them looking over the crates on the sidewalk. "Hello! What you buy today?"

Meg waved back feeling more certain he'd no longer call the police every time she picked up a piece of fruit. After she found what Mom wanted and bought the items, she handed Toby the change: twenty-six cents.

Toby hurried back outside, looking for what he might buy: a bunch of grapes, an apple or...maybe...

He picked up little orange fruit balls. "What are these?"

Meg shrugged. "Ask Stan."

Toby waited until Stan finished helping a customer before he held out his hand and asked, "What are these?"

"Kumquats."

"Do they taste good?"

"I like," answered Stan.

"Will I like them?

Stan shrugged. "Maybe. You buy one. If don't like, I give back money."

Toby paid six cents for one kumquat and wiped it off on his jeans. He shoved it into his mouth and crunched down. His lips squeezed tight; his face looked pained. He spit the kumquat onto his hand and shook his head. "Ewe! Sour!"

Stan tipped his head. "You like?"

Toby thought for a while. "I don't know." He popped his chewed kumquat back in his mouth. His face grimaced. "I'll buy one more."

He paid Stan for another one. After wiping it off on his jeans, Toby scrunched it in his mouth. He grimaced but said, "I like it."

Stan laughed and laughed. "You adventure eater."

"A what?"

"You try new food. You adventure eater."

"Is that good?"

"Very good." Stan handed Toby another kumquat. "For free."

7

FRIDAY MORNING. MEG HAD DRESSED and fixed Toby's breakfast when she received a text at 8:00.

Ms. Gillis: **I have your placement results. Come in this AM. Bring your laptop.**

Laptop? Dang! She had no computer or Internet access. Her last school provided a computer, but Ms. Gillis hadn't mentioned one would be available here. Plus, she'd promised Toby they'd spend the day looking through the stores around their new neighborhood. *Guess he's either going to school with me or we're making a brief stop in daycare. I know what he'll choose.*

THE BUS RIDE AND THE walk into the high school with Toby went well. The trophy cases and the long, wide hallway with the shiny floor fascinated him. He took off running down the hall. She shouted to him just before he ran into a teacher pushing a cart stacked high with books.

Meg hurried down the hall and apologized to the teacher, then turned Toby back toward the office area. He knew better than to take off. They exchanged knowing looks without a need for any discussion.

Four students sat waiting in the counselor's area. They

made room for them to sit. She pretended to read a paper she pulled from her backpack. It was a copy of high school info on dress codes, language, and expected courtesy she'd read earlier, but it helped her avoid conversation with nearby students. The fewer who knew she was deaf, the better. Over the years, she'd found pretending to read was a good trick when she wished to remain anonymous.

Toby was restless. He swung his feet and fidgeted, so she loaned him her phone to play one of the games she'd loaded on for him to use during moments like this. How he could be amused watching little colorful candies or brightly colored balls bouncing around for hours amazed her. For her, the phone represented her contact with the world, not a gaming toy.

Meeting with Ms. Gillis produced a mixed outcome. In Math she'd scored advanced placement. The disappointment came when she scored low in English, a favorite subject. According to Ms. Gillis, she'd keep her junior status if she proved she could keep up. She wished she could sink through her seat and become a small pile of dust to be swept away.

She took back her phone from Toby as Ms. Gillis invited them to sit.

Ms. Gillis: **We are a rigorous academic school. You need 24 credits to graduate. There's no space for electives.**

Meg: **I understand.**

The schedule looked straightforward. She'd have six periods, all required classes for juniors: Math, English, Science, PE, History, and CTE.

Meg: **CTE?**

Ms. Gillis: **Computer Technology Education. Open your laptop. We'll set your class logins. All teachers enter assignments to their online school accounts.**

Meg: **No computer. Is there a loaner?**

Ms. Gillis: **I'll check. Use CTE between 6:30 AM to 6:30 PM school days. I'll give you a priority permit. Also, use the public library for weekend connections.**

Meg's skin burned as though on fire when she revealed her family's lack of technology. Maybe Mom could find a way to rent a laptop or... She noticed Ms. Gillis staring at her. She straightened and waited for her next text.

Ms. Gillis: **Find study buddies. Use your interpreter, who'll arrive in 2-3 weeks at the latest. I'm sorry for the delay. Had I been notified by your last school…**

Meg nodded, beginning to feel like a bobble head doll. She watched Toby start to fidget. He wasn't going to last much longer without a distraction.

Another set of papers and another text.

Ms. Gillis: **90-minute classes change daily. Confusing, so keep these pages handy. Announcements and Assemblies, AM Advisory. Ask a student in each class to share their class notes with you. Any problems, contact me.**

She handed over a paper entitled Early Release for 2018-2019. She pointed toward Toby: **Your brother's Early Releases will be different.**

Meg's mind began spinning. Ninety-minute classes changing daily? Assembly and Early Release schedules?

Ms. Gillis watched Toby and frowned.

Meg followed her gaze. He was squirming and looked like

he needed a break. "I need to get Toby home."

Ms. Gillis handed over more papers and pointed to Meg's phone.

Ms. Gillis: **Keep school maps handy to locate classrooms and Advisory class. 2-hour late start schedule. ASB information. Your locker is #612. Bring your own lock.**

Meg looked up and spread her hand in surrender.

Ms. Gillis nodded: **It's a lot.**

Another text arrived: **Pay for lunches by check or credit card only. Free and reduced lunches need parent-signed form. Return them ASAP if you plan to use that service.**

When she looked up again, Ms. Gillis reached her hand across the desk to shake with Meg. "Come in any time. I want you to be succeed."

"Thanks."

Ms. Gillis: **Next Tuesday, Kick-off assembly. All classes will be each 35 minutes. I'll find a student escort for you.**

"Escort?"

Ms. Gillis: **To walk you to classes and lunch. I'll text you.**

Meg stood. "We need to go."

Ms. Gillis's smile faded. It looked like she'd just realized how overloaded Meg felt on receiving a seemingly unending pile of information.

She escorted them out the office door. Meg thanked her but kept walking until she and Toby were outside, where she sat down on a bench near the flagpole to sort out the papers. Classes, funny hours, and special dates and times. She closed her backpack, exhaled deeply, and pulled Toby to stand up.

"Let's explore our neighborhood."

MEG ONCE AGAIN TOOK THREE dollars from the family's miscellaneous expenses money jar and headed out with Toby. He'd done a fair job of waiting while she spoke with Ms. Gillis, plus riding the bus had been a highlight of his morning. Now it was Toby Time, a chance for him to dictate where they wandered.

Toby tugged on her hand as they approached the row of shops. "Let's stop at Stan's Market. I want more q-u-a-t-s. I have twenty cents."

On their arrival, they saw Stan outside, arranging last minute crates. "Hello! What you try today?"

Toby picked up three kumquats and handed Stan his two dimes.

Stan nodded. "You my young food adventure eater. I give you four for two dimes. Okay?"

Toby agreed and picked up one more kumquat as Stan hurried off to help another customer.

Toby signed, "Stan likes me, and I like him."

FOR THE NEXT HOUR, THEY peeked into shops. Most of the community store signs were written in Asian languages; few had English translations; they'd need to check out their front display windows and go inside to know what might be on sale.

Toby's favorite shop turned out to be Han's Variety Store. Back in Yakima, he loved the almost-a-dollar store with merchandise much like Han carried. Where else could a ten-year-old boy find hundreds of items to buy with his dollar-a-week allowance?

In Han's, Toby spotted a dusty Chinese Checkers game

box on sale for just under four dollars. He showed Meg the game and begged to purchase it.

She signed, "I only have three dollars. Sorry."

Toby scrunched up his face. "Will they keep it for me? Maybe we could come back to buy it."

"Ask."

Toby went to the counter and asked the woman. She looked puzzled and called her son to talk with Toby. The son shook his head. "You must buy it now. You'll need four dollars and fifty cents."

Toby put the checkers game back and hurried from the store. Meg followed. He turned toward their apartment without a word, but his face wore his disappointment like a mask.

Right then and there, she decided she needed a job so she could help Toby buy small things like the Chinese Checkers game. This move had been hard on all of them, but especially Toby, who'd lost his good friends, his acres of space to run around, and Gran. She'd been the rock they all clung to, the person who spent time with them every day while Mom was busy earning money to keep them safe and cared for.

Getting a job would be difficult. What could she do? When would she have time to work with all the school assignments coming her way? And...who'd hire a deaf girl?

8

MEG WOKE LATE. THE LIGHTS in the kitchen created shadows on the bedroom wall.

Daylight crept in along the sides of her new window shade. Toby lay crosswise in his bed, his feet dangling and his covers on the floor. The smelled of percolated coffee filled the room.

Her phone read 9:00. 9:00? She leaped to her feet and scrambled into her clothes. As she rushed into the kitchen, she saw her mom and Uncle Zach casually drinking coffee.

"Morning," they both signed.

"I'm late for school."

Mom stood to hug her and signed, "It's Labor Day. No school."

Meg let out a long breath and sat at the table with Zach.

"Hi, kid. Glad to see you're excited for school."

She stretched and yawned. "Right. You off today?"

Zach signed, "I am. Came to visit and help. Later go to the beach or exploring."

Mom signed, "I have today off as well. Let's explore *after* we finish up." She pointed to wooden panels leaning against the wall. "Zach bought this folding screen for your bedroom. Give you privacy after it's repaired and we find something to fill the open sections in the panels."

Zach opened the screen and grinned as it wobbled, refusing to stand alone. "A young lady needs her privacy," he signed and bowed with a flourish of his arms.

The screen had three panels of smooth dark wood with several missing hinges. Each panel contained carved scrolls and swirls around an open oval in the center. It *definitely* needed something to create privacy.

Meg hugged Zach, then Mom. "Thank you."

After Toby got up, the group sprang into action. Meg wiped down and waxed the panels, Zach replaced the broken hinges and Toby held his tools. Mom fixed pancakes for brunch and conversation began on how to cover the panels.

"What can I use?" Meg asked.

Mom suggested wood, paper, maybe drawings or fabric. "It's your screen. You decide. We'll need to borrow the manager's staple gun or small nails."

Meg sat staring at the openings, her ideas bouncing from one thing to another. Kelsey always looked stylish; if she was home maybe she'd have an opinion. It might be a way to discover where their friendship stood, if it even existed.

KELSEY LOOKED OUT THE FISHEYE in her apartment door when she heard the knocking. She saw Meg. The last time Meg had knocked, she'd left her to fend for herself.

Meg knocked again.

Kelsey opened the door.

Meg smiled and shared a text: **Hi! May we borrow a wood stapler or small nails to fix a folding screen?**

Kelsey typed on Meg's phone: **Sure. What's the screen look like?**

Meg hesitated, then waved her to follow. "Come see."

As Kelsey looked at the details on the screen, ideas floated into her mind and envy slid into her heart. The screen needed something soothing if it was to be a privacy screen. Maybe drawings if Meg drew, colorful wallpaper scraps, or fabric—definitely fabric. The light would shine through, adding extra beauty.

Kelsey: **Come to my room. I have a few ideas.**

Stepping into Kelsey and her dad's basement apartment surprised Meg by its differences and spaciousness. The walls wore bright colors; Meg's were a dingy tan. The remodeled kitchen contained a granite-topped island with 2 bar stools, new appliances, and a shiny linoleum floor, while hers was an open, tired-looking kitchen with Formica counters and only basic appliances. There was a hallway, a modernized bathroom and two bedrooms. Kelsey's father's room was a mass of clothes piled amid toolboxes, two-by-fours, and sheetrock. But Kelsey's room...

Walking into Kelsey's room she stepped into every teen girl's dream space: yellow and pale rose painted walls with floral wallpaper along the lower sections, sheer curtains behind deep rose fabric curtains, a large mirror at a dressing table, and a tall bookcase filled with books and wicker storage baskets. The plush, rose-colored carpet with swirls of gray made Meg want to dance across it.

Kelsey let Meg look over everything, sensing her fascination with the room. She tapped her arm and began texting.

Kelsey: **Dad remodeled our apartment soon after we moved in last year. He took part of the storage room to** make my bedroom. He promises to finish things, but he works 2 jobs, so it's taking longer than he thought.

Meg stepped close to one of the paintings on the wall.

Meg: I love the colors. Where did you get these paintings?

Kelsey: I made them.
Meg blinked. You're an artist.
Kelsey: I like color and art. Here's what I want you to see.

She pulled two baskets from the bookshelf and handed Meg several pieces of cloth. "For your screen."

Kelsey: They'll let in light and look like art rather than fabric.

Meg slid her fingers along each piece, feeling their varied textures.
Kelsey reached for a third basket and smiled.

Kelsey: Maybe add a string of colorful beads to reflect the light. Make your space even brighter.

Meg stared at the fabrics and the beads, uncertain of what to say next.

Meg: Where can I buy fabric or beads like these?"

Kelsey: Take any you like. I make purses, shirts, and jewelry to sell at school so I can buy a few nice clothes. I'm a fabric and bead hoarder.

Meg handed the fabric back to her and shook her head.

Meg: I can't take these. Could I buy some of them?

The sad expression on Kelsey's face surprised Meg.

Kelsey: Consider this my apology for not helping you on your first trip to school.

Meg felt a warmth grow inside her: **Thanks. Please, come help me fix my screen, if you have time.**

Kelsey nodded and blinked fast as she rubbed away tears forming in her eyes.

OVER THE NEXT HOUR, THE girls covered the open ovals with a pastel flowered fabric reminding Meg of Gran's garden. Kelsey picked out colorful complimentary beads as well as a few wildly colored ones to glue over the staples holding the fabric in place.

The additions made the screen come alive. Meg crossed her arms and tipped her head side to side. "It's beautiful. Thanks."

WHEN MEG AND HER FAMILY drove to Alki Beach, Kelsey joined them. They found a table and enough vacant sand to spread out blankets so they could stretch out to watch nearby groups of people and boats cruising around Elliott Bay.

Meg, Kelsey, and Zach even took on Toby's contest to determine who could stand in the chilly water the longest. Toby won with Zach a close second. Meg and Kelsey rewarded them with serious splashing, ending with all of them soaked and laughing.

After everyone dried in the sunshine, it was time to head home. Zach treated them to triple-scoop ice cream in waffle cones to officially end summer and this last trip to the beach.

EVEN THOUGH SHE WAS EXHAUSTED, Meg struggled to fall asleep. A combination of looking back to her time with Kelsey and her family on their Labor Day outing and looking forward, anxious about tomorrow and her first day of school kept her mind whirling. Thoughts jumbled together; worry circled through her mind. *Will Kelsey be at the bus stop in the morning? Will she help me find my classrooms? Will Toby like his new school? I can't even guess. My job right now is to get some sleep so I'm ready to take on every unknown. Tomorrow will probably be filled with a pile of embarrassments and errors, but I need to handle whatever happens.*

9

BY 5:45 MEG HAD DRESSED, checked her backpack, and made her favorite lunch: a PBJ sandwich with two cookies and a banana. *Comfort food is like bringing along an old friend, considering all the challenges ahead.*

At 7:10, she stood at the bus stop, watching the city wake up around her. A few minutes later, she became part of a dozen students and even more workers climbing on the bus. The students looked sleepy; the workers looked resigned. A day of unpleasant tasks and new experiences lay ahead. But where was Kelsey?

As she entered school, she still didn't see Kelsey. *Is she sick? Avoiding me? Do I care where Kelsey is? Yes, but I've vowed to be independent so it's just as well she's nowhere in sight.*

The main hallway of Sherman Harrison resembled an agitated swarm of bees returning to their shared hive. Nervousness oozed from the people around her. She knew from Kelsey to follow the crowd toward the gym. *Time to join the high school hive.*

She picked a seat up-front yet near the exit and waited to see what was planned for this early morning. The gym looked less than one fourth full. Only freshmen along with a few older-looking students were in the audience. Additionally, a band, cheerleaders, and a cadre of chatting students, probably ASB officers, faced the gathered students. A tall man wearing a suit with a tie in colors that matched a school banner approached the microphone.

Meg sat close enough to read his lips. "Welcome new students! It's time to start another great year at Sherman Harrison High School."

The band and the assembled returning students facing the newbies stood. Each put one finger to their lips. They moved their heads from left to right and back to the left before they took their finger down and returned to their chairs.

How strange. They looked like they were shushing the group. She'd need to find out what the movement meant.

Next, a cheer squad stepped forward and led a school cheer. Students stood and followed the directions on the poster: 'give us your best and loudest'. The risers vibrated with energy as the new students did their best to look like they knew what to do. When the cheer squad asked all freshmen to stand, she discovered she'd seated herself in their section. Too late now to move somewhere else.

Student after student spoke. The audience made the risers tremble with foot stomps before being dismissed to meet with Advisory teachers. Thank heavens Kelsey explained Advisory to her last night.

The band played as everyone dispersed into the hallways. Once the gym was empty, she made her way into the hall. Students wearing "Ask Me" badges stood at each intersection helping students find their way. Kelsey was one of the helpers. Here goes, she thought as she approached Kelsey.

"How can I... Meg? Hi. Glad to see you. Show me your schedule."

Meg held out the paper and Kelsey pointed her to the stairway. "Go up two floors. Room 302 is your homeroom. It's on your left."

Another student pushed up to ask Kelsey a question, so Meg walked away, up two flights of stairs, and found her homeroom. By then, all the front seats were filled, so she moved to an empty seat further back. There were a surprising number of new juniors. She shifted side-to-side, trying to look around them to lip read what Mr. Oberlander, the teacher was saying. He paced and turned around so much she had no idea what was happening, but she sat looking forward, pretending to know what he'd shared.

Next, the new students attended classes one through three, making the trek up and down the stairs and into and out of classrooms. Her earlier vision of bees returning to their hive changed to confused bees scurrying about, searching, trying out a new, unfamiliar hive.

When lunch time arrived, she followed students down the corridor, down the stairs, and into the cafeteria where people sat in cliques. Her guess: potential athletes in the middle of the room, girls in fashionable outfits and cheerleaders sat nearby, leaving the rest of the students strung out over a dozen tables in friend groups.

As she passed the popular girls table, she noticed Kelsey in their midst, chatting, gesturing, laughing, and whispering. Must be the junior and senior helpers she saw in the hallways. She caught Kelsey's glance, but it contained no invitation to join the table, so she headed for the benches outside the cafeteria. Sunshine engulfed the patio as she ate her sandwich which tasted like cardboard. Maybe she needed a different brand of peanut butter.

Afternoon periods mirrored the morning classes with overviews and various rules shared. For her last period, she was back in Mr. Oberlander's class for history, her least favorite subject. He handed out a suggested reading list, his available hours for student conferencing, and his grading criteria. It looked like every teacher wanted brief, personal summaries to know more about the students, but each used different questions. At this rate, she'd be up writing until after midnight *if* she could uncover what each teacher wanted.

THE RIDE HOME ON THE city bus gave her time to relax and close her eyes to screen- out the world. *Blah! So many identical rooms along so many identical hallways on so many levels with so many stairs. Who knew attending a large high school took so much energy? This was only the new students! Lots of freshmen, but why so many new juniors?*

Meg dropped her backpack onto the kitchen table. After she grabbed a glass of milk and a handful of cookies, she dumped everything out. What a huge stack of stuff, to sort through and so many brief personal papers to complete within the week or lose precious class points. If she believed the pages and pages of information passed out, missing deadlines would assure a low grade or failing a class.

Seeing Kelsey ensconced with the popular girls was off-putting. Still, Kelsey was her only almost-friend who could help her navigate the piles of information. It appeared she'd need to head down and ask for help before attempting to read her mountain of paperwork.

TOBY'S REPORT ON HIS FIRST day at school filled the apartment with excitement. He signed, "I love my teacher. She reminds me of Gran. She looks like Gran, but her hair is not all silver. She reads to us, and she never raises her voice."

Meg nodded. "I'm glad."

Toby frowned and signed, "I need crayons and pencils and a ruler and a whole bunch of other things. Can we go buy them today? If everyone brings everything by Friday, we get an ice cream party next week."

"After you eat your snack, we'll go. I need things as well."

The emergency money jar was close to empty after she took out the twenty dollars she estimated they'd need. The neighborhood variety store might not be the best place to shop, but she was too tired to ride another bus or to even try to locate a store with discounted school supplies.

They stepped into Han's Variety Store. They each grabbed a shopping basket and started down the aisles with their lists. Surprisingly, the store had a special display of most all they needed at sale prices. At checkout their purchases totaled twenty-three dollars including tax. She put back enough of her items to allow Toby to check everything off his list.

Meg's only expensive 'required' purchase Han's wouldn't have was a scientific calculator. That would set Mom back close to ninety dollars, but it would last through college. There was also the specifically formatted notebook required for CTE class only available through the school store at a cost of nine dollars. *Nine dollars for a notebook! I definitely need a job!*

AFTER FINISHING DINNER DISHES, SHE headed to Kelsey's apartment. Luckily, she was home and in a friendly mood. She invited Meg in and fixed a tray with chilled sodas and a plate of her mom's recipe for Choco-Nut bar cookies.

Kelsey didn't talk about her mom, but her face wore a

wispy expression whenever she said 'mom'. They must have been close. Mom told Meg she'd heard she'd died years ago. *How would I handle my mom dying when I was ten? Kelsey seemed resigned to just having a dad, but what option did she have? What would my dad have done if that had happened in our family?*

MEG TOSSED HER NOTEBOOK AND the stack of papers she'd accumulated onto Kelsey's spare bed. She sat down beside them and let out a huge sigh. "Can you help me? Please?"

Over the next hour, Kelsey shared important details like the daily schedules and made suggestions.

Kelsey: **Remember, today was a special schedule. You usually only have three subjects a day. They will be the same classes in the same order every other day. It's confusing at first, but you'll get it.**

Meg: **How long did it take you?**

Kelsey: **A week. Just my luck this year. I've got Spanish, not French, like I wanted.**

Meg: **What's wrong with Spanish?**

Kelsey: **French is the language of high fashion.**

Meg: **You want to design clothes?**

Kelsey stared into space for a moment and shrugged. Her faced clouded as her eyes scanned the design posters on her walls.

Kelsey: **I'd rather be the model wearing the clothes. 'Sil vous plaît'. That means if it pleases you. It would definitely please me!**

She sat quietly for a long moment, then shook herself back to her current task of helping Meg. As they finished sorting out Meg's mountain of papers, Kelsey grabbed Meg's hand and texted.

Kelsey: **Do you want to play school basketball?**

Meg: **Yes. Am I too late?**

Kelsey: **No. BB starts in Nov. It's competitive."**

Meg: **Fees?**

Kelsey: **ABS card ($90) + medical checkup + good court shoes.**

Meg: **Are games and events free with ASB?**

Kelsey: **Discounted. You'll also have class and lab fees. ($300)**

Meg's eyes widened at the total. With her scientific calculator she probably needed four hundred dollars. She *definitely* needed a job.

EACH STEP UP TO HER family apartment became a challenge and mirrored her school frustration. *When will my interpreter arrive? I'll be at a disadvantage until then. With all these costs, this year will become expensive, but hopefully I'm not a failing disaster.*

10

AFTER ANOTHER RESTLESS NIGHT, MEG woke in darkness. Her clock read 3:30 then 4:15, 5:24 and finally 6:00. Would each night be a repeat of sleeplessness? If so, she'd need to find a way to stay alert in her classes. Maybe she'd start drinking coffee. She shuddered. Even though she liked the smell of freshly brewed coffee, she couldn't understand how her mom and Zach could drink such bitter, brown sludge.

Yesterday on her own had been so confusing. Teachers must not have known she was coming because none saved her a seat up front where she could attempt to read their teacher's lips. *I hate feeling like the class dunce, sitting, watching, never participating as the school requests me to do. One good thing: even though teachers expect us to have and use computers, they still pass out work papers so I can almost keep up. At least I'm not pigeon-holed as the deaf girl, yet. That's coming; the shouting faces will begin once they know.*

KELSEY WASN'T AT THE BUS stop again today. *Strange. How is she getting to school? During the time working on the folding screen and sorting through class papers, Kelsey acted like a friend. Maybe our friendship only works when we're away from school.*

As Meg entered the school, the halls were so crowded they became close to impassable. She watched a minute, inhaling scents she'd not noticed yesterday or when she came to take her placement tests: sweaty bodies, hair spray, and food odors with an underlying scent of floor wax and disinfectant, not something the other students probably noticed. Together with the mobs of people, everything assaulted her senses.

Hurrying students rushed around her, then stopped dead in their tracks to chat with clusters of friends. No one noticed her lurching around them. She'd remained invisible in the throbbing mass of bodies a little longer.

Kelsey stood laughing and talking with a group of well-dressed girls and preppy guys, blocking the main hallway, causing Meg and others to scoot around them to reach their lockers or head to their first class of the day. Kelsey looked comfortable, energized, and animated with her friends. *A far cry from her interactions with me.*

Standing at her locker, Meg pulled out her schedule and the school map. *Here goes. Maybe I can get lost in the crowd for a few days.*

Seattle Schools - Sherman Harrison High School
Student Name: Meg Appens
Student ID: 417632-2018   Grade: Junior
Class Schedule for Semester One: Sept. 2018 - Jan. 2019
Advisory - 11:   Mr. Oberlander - Room #302

CLASSES	TEACHER	ROOM
1- Math - 11(Adv Placement)	Barkton	Room # 218
Advisory - 11	Oberlander	Room #302
2- English - 11	Vance	Room #111
3- Science -11 (Physics)	Dexter	340 A

```
Lunch One
4 - PE - 11(Life Fitness)    Young        Gym A
5 -CTE                       Carter       Tech Center
6 - History 11(American)     Oberlander   Room #302
```

So, I'll spend every day in Advisory with Mr. Oberlander, then head back there to end my day. Terrific. Why did her advisor have to be him? It's almost funny how they'd begin and end each school day together. He'd have ample opportunity to discover how much she disliked history.

Meg stashed her jacket in her locker, headed to his classroom as quickly as possible to grab a seat up front. Mr. Oberlander began talking something about a seating chart. He looked down at his desk and appeared to be muttering. The students began moving around. A girl stood beside her looking peeved. "Well? That's my seat. So, move."

Mr. Oberlander walked over. "Young lady. What's your name?"

Meg watched the irritated girl, unaware Mr. Oberlander carried his papers and stood speaking to both.

Mr. Oberlander moved in front of her. "What's your name?"

"Meg Appens, sir."

He looked over his list and back to Meg. "You're not on my class list. Are you sure you belong in Sophomore History?"

"Isn't this Advisory?"

Mr. Oberlander shook his head and moved on to speak with other students.

Those seated around her covered their mouths with their hands or turned to neighboring students. She assumed they were laughing at her, so she made a hasty retreat. Once in the hall, she leaned against the wall and took several deep breaths. *Dunce. Why does my schedule show Advisory at the top if it isn't first? It's where I started yesterday.* She headed down the stairs to the counseling office.

Ms. Gillis was busy, so Meg sat on one of the benches, waiting with other students. All sat focused on their cell phones, so she opened hers, hoping they'd continue to ignore her.

Thirty minutes later Ms. Gillis unraveled her error with the class schedule.

Ms. Gillis: **I'm so sorry. Your advisor's name is always listed above the daily class schedule. You start with Math, then go to Advisory. Your interpreter is expected to arrive next week. I'll contact a senior escort to help you until he or she arrives. It's the least we can do to help you fit in.**

Fit in? I'll never fit in. Doesn't anyone get it? I'm not... She stopped herself, knowing if she spoke what she was thinking, she'd appear ungrateful.

While they waited for the senior 'escort, or babysitter' they covered a few more details. Ms. Gillis promised she'd find her a loaner scientific calculator to use in Math and Science classes. Then she shared yet another paper, listing the year-long benefits of purchasing an ASB card. Then she waved Meg out to the hall to wait on a bench.

Once more, students filled the benches, waiting to talk with advisors and leaving. *This looks like a thankless job the first of the year.* She'd cross off school counselor as a possible profession.

Time dragged. When Patsy, a petite girl with a pixie haircut arrived, they returned to Ms. Gillis's office. Patsy would be allowed to text her during classes to keep her on track. This first week she'd also help Meg with the school's schedule of rotating classes, Advisory, and lunch procedures, reinforcing what Kelsey already explained.

Patsy and Meg would seek out a student in each class who'd share their notes and have them copied in the office. The accommodating student would retrieve them at the end of each day. Meg shrank into herself. Needing to approach a student to take on extra work didn't feel like a great way to win friends! Maybe Kelsey would help.

Today she'd follow a Wednesday schedule by attending odd numbered classes. She'd already missed Math, then skipped the last five minutes of Advisory, and now headed quickly to her last AM odd-day class, Physics.

Her head was spinning like a gyroscope, changing angles every few seconds.

Mr. Dexter, the Physics teacher, passed out textbooks and class information papers while talking and moving around the room, making it difficult to read his lips. Patsy helped her by texting and writing notes about what was said. Occasionally, she forgot Meg was deaf and attempted to whisper to her. Perhaps, for the time being, she'd still appear to fit in.

The morning had been a disaster. Since she doubted they did a slow start in AP Math, she was already behind. Now, sitting in Physics, the ninety-minute session ticked by as slow as a bad three-hour movie with poor closed captioning.

From the notes Patsy handed to her at the end of class, it was obvious she wasn't into Physics, but at least she tried. Meg thanked her but worried she'd also fall behind in this class.

After lunch with Patsy, they headed to period five, CTE.

Finally, a practical class. Computers were something she understood better than she'd ever understand History. Each student sat at an assigned computer carrel to use all year. Patsy also attended this class and promised to check-in each day after school.

On the city bus home, Meg closed her eyes and tried to relax. *I need to keep a positive attitude, but I need to know what happened in the classes I missed. Should I ask Kelsey? It depends on who she is today: the friendly, creative helpful girl or the aloof, I-don't-know-you girl she passed in the hall. Hopefully, she'll consent to help me locate reliable students who'll let me copy their notes and answer my questions until the interpreter arrives.*

MEG FIXED TOBY'S SNACK AND sat down to look through today's new pile of papers. The Advisory packet contained a notice from the Athletic department about sign-ups for the various sports, as well as a notice from the city sports leagues. Unfortunately, she'd missed fall sports deadlines; maybe she could still join a fee-free city-league team. With the weather about to turn chilly, playing inside, away from the upcoming rains, sounded like a good decision. It would mean Toby would be forced to stay in daycare any nights she'd be late. He deserved better, but didn't she deserve a chance to join a sports team?

Hopefully, she'd keep her grades up and be allowed to try out for basketball. It could help her secure a college scholarship. Dreams of being a starter at Sherman Harrison settled in, but, at such a large school with so many students available to play, making the team might be difficult. She'd work hard to change those dreams into goals; if she focused in history and aced her other classes, those goals could become her reality.

Toby and Meg sat at the kitchen table working when Mom arrived home with good news. She signed: "I've found a part-time job to fill-in the hours I'm short. A client of the insurance office needs a part-time bookkeeper. I'll work three nights a week, if I can find a sitter for Toby when you have sports."

Meg signed, "How did you know I was just thinking about sports?"

Mom stepped over to rub her back. Then she signed, "You are our first family athlete. I can't imagine you no longer wanting to play."

Toby looked up. "How late will you be at the new job? Do I have to go to daycare again? Can't I stay alone here in the apartment?"

Mom shook her head. "No staying alone. We'll find someone to come here. That's better, right?"

Toby nodded and went back to writing his spelling words in sentences.

Meg bit her lip. *I wish I could solve my problems by a babysitter at home rather than a babysitter at school. Patsy is nice enough, but she must be bored out of her mind, and she's missing her classes. At least she'll only be with me a few more days. I feel stupid for needing help. If only Kelsey... Time to go downstairs and talk with her one more time.*

Her frantic knocking on Kelsey's door emphasized how frustrated she felt. Maybe it was time to confront Kelsey and try to understand what was going on in her head.

Kelsey opened the door saying, "Hi! How's school going?"

Meg's face showed her answer.

Kelsey stepped back and let her into the living room, their *remodeled* living room.

Meg took out her phone.

Meg: **You avoid me. School has a wacky schedule. I'm behind. I need help. Please!**

Her entire body trembled as she waited for Kelsey to invite her to sit down. Meg inhaled deeply, trying to relax. "Sorry."
Kelsey stared out the window for along moment.

Kelsey: **I'm afraid to invite you to my group. It may push me out.**

Meg: **Why?**

Kelsey: **They only want the stuff I make and my help on their classes. They might not understand if we're friends.**

Meg stared at Kelsey, waiting for her to continue, to explain herself, but she didn't. A cloud of anxiety filled the space between them. Finally, she jumped up and waved Meg to follow. "Let's go to my room."
They sat on Kelsey's rug. She reached to Meg and spoke slowly. "I'm sorry. I don't know what to do. Can we be friends at home at least?"
Meg nodded.

Kelsey started texting: **I'll help you with school questions When we're home. The rest I need to figure out. It will take a little longer. I don't know what to do.**

Meg set her jaw, but nodded

Meg: **I get it, but I am already behind.**

Over the next hour Kelsey texted details, suggested reliable classmates who might lend Meg their notes and once again explained how the daily schedule worked.

Kelsey: **Friday's our only normal day. We have all classes,** first through sixth, in order.

She suggested Meg keep her senior helper until the interpreter arrived. As for the city sports teams., she encouraged Meg to sign up. She also explained where she was each morning.

Kelsey: **I ride each morning with my dad so we can talk. He works crazy hours. You could ride with us.**

Despite her irritation, Meg stared at Kelsey before she replied.

Meg: **What about your in-group at school? What if they saw me riding in your car?**

Kelsey squirmed, looked down at her hands and shrugged.

Meg: **I'll take the bus.**

The girls located Meg's class assignments, but Kelsey kept eyeing the clock.

Kelsey: **You need to let the teachers know you're deaf, so you'll have a seat up front. Write a note. Get the seat you need. Some guys will be upset about moving, but you need to take care of yourself.**

Meg: **May I double check my assignments on your computer?**

Kelsey: **Yes, but it's better if you use the computer lab. At the end of CTE, check your assignments. Teachers stay 40 minutes after school for kids to ask questions. Carter keeps CTE open til 6:00 school days.**

FEELING CONFUSED BUT GLAD FOR Kelsey's suggestions, Meg returned upstairs. She should have thought of them herself, but she wasn't thinking clearly. Tomorrow, she'd make a better start with Advisory and her classes. No! Advisory was only first on even days. She stopped and entered the order of her classes for both even and odd in her phone, hoping she'd get where she needed to be on the right day and at the right time.

She checked the clock: 8:00. Sitting beside Toby at the kitchen table, she got to work, knowing she'd be up late because of the time she'd spent with Kelsey. She grudgingly acknowledged that Kelsey had been right; she needed to stand up for herself. Nobody could or should need to do that for her.

11

WEEK TWO. MONDAY. ODD CLASSES only. Meg sat in Math class, working on the final unit test problem. She nodded when the teacher tapped her hand and pointed to the clock. Ten minutes to finish.

In five minutes, she finished, closed the stapled pages, and sat waiting to be dismissed and turn in her test. Not having an interpreter yet made each day a challenge since Patty, her senior helper, had gone back to her own classes.

Today marked a month since her family had migrated across the Cascades. So far so good. Mom liked her jobs, Toby liked his school, and she was settling in.

THE MAIN HALLWAY WAS CROWDED as usual as she headed to the locker across the hallway from Kelsey's. The fact that they were both extra tall girls, their walking together didn't go unnoticed, but as she'd anticipated, few stopped to chat when Meg was with Kelsey. She knew she'd been pigeon-holed as different, but her skill at lip reading gave her a distinct advantage she'd not yet openly shared.

As for her classes, she loved everything except history. Who cared what happened one or two hundred years ago? How could it impact her life? The world had changed in a thousand ways since then so how could they possibly have any connections?

Until this fall, she'd attended a small private school for deaf kids. Her mom worked there as the receptionist, which allowed Meg a monthly discount in tuition. But after 10th grade and because Gran had died, her mom needed to find them a new home and a new job, and Meg needed a high school. Seattle offered ways to fill their needs.

Their inexpensive apartment near Mom's work removed the need to purchase a car. Even a clunker would stretch their meager savings beyond its limits. Luckily, Seattle had good bus service, and their neighborhood supplied the basics they needed.

MEG LOOKED FORWARD TO THIS Friday. Teacher's had meetings, so students had the day off. She'd enjoy sleeping in, extra time with Toby, and time to get caught up. As she set the table for breakfast, Toby wandered out, rubbing his eyes. "Do I need to go to daycare today?"

Meg shook her head and signed, "Nope. Today we'll explore more of our neighborhood. Okay?"

"Can we go to Stan's?"

"Maybe. After we eat, do chores and I do my homework. Also, I promised Mom I'd go through this junk box. Won't take too long."

Toby cleaned up their bedroom while she tidied the kitchen area. They took a load of laundry to the basement to wash and dry. She had one small task left: tackling the junk box. She dumped its contents onto the kitchen table, spreading out its hodgepodge of items. *What on earth? Why did we bring these odds and ends from Gran's all the way to Seattle?*

She ran her fingers through the mishmash of unused band-aids, chipped marbles, broken pencils, last year's pocket calendar, grocery receipts from the farmer's market in Yakima, Toby's wheelless toy car, two tubes of lip gloss, an expired coupon for a dollar off a bag of potatoes, assorted rubber bands, bread ties, a wad of yarn, several coins, a broken bracelet, and stacks of used and unused post-it's.

A small keychain caught her attention. It held Gran's key for the barn. Meg had given the keychain to her years ago. She'd said she liked how the tiny plastic Rhode Island Red chickens clustered together, like a family. "They remind me of the first chickens I had as a young girl."

Meg removed and tossed away the key then hooked the keychain on her backpack hoping it would be a good omen. In the least, it would be a conversation starter.

She tossed the loose change into their emergency fund jar and started to brush everything else into the kitchen garbage can when she spotted an envelope addressed to her mother. The canceled stamp showed it was mailed two years before Gran died. The return address was missing, but it was her father's handwriting.

Should she look inside? It had already been opened. She set it aside as she dumped the rest into the garbage. Every few minutes she looked at the envelope, debating whether she should look inside or give it to her mother. Temptation won. She picked up the envelope, opened it, and unfolded the letter.

Her hands shook as she read.

2/14

Della,
I know you're disappointed in me. In some ways I'm disappointed in myself that I didn't do a better job of

making our marriage work. You wanted a home and a family. Being married worked for a while but I wanted my freedom to travel and perform again. I don't want to be tied down to kids and working to keep Mom's farm above water.

Stay as long as you wish. Once she's gone, I'm selling the farm and using the money to support restarting the band. You probably squirreled some money away so you'll be fine without me.

Tell the kids whatever you want, but don't promise them I'll be around. It's not something I want anymore. You always expected too much from me.

Hal

MEG FLOPPED DOWN ON THE couch and reread the letter. Tears slid down her cheeks. *So, dad never wanted me or Toby. Or was it just me? Maybe he saw me as damaged.*

As she refolded the letter and closed the envelope, her mother walked into the apartment. "Hi, honey. Surprise! I'm off early today. How's...What's in your hand?"

"A letter from Dad to you. I read it, but...."

Mom set down her bag of groceries and signed. "Oh, honey. I never wanted you to see that." She sat down and held Meg's hand, then signed, "Your father was upset when he wrote it. He was mad at me, at the farm, and maybe the whole world. I don't think he truly meant what he said."

Meg signed with angry force, "Yes, he did, Mom. It says he didn't want us. Or was it he didn't want me 'cuz I'm deaf?"

Della put her arm around her and held her as she cried.

Meg straightened. "Why didn't he want us?"

Della wiped away her tears with a tissue then signed, "Your

dad was, is, a good man. He wasn't happy working a regular job and managing Gran's farm, He wanted to get back to the band. He didn't know how to be a husband or a father. Gran knew it. She warned me, but I thought he'd change. He said he'd try, but he couldn't manage it, so he left."

"Do you ever speak with him?"

Della shook her head. Her hands remained relaxed as she signed, "Once Gran died, he came back only long enough to sell the farm, and disappeared again."

"What did I do wrong?"

Mom's eyes showed her sadness. "Nothing, honey. None of us did anything wrong. He wanted to be free, to live his life as a musician. He's doing what he wants and needs to do. Now we need to do what we want and need to do. Understand?"

Meg's hands flew through her signing. "Dad said you saved money, so he didn't leave us anything. Is it true? Is that how we moved to Seattle?"

"No, honey. I didn't set aside any money. I didn't think I needed to. Gran's will gave us a thousand dollars, but it wasn't enough to live on, or even rent an apartment for very long. My good friend Nora knew I needed a job. Her cousin lived in Seattle and needed a bookkeeper, so we moved here. This apartment is close to his office, so we'll be living here until we can afford something with more space, maybe separate bedrooms for you and Toby."

"And one for you, too," Meg added.

"I'm setting aside the wages from the part-time job to help us get there faster."

"I could get a job after school. Toby could stay with someone around here."

"Your job is going to school and doing your best. It's my

responsibility to earn money to support us. Don't worry; we'll be fine. Do you have more questions?"

"No. I'm fine. Thanks, Mom. Are you going to tell Toby about the letter?"

"No. Let's wait. He's too young to..."

Toby walked into the room and stopped. He signed, "I'm too young to do what?" He gave Mom a hug.

"You're too young to stay alone," Mom said. "We'll try to find someone nearby to watch over you after school when we're both away from the apartment."

Toby looked from Mom to Meg and back to Mom. "Was Meg crying?"

"She's tired, and she feels sad." Mom straightened. "How about we cheer her up? Our cookie jar is getting empty why don't you two bake cookies while I check the mail and start dinner then we'll have time to play cards."

'Cookies' was a magic word for Toby. He immediately began getting out the cookie sheets and putting on his child-size apron. Meg took a minute longer to shift from thinking of her dad to overseeing making cookies. Someday in the future, she wanted to have a larger conversation with her mom. But very soon, she needed to talk more with her about the information sheet she kept folded in her pocket.

COOKIE BAKING REPLACED THEIR TRIP around the neighborhood. Meg promised Toby they'd go out exploring another day when they had more time.

Even after dinner, the smell of fresh baked cookies still filled the air. Meg sat on her bed, looking at Monday's home-work, mulling over the idea of getting ahead on her classes. She slipped her hand into her pocket, pulled out the paper, unfolded it, and felt her enthusiasm drain away.

Yesterday, Kelsey shared information about high school expenses she'd not anticipated needing to pay, especially if she intended to try out for basketball. Typical Kelsey, she'd divided the list in Must Buy if she wanted to participate in activities and sports and Want to Buy: things Kelsey thought she might include, as money allowed.

MUST BUY:	WANT to BUY
ABS card $90	prom dress $20-80
physical for sports $50	school photos $20
sports fees (each) $70	buy annual $25
lab fees $20-50	scientific calculator $80
sports shoes $100	computer $200
$330- 360	$345-405

Kelsey: **If you want to fit in, you need to join in. That's why I sell jewelry. I ❤ school annuals and activities and the dressy dances. Secret: I make my own dresses, but please, never tell anyone, K?**

Meg: **K.**

Kelsey: **Put the calculator and the computer on your Must list. The pub library computers are old so use CTE when you can. Best to have your own.**

Meg signed off, revised her list, and slipped it back into her pocket. Mom would faint when she saw all the fees. Finding a job on weekends sounded like a partial solution, but what was she qualified to do?

12

FOR THE DAYS MEG STAYED after to use CTE or attended volleyball camp, Mom needed a sitter. One day a solution arrived at their door.

Toby raced to Meg and signed someone was at the door. Together they opened the door to a very short, older woman leaning on a gnarled wooden cane.

"Hello. I'm Ms. Iris. I live down the hall. I'm sorry to bother you, but is this your package? I found it at my door." The woman held out the package like it contained a live venomous snake.

Meg looked at the return and the name and address on the package. "No. You'll need to ask the manager."

Ms. Iris looked tired and slightly distressed. "Those steps are trouble for me. Do you think this lovely young man could take it down to him?"

Toby reached for the box, but Meg stopped him. "Yes. We'll take care of it."

"Thank you so much, my dear. I've been meaning to come and meet you ever since you moved in, but I haven't made it until now."

Mom appeared on the landing with a bag of groceries. "Invite her inside, kids."

Ms. Iris straightened and walked into the apartment. Mom set down the groceries and took off her jacket. "I'm Della Appens. These are my two children, Megan, and Toby. Please. Sit down. I was about to have a cup of tea. Will you join me?"

Toby gathered up his and Meg's homework and disappeared into their bedroom. Meg set the kettle on the burner and got down two cups before she joined Toby. Both would have loved to know who the lady was and what was being said, but homework called, and Mom insisted they follow their daily routine.

As it turned out Ms. Iris was a retired schoolteacher who'd lived in the building for several years. She spent much of each day doing word searches and checking her deceased family and friends on Ancestry. She also enjoyed babysitting her great-grandchildren and for friends, as well as for people living in the building.

After a late dinner, Mom sat down with Meg and Toby and signed, "Ms. Iris watches several children in her apartment. She's given me the names of two families she works for that have kids Toby's age. I've called them. They say she's kind as an angel."

Toby bounced up and down as he signed, "Can she be my sitter?"

Mom grinned. "Yes. I've asked her to watch you as a trial visit tomorrow and the next day for the hours before Meg gets home. If things work out, we'll use her for days when Meg or I am late. Toby, you won't need to go to the daycare except for emergencies. Ms. Iris will fix snacks for you and the other kids she watches. After homework, you'll have time to play with kids your age."

Toby jumped up and ran around the apartment, gathered up his homework, a favorite game, and his jacket. "I'm ready. When can I go to her apartment?"

Mom laughed. "Tomorrow. Now, let's get back to finishing your homework and then into the shower. It's almost bedtime."

THE TRIAL RUN WITH Ms. Iris was a huge success, Toby couldn't stop talking about her, the toys, and all the books in her apartment. "She even has a spare room where we can put down a racetrack, and we don't even need to put it away when we go home. When can I go back?"

Meg was relieved once Ms. Iris started watching Toby. Having the time to participate in the city volleyball league gave her the chance to be active and meet other girl athletes. Once they understood she was deaf, they found ways to get her attention and take advantage of her skills. Once the high school team basketball tryouts arrived, she'd be ready to try out, hopefully she'd make the team.

Ms. Iris keeping Toby also meant Meg could stay after school and use the Tech Center for projects and assignments. Without an interpreter, the freedom to stay after school provided a way to keep up *most* of her class work.

Ms. IRIS APARTMENT BECAME TOBY'S second home. After school, he and two other kids from his class scampered up the stairs and knocked on her door. They listened for the sound of her cane and her footsteps crossing the wooden floor, followed by the slow process of her unlatching a series of locks before she could open the door and let them in.

Some days, Toby knocked and pretended to be an alien wanting to get inside. Other days, he or the other kids changed their voices to sound like lost kittens. Ms. Iris loved their antics but always made certain who was there before she opened the door. In fact, they used a secret password: Lulu Belle, and a secret signal of three knocks, a pause, and three more knocks.

"Now, Toby, any other time you need me, remember to knock, then say the secret password. I'll let you in quick as I can. You never know when you might need help."

Ms. Iris's wide variety of toys entertained her great- grand-children and her 'young friends' as she called the children she watched. Toby could play with any toys whenever he stayed with her, which was at least three days a week. His favorites remained the gigantic box of Legos and an ancient box of Lincoln logs. He mixed them together to create villages for his toy cars, half of which he now left with Ms. Iris. Other 'young friends' left theirs as well, filling a communal box with assorted vehicles.

After she fixed snacks, it was homework hour. She had a large kitchen table with space for all her 'young friends' to sit together but work independently on whatever needed to be done. Her couch became her help desk for times they needed assistance. Later, she left the children to play in the spare room, checking in on them from time to time to make sure they were safe.

Half an hour later was story time with the children seated around her, listening to stories and singing silly songs. Their favorite books to be shared again and again remained *The Boxcar Children* and *The Magic Treehouse* stories. This lasted until parents began collecting their children.

Ms. Iris represented a true blessing for the Appens and many other families.

13

THE INSTANT MEG SAW HER interpreter she knew disaster was about to strike.

She blew into the room like a girl crashing a party. Her ratted black hair stuck out in all directions and her jacket was buttoned crooked. But her smile was disarming.

The young woman was ninety minutes late for her meet-up with Meg in the counselor's office. Ms. Gillis stepped back as the young woman swept into the office and flopped down in a cushy chair behind the straight-backed chair where Meg sat waiting.

She let her book bag drop, exploding across the floor, spilling out an assortment of items: a wallet, a cosmetic bag, a hairbrush laden with stray hair, two chick-lit novels, a bag of trail mix, two bottles of nail polish, a ring of keys, a handful of hair scrunchies, a collapsible umbrella, three file folders, numerous rumpled papers, a package of apple and cinnamon instant oatmeal with a plastic spoon taped onto the side, and assorted pens and chewed pencils.

She pawed through everything until she found what she needed; then she stuffed everything back in her bag. She stood and handed Ms. Gillis her certificate. "Where do I sign up and where's my client?"

Ms. Gillis paused then made introductions. "Ms. Louise Feld, this is Meg Appens. She's a junior and..."

Louise stepped forward, cracked her wad of gum, and reached out to shake Meg's hand. "Very... glad... to... meet... you.

The way her neck muscles strained, and the slow way her mouth opened and closed, Meg felt positive Louise was shouting. The way Ms. Gillis drew away from Louise confirmed her observation.

Ms. Gillis straightened an already straight pile of papers on her desk and reached for a folder labeled 'Meg/Interpreter'. "Let's begin." She motioned Louise forward to sit beside Meg then handed her the folder. "These are our expectations and our code of conduct you are to follow as long as you work with Meg."

Louise nodded.

"First, you must arrive on time to walk with her to classes before the tardy bell sounds. Once you arrive to a classroom the first time, introduce yourself to the teacher and find out where you are allowed to stand for signing. Make sure Meg has a seat in the front row of every class.

"Second. You are expected to interpret *details* of what is said in class, especially when the teacher has turned away, preventing Meg from reading his or her lips."

Louise looked at Meg. "So. You...can...read...lips?"

Meg nodded, hoping her irritation with Louise didn't show.

Louise signed, "Cool."

Ms. Gillis continued: "Three. It's your job to be certain she has *all* assignments. Some teachers move around while giving instructions. Record all directions given out."

"Got it. Should I write this down?"

"Please."

Louise dug out a paper and pencil. "Can you go back and repeat everything?"

Ms. Gillis repeated her comments and went on. "Four. Sign in and out at the main office each day. Your hours will match Meg's except for lunch which is your break. Please eat on campus. There's not enough time for you to leave and get back before our afternoon classes begin. Any questions?"

"Just one. How often do I get paid?"

Ms. Gillis looked from Louise to Meg and back to Louise before she answered. "The last school day of each month. Any other questions?"

"Does the lunchroom serve lattes?"

"No. Now, please sign these forms. Today is Tuesday so you both need to get to Meg's English class."

After Louise signed all the paperwork, including the code of conduct form, Ms. Gillis opened her office door. "A reminder: the first two weeks are a trial period for your services. When you have questions, you're welcome to make an appointment to speak with me. Mostly, however, you need to ensure you're meeting Meg's needs."

Meg signed, "English class is half over. We need to hurry."

Louise snapped her gum, then signed, "Let's get going!"

As they entered the English classroom, Mr. Vance looked up and stopped his conversation with the class. "May I help you?"

Louise hurried forward and shook his hand. "I'm Meg's interpreter. She's deaf." Louise scanned the room and turned back to Mr. Vance. "She needs to sit up front so she can see better. Where do you want me to stand?"

Mr. Vance explained what was happening to the class. He asked a student seated in the front row to move to an empty seat in the back and nodded to Meg to sit down.

Meg felt eyes burn into her back as she sat in the prime seat in the classroom. *I'm not making friends with Louise's abrupt manner.*

Louise waved to the class, then turned her attention onto the teacher, who returned to the lesson, then began giving out instructions for the first writing assignment: "Think about how you will write your autobiography in one page. Include information about yourself to interest your classmates."

Mr. Vance turned to write the due date on the board. It appeared he continued talking while his back was turned. Meg watched Louise watch him. She wasn't writing down anything or signing what was said.

Mr. Vance pointed to the posted calendar. "It's due in two weeks and accounts for 1/4 of your term grade. I'll post the details and the rubric online. Read and follow them."

The bell rang. He looked over the class and nodded. "Class dismissed."

The students hurried out of the room. Meg and Louise followed them. "How was that?" Louise asked.

"Not great. I think the teacher shared more details than you signed. Did you write them down?"

"Oops. Next time." Louise signed. "I usually edit. Just share the highlights, not every single detail. Is that ok?"

"Not really. Please share the details or sign them to me."

Louise rolled her eyes. "You're kind of fussy, aren't you?"

Meg hesitated before signing her next comment; she needed to address Louise's aggressive manner with the teacher. "I'd like to sit to one side in my other classes so I can see more of what is said when teachers turn away. Also, please talk more privately when we go into my classes. Most of the students don't know I'm deaf."

"How come?"

"I don't want them to think I need special treatment."

"But you do. I'm supposed to get you what you need."

"I know, but please do it quietly and privately."

Louise squinted and scrunched up her mouth like a sulky teen television brat and answered. "Okay, boss."

Luckily, after Science came lunch, giving Meg a break from the slap-dash signing and from Louise creating a distraction. While Meg ate lunch, Louise wandered off to scan the cafeteria food service offerings. She returned with a can of juice and a banana. She flounced down beside Meg and stare around the cafeteria, avoiding speaking with her.

As they entered PE class, Meg felt relieved. Louise didn't need to ask for favors. But Louise took it upon herself to pull the teacher aside, talk to her for at least five minutes, constantly pointing to Meg, drawing the waiting students to follow her pointing. Standing mere inches from Ms. Young, she began signing the directions for today's PE activity, moving her hands like a symphony conductor. Her paisley dress and her bright red nail polish made her signing gestures difficult to distinguish from her outfit. Her exaggerated moves ended with unnecessary flourishes. After weeks of Meg effectively faking what to do, today proved a true disaster; she felt exhausted watching Louise sign.

If the floor had a soft spot where Meg could drop through, she'd have taken it. Louise *may* have had good intentions, but she didn't possess much common sense. For being a certified interpreter, she didn't listen well. Meg chose to ignore her in favor of watching the others in class and copying their movements. That worked moderately well until she noticed Louise staring her direction and shaking her head.

Louise marched up to her and, in front of the class, began a viscous tirade of both speaking and signing her displeasure with Meg's inattention to *her* directions.

Before the end of the day, people in heads-together conversations pointed toward Meg and her new human appendage. The days of her blending-in crashed to an end. Would her status skyrocket or dip below zero? By the end of the week, she'd know if she could survive Louise.

MEG LOOKED OUT THE APARTMENT bathroom window, hoping to see Kelsey in the alley shooting hoops. Finally, she arrived! She had a good eye and aim from the right post position; her left side was less accurate. With Meg's long arms and her dominant left side, they'd make a good pair if they ever played on the same team at the same time. She fed Toby his afterschool snack, grabbed her basketball, and they headed out to join Kelsey.

"Lift your shooting arm higher," Meg called out.

Kelsey did and swish. She made her shot without disturbing the net. She grabbed the rebound and shot it to Meg. "Thanks."

Meg passed the ball to Toby, who ran, jumped, and let it fly, reaching halfway to the hoop. The threesome passed both balls and shot for several minutes, enjoying the chilly air, the silliness of using two balls simultaneously, and the camaraderie of fellow basketball enthusiasts.

As the light began to fade, Kelsey held her ball and tossed Meg's to Toby. He kept running around, shooting baskets while the girls sat against the wall and pulled out their phones.

Kelsey: **Want to talk about it?**

Meg waggled her hand and shrugged.

Kelsey: **I bet it's your interpreter. Most people thought you were shy. Guess her being at school changes things.**

Meg: **Louise is terrible. I'm definitely an oddity now. People ignore me or stare or shout at me.**

Kelsey: **That's crazy. Why...**

Kelsey saw Meg's distress without saying another word. *Should I talk with my friends, see if they'd allow Meg to hang out with them? What will her being around with Louise stuck to her like glue do to my being included in their little confidences? I doubt Louise can keep a secret. Glad I don't have to cope with her every day!*

Meg pocketed her phone then picked up Kelsey's ball and tossed the ball to Toby with such force it sailed over his head, bounced off the building, flew against the dumpster, and rolled to a stop by the alley doorway.

Kelsey saw Meg's eyes glisten, but no tears fell. She tapped Meg's arm and pulled out her phone again.

Kelsey: **There's a football game Friday night and a dance after. Do you go to dances? I mean can you hear?**

Meg felt a tiny shift in her relationship with Kelsey. Just the way she asked questions was changing. Maybe she cared a little, or she was filing away details to share with her group.

Meg: **I hear very loud music and feel the beat pulse.**

Kelsey: **Come with me to the game and the dance? My dad loves football. He'll drive us, watch the game, and pick us up after the dance.**

Meg tucked away her phone, grabbed up a ball, and bounced it, giving herself time to think. She nodded then flung the ball against the wall, retrieved it, turned, and shot from three-point range. Swish.

Kelsey grabbed Meg's sleeve. "Are you angry with me?"

"What?"

"You're acting angry."

"I am?

"Yeah."

Meg looked away then turned to face Kelsey, her hands rigid against her statue-like stance. *Am I angry? No...maybe ...I don't know.*

Kelsey watched her, waiting for an answer. When none came, she walked inside and down the steps to her family apartment leaving Meg to round up both balls and gesture to Toby to head in.

Meg exhaled deeply as she climbed the stairs to their apartment. Maybe she was angry, but was it with Louise or herself? She'd need to handle it before school tomorrow.

DURING DINNER, SHE PICKED AT her food, then helped her mom clean up the dishes before taking herself off to do homework on her bed, behind the folding screen.

Meg thought about her conversation in the alley. *Kelsey's been hot and cold as a friend. One minute, she helps me decorate the folding screen or shoot hoops. The next she ignores me at school. She zeroed in on my anger before I identified it. Is she right when she says everyone thinks I'm angry? Is being the only deaf student in school changing who I am and how I act? Maybe.*

She slammed her history book closed and flopped back on her bed, wiping her eyes.

Mom appeared beside her bed and signed, "What's wrong, honey?"

She signed, "Nothing. Everything. Why couldn't Dad let us live in Gran's house? What made him so mad he left us?"

Mom sat down beside her. "Your dad needed a change. There's nothing we can do about what he needed for himself. We must take each day as it comes, try to move forward, and take care of ourselves."

"What makes us so unlovable?"

"Your dad still loves you and Toby. Things will get better. Once the kids at school get to know you, they'll see the talented young woman I know."

Meg nodded and let her tears flow as her mother drew her snugly into her arms.

14

MEG FIDGETED AS SHE DRESSED for school. Would Kelsey talk with her friends, really? Friday's football game was creeping closer. Did she even want to tag along with Kelsey's group?

Meg's stomach gurgled. Was it hunger or nervousness? She opted to skip breakfast but grabbed a snack as she made her lunch before hurrying down the stairs. Kelsey sat on the bottom step. As Meg arrived, Kelsey stood up.

"What's the sign for good morning?"

Meg showed her.

"What's the sign for I'm sorry?"

Meg's hands flowed.

Kelsey signed, 'I'm sorry', then picked up her backpack and held the door open for Meg to exit the building. They arrived at the bus stop as the line of workers and students stepped on.

Kelsey slipped into the first empty seat and beckoned Meg to join her. They sat side-by-side in silence, watching the city views slide by.

ONCE OFF THE BUS, KELSEY stepped aside and pulled Meg's arm to stop before she headed up the front steps to the building. "I'm sorry," she signed a bit clumsily then confessed aloud, "I'll talk with them today."

Meg nodded and walked off, focusing on Friday's football game and dance. *If they don't want me around, should I go alone, or would that look desperate? What if I go with Kelsey and the group rejects me or makes fun of me? — Why is this so complicated?*

As she waited for Louise by the office, she watched students surge through the main hallway, laughing and talking, pushing and shoving their way to classes. *Do any of them ever feel isolated or worry about having friends? Do they ever look around to notice the kids who were excluded from groups or kids they never speak to? Probably not. Do I ignore people? Maybe.*

HAVING LOUISE ACT AS HER interpreter continued to be a disaster. Without Kelsey's help, she'd have missed vital details since she'd forgotten about teacher office hours. Louise called Advisory and teacher hours a dumb waste of time. Plus, she failed to record any mention of make-up or extra credit assignments.

Her class notes made Meg think she'd be better off without Louise's fumbling, inaccurate flourishes while signing. She looked and acted more like an actress than an interpreter. Her skirts? Way too short. Her blouses? Too sheer or low-cut. Her makeup? Too exaggerated. Her signing gestures? Way too flowery to be the words spoken in the classrooms. Didn't Louise realize she was not auditioning for a role in a 'B' movie or TV a crime show?

Was there any solution? Would telling Ms. Gillis how inept Louise was get her fired? Did she deserve to be fired? Probably, but I'll give her a few more days before I decide. Without her, it could mean no interpreter for the rest of the year.

Louise raced into the building like her hair was on fire. "Sorry," she signed. "Locked myself out of my car (or was she saying something about a cat?) "Had to take a bus (or did she mean a trip?)"

Much of what Louise shared bordered on confusion and inaccuracy.

The rest of the day, Louise didn't improve. Meg's lunch on her own felt like a vacation until she saw Kelsey sitting with her friends. *I don't care if Kelsey's group doesn't want me around. No. That's a lie; I care. Maybe Mom and Toby will come to the game with me. Probably not. Am I angry with Kelsey or myself?*

She bit into her PB and J sandwich and looked away from where Kelsey sat, but her eyes crept back toward them. Her heart raced as she watched them talk and turn to stare at her. She packed up her lunch and moved herself further away to sit with her back to them.

"May I sit down?"

A long pair of legs in jeans stood in front of Meg. She looked up and up.

"May I sit down?"

She nodded. It was the guy from the counseling office, way back when she first arrived at Sherman Harrison.

He set down his lunch tray and sat down before swinging his legs over the seat, directly across from her.

Meg felt a tingle of excitement; someone wanted to sit with her. She dipped her head and took a bite of her sandwich before she looked toward him again.

"I think we're in English together. Mr. Vance. Second period? Right?"

She nodded, took out her phone, typed a message and turned it so he could read it.

Meg: **I sat behind you.**

He nodded, kept hold of her phone and entered his number. He wrote a message before handing it back to her.

Eli: **Meg, right? How do you like Mr. Vance?**

She nodded, texted him at his number, and looked up.

Meg: **I like his jokes.**

Eli: **What's with the crazy lady up front, waving her hands?**

Meg: **That's Louise, my interpreter. She's a bit unusual.**

Eli: **I'll say. I'm Eli Johnson.**

He reached out his knuckles for a fist bump. As she bumped her fists against his, heat moved up her neck and spread onto her face.

He took a monstrous bite of his burger and asked something muffled by the food in his mouth. Then he laughed.

Eli: **Are you coming to Friday's game?**

Meg: **Maybe. Are you?**

Eli: **I'd better be there. I'm the quarterback.**

The heat on her face intensified, as if to burn away her skin. She smiled.

Meg: **I guess it would be a problem if you stayed home.**

Eli nodded, inhaled the rest of his burger, and gulped down two cartons of milk. He wiped his mouth on his sleeve and texted before he stood.

Eli: **See you there. Save me a dance.**

Poof, he was away like a rocket, or maybe she should say like a quarterback ready to toss a game-winning pass.

She felt a happy bubble travel from her toes to her chest. *Eli Johnson, the Sherman Harrison quarterback, sat at her table and talked with her. Wait 'til Kelsey hears about this!*

KELSEY AND THE ENTIRE SCHOOL knew about Eli sitting at her table during lunch. Only Kelsey had access to the details.

Kelsey: **So. Lunch with Eli Johnson? Dish.**

Meg: **Dish?**

Kelsey: **Tell me about eating with Eli. Spill.**

Meg: **We agree. Mr. Vance has good jokes. He asked if I was coming to the football game.**

Kelsey: **Are you? My friends want to meet you, especially after Eli Johnson ate lunch with you.**

Meg grimaced at Kelsey. Was she joking?

Kelsey: **They want to meet you. Show me the sign for absolutely.**

Meg showed her the sign.

Kelsey signed 'absolutely', then headed to her next class.

Meg floated through her afternoon classes, then sobered when she saw Louise flirting with the cute guy who sat next to her in CTE. She sat down and pretended to be busy until class started. *Louise can massacre ASL as much as she wants today. I'm going to ignore her. I'll check today's assignment online before signing out.*

A BRISK BREEZE SWIRLED AROUND the football field Friday evening as the band marched and the cheer squad performed midfield. Meg tucked the blanket under her legs, pulled Toby close, and signed, "Are you warm enough?"

Toby nodded but leaned into her. She was glad to be out with Mom and Toby; much safer than being with Kelsey's crew and way less intimidating. Seeing them, maybe meeting them at the dance would come soon enough. Shortly she'd learn if they'd accept her or see her as a charity case to be tolerated.

Mom touched Meg's hand and signed, "This is a good idea. It's great to be out in the fall air. Reminds me of Gran's harvest celebration."

Just then the band formed a giant S and H on the playing field. Everyone stood and turned to face the large flagpole by the side of the field for the national anthem. Minutes later the teams stepped onto the field.

Meg spotted Eli on the sidelines, warming up. He threw the ball with a lot of force and didn't look any place beyond the targets of those tosses.

She knew little about the game of football, so she contented herself by watching the two teams crash into each other and push each other around like arguing brothers. She lost sight of Eli except when he moved back and tossed the ball to a player who tried to race closer to the end of the field. Dad would have probably loved watching the game, but she didn't know where he'd landed or if he even cared about football anymore.

Suddenly, everyone in the stands stood and danced around. "Big score," Mom signed.

Meg stood so she could see the field. Students cheered and did the strange action they'd done in assembly: a kind type of quiet signal with their fingers to their lips, moving from left to right. She still needed to ask Kelsey about it.

Eli was being patted on the back by teammates as a kicker sent the ball through the posts at the end of the field. Soon the game settled down to both teams running back and forth and exchanging the ball with long kicks. Final score: Fishermen 7, Visitors 6.

MEG WALKED MOM AND TOBY to the street, where they caught the city bus home. "You'll be okay riding home with Kelsey?"

"Yes," she signed. "Home before 11:00, unless we go for ice cream after the dance. I'll text you."

She watched them step onto the bus; then she turned back toward the school cafeteria. The lights had been dimmed; students milled around in small groups. She looked for Kelsey but didn't see her at first. Then she spotted her, standing with several girls who weren't paying much attention to the music she felt vibrating through her body. The student gyrations in the open area resembled the ones she saw on the TV teen shows; few students moved as couples, opting to freestyle *near* others without any touching.

Eli stood with a small group of guys, probably reliving the game. A cluster of anxious-faced girls headed their way, shyly looking at them and moving closer and closer with fake nonchalance. So-o obvious.

The players appeared to enjoy their attention; some walked out to dance with the bouncing mob in the center of the cafeteria-turned into a dance floor.

As she watched, Eli pushed through the assembled girls and headed toward her. "You're here. Did you go to the game?" he mouthed slowly.

She nodded. "You played very well."

"Thanks. Do you want to dance?"

"Sure." A sudden bravery and playfulness ran through her as Eli reached for her hand and led her onto the dance floor.

THE MUSIC CHANGED FROM STRONG, fast vibrations to a faint, slow beat. One of Eli's arms wrapped around her waist. The other took her hand in his as he stepped slowly forward and back and then side to side. He pulled her closer and put his cheek against hers. She could feel his breath on her face.

Did she like his closeness? She couldn't decide, but probably not. No one usually stood this close, touching her face, her back, and her hands except her family. She stepped back from Eli and smiled as he looked down at her.

When Eli stopped moving, he walked her back to join Kelsey's friends. Before he left, he mouthed, "Thanks for the dance."

The cafeteria quieted as a group of students took over making announcements and exciting the crowd to clap and turn to each other to chat. Kelsey's friends stared at Meg, waiting. What did they want from her?

"Eli, huh?" Kelsey said as she nudged Meg. "Nice going."

The group of girls leaned close, waiting for her to share something. She crossed her arms and looked down to the floor. When she said nothing, the group pulled back and began a conversation as the DJ began spinning music with a throbbing beat once again.

Meg moved to an open table to sit and watch the dancing. She noticed Eli danced with a couple other girls, but he didn't dance cheek-to-cheek with them. She felt a tingle of smugness lighten her mood. It appeared Eli liked her.

THE RIDE WITH KELSEY AND her dad was subdued. Once they returned home, Kelsey invited her to come to her bedroom, where they sat facing each other to text.

Kelsey: **Eli? How do you know him?**

Meg felt her face heat up: **Mr. Vance**

Kelsey made a strange face Meg couldn't interpret

Kelsey: **Girls will be jealous of his sitting and talking and dancing with you. He's popular. He's always looking for compliments. Be cautious, Meg.**

As she headed upstairs, she wondered what Kelsey was trying to say. *Is she jealous Eli sat with me? Maybe. Sitting at lunch with Eli was private. I don't intend to share any dance details with Kelsey, at least not yet.*

The stove light was on as she tiptoed into the apartment. Her mom woke up, stretched, and signed, "How was the dance?"

"Fun. I even danced."

"Good, honey. Have a good sleep."

Meg straightened Toby under his covers, then sat on her bed, replaying her dance with Eli. That's when she noticed a flashing light outside her window. It came from one of the taller buildings a couple of blocks away. The flashes blinked in an irregular pattern, probably a little kid sneaking a flashlight in his room and playing way after bedtime. She hoped Toby wouldn't get any ideas about copying the behavior. He had such an active imagination he'd likely want to trade beds so he could be next to the window and try it himself.

15

MEG'S LOCKER COMBINATION WAS EASY. Since she had to bring her own lock, she made the combination 4002216: her birth date, backward. The hallway lockers were squishy before school. Kids jostled for space to open their doors wide enough to put in jackets and take out textbooks needed for their morning classes. Lunch time had two sessions, so the crush of hurried, sweaty bodies lessened. Many students gave up and carried their textbooks all day, every day. With her schedule, she discovered she had time to stash morning materials and grab her afternoon needs.

Her biggest problem at the lockers was not knowing when someone approached. As Kelsey headed off the class, she handed her a small package with a note attached:

> Hang this mirror on the inside of your locker door. It's magnetic. That way you won't be startled when someone comes up behind you.

MEG APPRECIATED KELSEY'S CHANGED ATTITUDE since the dance, but she detected a bit of jealousy over Eli's attention, from both Kelsey and her group. She enjoyed a moment of satisfaction that maybe they saw her as a regular person.

Perhaps it would become a permanent improvement.

Having the mirror not only gave her a way to check her togetherness, it also provided a view behind her, allowing her to eavesdrop on conversations.

The locker belonging to Kelsey's friend, Genna, was directly across the hallway. As a member of the cheer squad, she often 'held court' by her locker with other squad members and the 'in' crowd, unaware that Meg observed her conversations via the mirror.

When Meg saw Genna's reflection, she stopped to watch her gesture and point with exaggerated, floppy mock signing. The gathered students laughed and joined in the performance. When popular guys joined the group, the mocking became a comedic commotion. Her confidence sank like a boulder dropped in deep water. So much for fitting in.

As she continued to watch their antics, Eli approached the group. Would he join in mocking her when he thought her back was turned? She watched and waited.

Eli faced away from her, but she noticed the strained cords in his neck. His arms flailed around before he stomped away. It looked as if he'd been angry with them, but, since he didn't stop to speak with her, she wasn't sure. Her worry lasted all day.

Meg missed him at lunch but found a note taped on her locker:

Meet me at the flagpole after school. E.

A CHILLY WIND BUFFETED MEG as she paced around the flagpole waiting for Eli. Since the dance, he took a few minutes each day to meet her after school, hold her hand, and make her laugh at his corny jokes before he raced off to football practice.

At first glance, today was no different. Eli waved and pulled out his phone as he walked closer. She waited for her phone to vibrate.

Eli: **What do you call a cat stuck in a tree?**

Meg:**??**

Eli: **A Cat-tas-tro-tree**

They stood inches apart, smiling and watching each other's eyes.

Eli: **How are you today?**

Meg: **Missed you at lunch.**

Eli: **Met with my math teacher. I need a tutor.**

Meg: **I could help. I ❤ math.**

Eli: **Not surprised. I'll share sports pointers to pay you back.**

Meg's nose scrunched up at the suggestion.

Meg: **How about help with history? Meet at the library down the hill after dinner? Unless you have a game or a date.**

Eli tipped his head and stared at Meg before he replied.

Eli: **A date?? You're the only date I want. See you at the library. We need to talk.**

Meg: **6:30 at the library.**

Eli grinned and hurriedly kissed her cheek before racing away.

The kissed spot on her cheek heated up but soon gave way to the swirling chill of the wind. *What does he want to talk about? Does he know I watched Genna and the crowd mock me?*

That's too embarrassing to bring up. But what else could it be?

Since she'd missed the bus and because it was a crisp autumn day, she opted to walk home rather than stand around shivering half an hour for the next bus. Her brain rambled through a mixture of thoughts. *Should I share anything with Kelsey about my time with Eli? Maybe not, especially after today. He's acting jumpy and a little anxious. Maybe he's ready to move on, but he just said he only wants to date me. Having him in my life might be more trouble than it's worth. I'll wait to worry about this boy-girl stuff until after we talk tonight.*

Meg picked up Toby from Ms. Iris's apartment, and they settled down to family chores. Toby completed his job of taking down the garbage and bringing up the mail before he set the table for dinner. She gathered and sorted laundry, tidied their apartment, and started dinner. Mom's second job provided extra spending money, but Meg still felt she needed to find a job to offset her high school fees, especially if she made the basketball team and needed good court shoes.

After dinner, Meg hurried to the public library and waited for Eli. 6:30 passed, then 6:45 and 7:00. No Eli. Either he'd gotten busy, forgot or… maybe this was him breaking up with her. When he didn't show up by 7:25, she finished her work and headed home. Disappointment tumbled inside her through bedtime and crept into her dreams, which slid into nightmares.

The next morning Mr. Vance stood at the board with his back to the class writing and talking as usual. Louise stood to one side interpreting. Sometimes, she was hard to understand, but Meg was becoming adept at filling in missing details.

"Interesting stories...Most loved ... Pets and Summer."

Sounds easy. Having Belle as her pet calf on Gran's farm was a different kind of story. She might even get extra points for writing about the funny way Belle followed her into the kitchen and tried to go up the stairs to her bedroom.

Even with Louise's pathetic notes, Meg knew she'd complete her first English assignment early. She was surprised Mr. Vance allowed them to start the year writing about their pets and their summer. She hadn't been able to share such simple stories since grade four. Maybe moving into the city and attending a large school would not be as difficult as she'd imagined. Once he returned their papers, she'd know what she needed to work on to keep an 'A' or a 'B'.

Lunchtime she sat at an empty table, watching for Eli. He hurried in, handed her a folded paper, and rushed off.

> *Sunshine could never be so bright*
> *As your touch, but will it burn me?*
> *Moonlight could never be so light*
> *As your smile, but will it soothe me?*
> *E*

She read and reread the poem, trying to understand what Eli was trying to say. She'd need to wait until they met at the library Saturday to ask him, if she felt brave enough. Their working together created a triple advantage for her: he'd get caught up in Math, she'd get caught up in History, and they'd have time to get to know each other.

Trying to explain Math concepts would be a challenge since he didn't know sign. Luckily, Math was a visual subject. Too bad History involved reading and sorting out which events were most important. However, the thought of spending time with him away from school created butterflies; she hadn't anticipated their wings beating so furiously, especially when she still had no idea what he wanted to talk about.

SATURDAY NOON AT THE PUBLIC library. Eli was hours late. Meg fidgeted as she sat in the teen section, working, but waiting. She'd finished her math, read the Physics assignment, and started answering the assigned chapter questions. Maybe he wasn't coming. She could have taken Toby to Stan's Market as planned.

Eli approached the table where she sat. He looked exhausted. "I overslept. Sorry."

She nodded and watched him unpack his backpack and settle into the seat next to her. His arms were bruised. The side of his face as well. She pointed to the bruises.

"Football. We won."

She resisted the urge to touch his bruises, the way she'd touch Toby's. Eli was slowly making his way into a caring place inside her, one usually reserved for special friends and relatives. Was the feeling mutual?

Their time together passed quickly. Eli helped her with history by pointing out key paragraphs in the latest assignment. He wrote notes to her about the author's intent, explaining the importance of the time period. She laid out his math problems in their extended form, drew arrows, and wrote brief notes to him. When she checked her watch, it was three o'clock, the time she'd promised to be back home.

Eli dropped her off, but his earlier request to talk with her remained unmentioned.

ONE WEEK LATER, AFTER MR. Vance finished his latest lecture, he passed out the class biography papers. When she opened it, her eyes widened, and her pulse quickened. 'F'

Meg slammed the pages closed and looked around. Had anyone seen her score? She trembled as she reopened her paper and read the red pen comments covering her work: Not appropriate topic, Needs to pay attention in class. See me after class or after school.

As the room cleared, she and Louise stood beside Mr. Vance's desk. He looked at Louise and then at Meg. "Ms. Feld. How did Meg know to write about her summer and her pets?"

Louise flirted with him in her perky, head-twisting manner. "I told her, of course. She can't read your lips when you face the board."

"Ms. Feld. What I said was *do not* write about your summer or your pets. Perhaps *you* should rewrite this paper."

Louise bristled and thrust out her chin. "I'm not allowed to write for her, just interpret what you say. If she made mistakes, it's her problem."

Mr. Vance shook his head, pulled his lips tight, and turned to face Meg. He spoke with her slowly and with calmness while Louise signed to her. "This was not your fault, but you need to redo this paper. You have one week to write one or a maximum of two pages. Pick a personal biographic topic you are willing to share aloud with the class. Do *not* write about your summer or any pets. Any questions?"

She shook her head.

"Come in during my afterschool hours for help and check my assignments online every day." He looked at Louise and back to Meg. "You need to take responsibility for your assignments."

Meg nodded and quickly left the room before she lost control.

In the hall, she glared at Louise's perky face, which showed no remorse for what had happened. What a nightmare! How had she gotten the assignment backward? Perhaps most of the rest of her signing was also wrong. Time to follow Kelsey's advice to daily double check assignments on her own and get notes from a reliable student in every class, especially English and History.

Louise disappeared while Meg ate lunch. When she rejoined Meg, she walked ahead of her all the way to PE, preventing Meg from confronting her. With each step closer to PE, Meg's anger rose. At the door to the locker room, she grabbed Louise's arm, pulling her to a stop and signed, "How did you make such a big mistake in my English class?

"I just signed what he said. He must have misspoken."

"No. He's the teacher. Please be more careful. Get the details, especially in English and History."

"Okay. I'm just saying —"

Meg hurried away from Louise to change for PE. At least over the next eighty minutes, she could burn off some of her frustration as she worked through the class conditioning circuit.

Luckily, Math class was easy and straightforward. She was getting 'A's' and extra credit for completing *all* the problems at the end of the chapters. Maybe she should be doing more than was assigned in *every* class. She'd get Mr. Vance's English assignment done first, then work through her other classes to make certain she'd not missed other assignments before it was too late to turn them in.

Meg sat tapping her pencil on the desk, deciding what she felt comfortable sharing about herself. So far, she was still an oddity with few friends: Kelsey and Eli her most treasured. She started her rewrite. Sharing whatever she wrote aloud was the kicker. Speaking with strangers tired her, but no way would she let Louise speak for her and ruin this chance to introduce herself to her classmates the way she wanted it done.

She allowed her ideas to percolate for two days before deciding she was ready to write about her journey into silence. *Might as well see where it goes.*

MEG SET HER FINISHED PAPER into Mr. Vance's turn-in tray. She'd processed and printed two copies at the public library last night. Now the wait began. Putting herself and her ideas on paper was a risk she needed to take, regardless of how it improved or permanently destroyed her acceptance at Sherman Harrison.

During the evening, she and Kelsey texted back and forth from their apartments about their day and the redo of their autobiographies.

Kelsey: **I hated writing about myself. Writing about crafting jewelry sounded show-offy so for my rewrite I changed to write about moving here. Now it sounds dull.**

Meg: **Mine's about being deaf.**

Kelsey: **Sounds brave. Glad you wrote it?**

Meg: **Not sure.**

Kelsey: **Want me to read it tonight?**

Meg: **No. I want you to hear it in class; then maybe you'll let me know what students are saying about it?**

Kelsey: **Got it. Off to more homework. Later.**

OVER THE NEXT FEW DAYS, students in Mr. Vance's class shared their life stories aloud. He sat at the back, writing notes but not asking questions; he left that to his students. The presenters shared a variety of topics: an accomplishment, a trip influencing their life, loss of a special relative, and so on. They each handled a handful of questions, then sat down with sighs of relief. Louise held her position off to the side through every speech, performing with flourishes and odd bits of information Meg no longer believed to be the truth.

On Friday, when Meg's turn arrived, Louise perked up, stepped toward Meg, and waved to the students. Meg glared at Louise and signed "I'm doing this myself."

Louise grimaced, then shrugged, and sat down in Meg's seat. Her lips formed a perfect, practiced pout.

Meg looked around the classroom, avoiding Eli's and Kelsey's smiles. Once she'd decided to sign and speak for herself, she knew she needed to avoid looking at Eli if she wanted to keep her concentration on her paper. Besides, he'd not been around or texted or called her lately. Maybe he didn't care what she had to say.

Her hands felt slick with sweat; her heart raced as if she'd completed a marathon. Louise sat back with her arms crossed, looking defiant instead of supportive. Meg set her pages on the lectern. She began reading aloud and signing simultaneously.

```
    When I was little, I could hear
everything: TV cartoons, my mom calling to
me, rain on the window, the phone ringing,
and the neighbor's cat scratching on our
door to get in. But that changed.
    I became ill with a disease called
meningitis. It comes from a bacteria.
Usually babies and teens get it, but I got
it when I was five.
```

Mine started with a fever, nausea, and
a headache. The light bothered my eyes.
Mom took me to the doctor, and he sent
me to the hospital. I stayed in intensive
care for several days. They gave me and my
family medicine. It took weeks for me to
feel better.

Soon after, the world became quiet, like
all sounds were turned down to low. In a
few weeks, everyone and everything grew
silent.

Now, I hear only extremely loud sounds
like fire and police sirens when they are
close by. I feel bass music like at the
school dances or a street jack-hammer
pounding near me. The rest you hear is
totally silent for me.

Sometimes, I feel alone, bullied, and
mocked. It's not pleasant.

I've learned to finger spell, use ASL to
talk with my hands, and I also read lips.
I often know what you are saying about me,
even from a distance.

I'm the only deaf person in this school,
but there are many famous deaf such as
Helen Keller; actor Marlee Matlin; the
model,actor, and deaf activist Nyle Di
Marco; the deaf writer and rapper Warren
'Wave' Snipe.

I want you to know I am not disabled.
I can do anything you can do, except hear.
My sense of smell and other senses are
stronger than most of yours.

I've been told people used to chant
this rhyme: 'Sticks and stones may break
my bones, but words will never hurt me.'
But that's not true. Words *can* hurt and *do*
hurt, even when people are deaf.

When she finished, the class sat motionless, staring at her.
It appeared she'd spoken too freely. She braced for an awkward
silence during the five minutes allowed for questions.

Seconds passed like hours. Suddenly, a sea of hands rose. She looked around. Mr. Vance began calling on her classmates. Meg called up Louise to sign the questions to her. As a spur of the moment decision, she decided to continue signing and speaking her answers to all questions. Louise looked miffed, but she did her part. However, she gave Meg a look that would have withered her had she not been so determined to control her project.

"What is it like being deaf? Do you hear any noise around you?"

"It can be peaceful. Sometimes, it's lonely because people leave me out of conversations. They think I have nothing to say, but I have a lot I like to share."

"Do your parents sign?"

"Yes. My mom, my brother, and my uncle sign ASL. That's American Sign Language. It's considered a world language. Some schools teach it like they teach French, Russian, or German."

"Do you miss hearing?"

"Sometimes. I would love to hear my mother's voice and listen to Toby playing space wars. I'd like to hear them say my name. Most of all, I miss hearing my family say, 'I love you.'"

"How should we let you know we want to talk to you?"

"Tap my shoulder to get my attention. Better yet, stand in front of me so I can read your lips. Also, speak clearly but don't shout and please, don't cover your mouth when you talk."

As the question time was ending, Eli raised his hand. "Can you teach us a few simple signs?"

She looked to Mr. Vance. "I imagine you mean swear words."

Smiles and laughter greeted her.

Mr. Vance frowned, then smirked. A twinkle lit his eyes, suggesting she be careful.

Meg shared, hello, thank you, good, and laughing. "This last word is what I use when I'm angry."

SHE SMILED INWARDLY. NO ONE except Louise would know that she'd signed peanut butter. Finally, she'd had the last word in a room full of hearing students, and it wasn't even close to a swear word. She expected to see it in use around the school very soon.

Mr. Vance stood and walked forward. He spoke and signed "Thank you".

To the class he said, "Meg brought copies of the ASL hand-signing alphabet for each of you. Take one at the end of class if you're interested."

The students clapped as she collected her notes and returned to her seat. A moment of success traveled over her like a silk ribbon sliding across her arms, winding her into a comfortable cocoon. Shortly she'd know how her story affected her acceptance in the school.

Louise returned to the front to interpret the other life stories for Meg's benefit. A bubble of laughter rose as she admired her own bravery to speak without Louise's over-the-top theatrics and her clumsy interpretations. There was no doubt the outcome from her talk would be completely different if she'd let Louise present her paper.

AS MEG LEFT THE ROOM, she sent a quick text to Mr. Vance.

Meg: **I signed peanut butter not a real swear word.**

On her way to Physics class a light tap on her shoulder stopped her. She turned. It was Eli.

"Nice talk."

Her cheeks warmed as she nodded and signed 'thank you'.

"Are you coming to the next football game and the dance?"

She shrugged but grinned and waggled her hand side to side.

Eli gave her thumbs up and turned back toward the main hall to head to his next class. Over the past two weeks, he'd still not explained why or what he wanted to talk about with her. Maybe the moment had passed.

The rest of the afternoon, several students stopped her. She watched the way their throat muscles moved and tightened indicating many of them were shouting to her, as if that helped her understand what they asked. She nodded as best she could in the chaos of hallway student traffic and patiently signed and orally answered their questions. Often, she suggested they text her after school if they had more questions. That usually ended any communication. By after school, many students moved on to their other lives of being independent teens with jobs or sports team practices or family responsibilities.

BACK AT THE APARTMENT SHE and Kelsey went to the rooftop, sat under blankets in the lean-to, and pulled out their cell phones.

Kelsey: **Your talk was great.**

Meg: **THX**

Kelsey: **My friends think you're brave to share about being deaf.**

Meg: **Felt strange**

Kelsey: **Glad it's over?**

Meg: **Yes. Think anyone wants to learn to sign?**

Kelsey: **Yes! You could teach a class. Talk with Ms. Gillis.**

Meg nodded to Kelsey and changed the subject.

Meg: **Can I ride with you to the next football game and dance?**

Kelsey stared at Meg and grinned. She mouthed, "Eli?"
Meg dipped her head and nodded. When she looked up, Kelsey was grinning.

Kelsey: **Guess the rumors are true.**

16

SETTLING INTO A LARGER HIGH school kept her on her toes. Dealing with Louise discouraged her. She suffered every day from misinterpreted and missed directions. Then she received a note during Math class.

> For Meg Appens:
> Report to the counseling office during your lunch break.
> Ms. Gillis

MEG WARMED A COUNSELING BENCH for several minutes before entering Ms. Gillis's office.

Ms. Gillis took out her phone. **"How are you settling in?"**

Meg: **Not great. Louise gets information wrong and leaves off details. Sometimes she's late.**

Ms. Gillis handed her a printout

Ms. Gillis: **I'll speak with her. You're fine on quizzes but missing assignments in some classes. What's going on?**

The list of missing or incomplete assignments filled a page.

Meg: **I didn't know about some. Mr. Vance let me redo my bio. I got B+ instead of 'F'. I spoke and signed it to the class.**

Ms. Gillis: **Good. Do you check class assignments daily?**

Meg ducked her head and exhaled before answering. She hated disappointing people like Ms. Gillis who believed in her.

Meg: **During CTE. No home computer yet.**

Ms. Gillis: **I'm so sorry. I haven't pursued finding one for you to keep at home. New student progress report next week. Bring it in. You'll have 1 week to finish missing assignments. I'll set up an appointment with Ms. Feld.**

Louise and Meg encountered each other outside the main office. Louise signed, "Morning? or should I say afternoon?"

Meg didn't stop to acknowledge her.

Louise hurried after her, spilling her grande latte as they headed to PE class.

As they entered the gym, Meg handed over her excused note from Ms. Gillis and waited for Ms. Young to tell her if she should suit-up or sit out the rest of class.

Louise caught up and signed, "What's wrong?"

Ms. Young pointed to the bleachers; she was to follow sitting-out protocol: sit, watch, and write three detailed observations. Today that felt like a good idea. It might give Louise time to figure out how angry she was without needing to speak with her.

She couldn't concentrate in CTE, but she managed to survive, anxious to head home to work on her missing assignments. Her sadness and self-disappointment about so many missing assignments turned to anger with Louise. She hurriedly left Louise chatting with students, raced out of the school, and boarded the city bus to get home and get busy.

Suddenly, she stopped her wild mental ranting and faced the truth. *I haven't checked my assignment every day. That's my responsibility. Being overwhelmed is no excuse. The way Louise confuses things, I shouldn't expect she's accurate about anything. I'm the one neglecting responsibility. I feel worse than the time I had a dozen hornet stings.*

As she organized her assignments, she received a text.

Kelsey: **Want to study together?**

Meg: **Can't**

Kelsey: **What's wrong?**

Meg: **Everything. Missing assignments.**

Kelsey: **What about Louise?**

Meg: **Total ditz. No help.**

Kelsey: **Want me to pick up your assignments?**

Tears flooded Meg's eyes. She wiped them away with her sleeve.

Meg: **No, but thanks. My job.**

THE NEXT DAY, LOUISE WAS a no-show, making it a good day to stay after school and talk with her teachers to discover how bad things were. First, she'd call her mom to arrange for Toby to stay longer with Ms. Iris. He always loved having her undivided attention.

She visited each teacher, texted her concerns, and made promises to get caught up. Totally exhausted from facing each teacher, she raced to catch a bus and got home with barely enough time to rush through their chores before Mom got home. For some reason, her jump-around brother acted unusually quiet; she'd need to find out why later.

HER TEACHERS FOR THE MOST part appeared to understand her dilemma. Most provided ways for her to make-up missing assignments, except her Physics teacher. Ms. Niven shook her head and said it was too late for any possible ways to improve her grade. She left that classroom disappointed. She should never have trusted Louise once she realized how carelessly she signed conversations. Mom would *not* be pleased.

It turned out Mom was fine. She understood what had happened. Toby was the one who failed to forgive her. She'd forgotten this was the day she'd promised to take him to the nearby bookstore to spend his allowance. When Toby brought it up at the dinner table, Meg closed her eyes and shook her head.

Much as she tried to gentle his mood, he refused to look at her or speak to her the rest of the evening. When she tried to give him a goodnight kiss, he pulled away and covered his head. His shunning hurt more than any missing assignments ever could.

MEG WORKED AT A FEVER-PITCH to complete as much as possible, working night after night 'til midnight before crashing into bed and falling asleep instantly. Each late assignment she completed made her feel better about herself but more and more angry with Louise. Monday morning, Louise would wish she'd stayed home.

LOUISE SAUNTERED INTO MAIN CORRIDOR of the school as

the last bell sounded. She was late, making Meg late as well. But today Meg didn't care. She stood with her arms. crossed, glaring at Louise.

"Let's get moving," Louise signed. "You're late to math. Well, I'm late too, I guess." She pressed on one of her saccharine grins. "Long line at the latte counter today. Must be the cooler weather. Gotta get my morning boost, right?"

Meg continued to glare at her and didn't move as Louise started toward the math classroom.

"Meg? Come on!"

Meg shook her head. "Ms. Gillis is expecting us."

ONCE THEY SAT DOWN, Ms. Gillis handed Louise a copy of Meg's missing assignments. "How do you explain these?

Meg focused on their lips, every gesture, and every blink to grab every detail of every word.

Louise looked at the paper then handed it back to Ms. Gillis. "I guess Meg isn't doing well." She shook her head with a sympathetic look on her face. "Must not be turning in her work on time. I'm doing my best to help her succeed, as much as she's capable of doing."

Ms. Gillis stared at Louise. Meg watched her jaw tighten. "She says you've not given her the details the instructor shares when he or she is turned away from Meg's view."

Louise straightened. "I'm doing my best. I can't make Meg into a stronger student than she is. After all, she's deaf."

Meg followed the exchanges. Her heart raced. She felt certain her blood pressure rose with each excuse Louise offered. *I've been so blind. She didn't care about me to notice I'm a capable person.*

Ms. Gillis stood and reached her hand out to Louise.

"Thank you for your service. You will no longer be needed at Sherman Harrison."

Louise looked shocked. "Does being here now count? I mean, do I get paid for coming today?"

Ms. Gillis guided her to the office door and opened it. "You'll get the pay you've earned. Goodbye, Ms. Feld."

As the door closed Meg began to cry. Ms. Gillis put her hand on her shoulder and sat down in the chair Louise recently vacated. When Meg looked up, Ms. Gillis was smiling.

She pulled out her phone and waited for Meg to do the same.

Ms. Gillis: **Don't worry. I'm searching for a new assistant; someone who cares. Turn in as many missing assignments as possible by Friday. It will be OK.**

OVER THE REST OF THE week Meg noticed her teachers seemed more attuned to her needs, giving directions, and sharing homework assignments while facing the class. By Friday she'd made up two-thirds of her missing assignments and felt an additional shift in the way teachers treated her, showing her more kindness and patience. She went home hopeful that her delayed progress report would show her sincere effort. She'd put too much faith and trust in Louise. She should have paid closer attention to details. Hopefully, her schoolwork would improve with a different interpreter and her being more proactive about checking on assignments.

17

ZACH SPENT MOST OF HIS days off with the Appens family. He'd arrive before noon on Saturday and the four of them would plan an outing around Seattle. On nice days they'd visit the Seattle Center, the Woodland Park Zoo, the Sculpture Garden, or Alki Beach. When the weather turned iffy, they'd head indoors to the Pacific Science Center, the Burke Museum, the aquarium, or to a movie, his treat.

Meg loved having Zach around. He always brought energy and fresh donuts from *Dream Creame Knots*. Toby enjoyed having a pretend big brother to play catch, cards, rough house with, or help plan his homework projects such as building a diorama. Other times, Toby gleefully became Zach's assistant like handing him nails and helping sand when they rebuilt Meg's privacy screen and crafted a bookshelf for the living area.

WITH HALLOWEEN MERE DAYS AWAY, Zach arrived on the weekend with a giant pumpkin. As they ate sandwiches, they planned their carving design.

Toby rubbed his hands over the ridges. "This should be a pirate or maybe a mad scientist. Can we save the seeds like last year at Grans? They tasted good with salt on them."

"Of course," Mom answered as she cleared the table and spread out newspaper.

After finding a place to admire their finished, four-eyed pirate with his two angry mouths, they picked up their carving debris, ready for today's jaunt to the Halloween Super Store. The walk downtown took them to the usually empty shop next to the Army Surplus store, a favorite family, rainy day destination. They roamed both stores for an hour in search of costumes but ended up returning home to rummage through the family's costume box.

Toby became a zombie ghost with bloody red paint dripping from near where his mouth should be. Meg took an ancient sleeping bag, cut open the bottom, glued on colorful felt circles, and became a tottering bag of candy.

Kelsey had warned how people of all ages in Seattle got crazy for Halloween, so Della created a hint of a costume since it was expected at her office. She became a princess by donning an old tiara while trailing a long piece of green chiffon.

BEFORE ZACH LEFT, THEY SHARED a family meal with each person responsible for one dish. Toby helped make a salad, Meg steamed veggies, and Mom handled the main dish, a similar division of duties they'd had at Gran's. Continuing the tradition helped hold her close.

Zach set the table and started laughing. He waved to Meg to get her attention, then signed, "Do you remember the time I came for a visit, and we took all of Gran's kitchen towels and hung them all over the kitchen? I thought Gran would strangle me."

Meg signed, "She loved your tricks. She missed you when you left for training. When you couldn't come home, you always called her. It's nice you're close to us now."

Zach came around the table and hugged her, causing her to lean into him as she bottled up tears. The memory of losing Gran and moving away from the farm still created a rush of sadness in moments like this.

AFTER DINNER, ZACH OFTEN ENDED his stay by sitting with Della to watch local evening news. Tonight's news shared details about the upcoming renovation of their neighborhood, the International District.

"And there you have it, folks. The already cleared away buildings will soon include an implosion set for spring. Once the century-old buildings are stripped of interior furnishings, windows removed, and security fencing placed around the block, they will be demolished, replaced by a state-of-the-art athletic complex. Watch for updates as they become available. This is Ray Reece reporting on location. Now, back to the studio."

"That's near here, isn't it?" Zach asked.

"Yes. The buildings are next to my part-time job office. Our building is due to be demolished soon, so I'll be out of a job if the owner moves out of town. The office rents around here will be going up as they gentrify more and more of downtown."

"Could be interesting to watch such tall brick buildings come down. Hope I'm here to see it."

Della looked up with a questioning expression. "Are they moving you away?"

Zach shrugged. "It's the Army. They can do whatever they

want. I'm hoping to stay around here permanently. You're my only family, Della. Being transferred away would mean I'd miss watching Meg and Toby grow up and maybe miss seeing you find someone to love and support you."

Della took Zach's hands in hers. "We all hope you'll be around the Seattle area as long as we're here, which I'm hoping will be a very long time."

As Zach was about to leave, something outside the window caught his attention. "Did you see that?"

"What?" Della answered.

Zach hurried to the living room window. "Flashing lights. Come take a look." He signaled to Meg to join them at the window and pointed. "There! In the tallest building. I thought I saw flashing lights."

"I see them," Toby said and pushed to stand next to the window in front of Zach.

They stood together by the window, waiting for the lights to flash again but nothing happened.

"Must have been kids with flashlights," Mom said.

Meg signed, "I saw them a couple weeks ago. I thought the same thing. Kids like Toby, playing around."

Zach checked his watch. "Got to go. Toby, I'm giving you a job. Let me know if you see the lights again. We may have a Halloween mystery to solve."

Zach hugged Meg and signed, "I'll try to be back for Halloween, but I may have maneuvers into November. I'll call when I can. I'm planning to be here for Thanksgiving with Hawaiian Sweet Rolls and a tree of Brussels sprouts."

Toby's face changed from excitement to a grimace. "Do you have to bring Brussels sprouts? They taste like yucky cabbage."

Zach ruffled Toby's hair. "If you mind your mother and Meg, I'll bring the yummy ones." As he reached for the doorknob, he added: "Take care of each other."

Toby saluted Zach, who returned the salute, kissed his sister's forehead, and was gone.

Every time Zach left, the apartment felt empty. His good-natured teasing and his presence brightened every corner. As long as Zach stayed around, Meg felt their lives would be okay. She looked at the pumpkin sitting on the counter. The mischievous pirate's dual grimaces would be a quirky reminder of his visit. *Return soon, Zach.*

SHERMAN HARRISON HIGH SCHOOL ALLOWED costumes the last hour of the day for their Halloween assembly and for the afterschool dance sponsored by the parent group. Meg slipped into her costume, but she planned to watch the happenings from the sidelines.

After the hallway hubbub of students stepping into costumes and getting seated in their class groups, the band played, the dance squad performed, and students read short blurbs she guessed were scary stories. Then, class by class, costumed students paraded around the edge of the gym and before a row of teachers holding clipboards and acting as costume judges.

Kelsey grabbed Meg and pulled her into the junior class line as their turn began. Being in costume gave Meg the courage to relax and join in the fun. Dressed as a pack of candy bits had been Toby's idea. It hid all but her feet and her masked face.

When the walk-around ended, she and Kelsey both placed in one of the school's dozens of categories for each grade.

Meg received a yellow ribbon and Kelsey a blue one for their creative designs. They stood with a third student to school applause, laughing to themselves. *Who knew an old sleeping bag could win as a creative costume?*

Eli must have had a body-covering costume because she couldn't pick him out. With masks removed, she saw him smiling at her. He'd worn brown felt shaped as a pack of M and M's. They both laughed at their candy-inspired costumes.

Many teachers got into the spirit of the assembly and donned costumes: Stuffy Mr. Oberlander dressed up as a text-book. Mr. Vance hid inside a long yellow pencil costume. Slim Ms. Gillis transformed into a plump, red strawberry with a green stem-shaped cap. Only Ms. Young shunned the spirit of the assembly, or else she was dressed to resemble a PE teacher, whistle and all.

During the afterschool dance, teachers and students formed groups for photos taken in front of a harvest scene. Meg and Kelsey took crazy poses for their duo. Eli pulled Meg in with him and another candy-inspired costumed stranger for their shot.

Dancing in costume confined her movements to stepping from side to side, but she danced with Kelsey, Eli, and a dozen other masked students. The band played loud music thumping with energy she felt traveling up from the floor. Being hidden but in plain sight helped her fit in more than any other day at school. Maybe this was a sign of changes coming where she'd blend in more naturally; or maybe fitting in would always require a mask.

THE RIDE HOME FOUND THE city buses filled with all kinds of costumes. Riders were asked to remove their masks while on the bus for safety's sake. Her driver handed out fun size candy bars to each rider as they entered the bus. Everything about today felt fun and funny.

At dusk, Meg took Toby trick-or-treating along the neighborhood streets. A Halloween spirit settled over most businesses. Han's Variety store gave out baseball cards or superhero cards, your choice. One insurance agent handed out pencils and pads of paper with their business information prominently printed on each page. Even the lady who ran the flower shop passed out treats. Still others handed out coupons inviting trick-or-treaters to return another day and receive a discount on a purchase.

Stan's Mini Market handed out small kumquats or boxes of raisins. Toby was in heaven when he saw the overflowing basket of kumquats. By the time he'd arrived the boxes of raisins were gone, but Toby didn't care. Stan gave him a handful of kumquats saying. "You come tomorrow. You take my leftovers, free."

Excited and exhausted, Toby returned to the apartment. Luckily for him and everyone else, they all had the weekend to recover. But his evening lasted longer than expected and with a surprise. Back early from maneuvers, Zach arrived unexpectedly.

As Toby got ready for bed, he repeated his nightly ritual of checking for the flashing lights. Tonight, flashing resumed. He shouted, causing his mom, Zach, and Meg to rush into the living room.

"Look! See the flashing?"

Zach patted Toby on the back. "Good job, Toby. I think we

have something more than kids playing with flashlights."

"Do you think it's ghosts," Toby asked.

"No. It's something much more interesting. Someone is signaling Morse Code."

"Huh?"

"Let me show you." Zach grabbed a piece of paper and a pencil then sat with Toby at the kitchen table. "Each of the flashes represent a letter of the alphabet." He drew:

—   ——••—   —••   —••—— "This spells Toby."

"Really? Can you teach me how to write this stuff?"

Zach nodded. "Next time I'm here. In the meantime, keep watching for the flashes. Become a code detective and make a list of the days you see signaling."

18

EACH NOVEMBER AFTERNOON, weather permitting, Meg hurried to the alley to practice shooting: alone, with Toby, with Kelsey, or with both. Perhaps by spring, she could add another favorite player, Eli.

Today, she played horse alone, shooting from as many locations as possible in the skinny, makeshift basketball court. It allowed her to release pent-up energy from sitting in classes all day. Hopefully, her newly allowed extra credit in Physics and her daily performance in her other classes would keep her on track.

Thanks to Ms. Gillis, her classes progressed well. The basic computer she'd been given for keeps through a local business-man's service club helped her stay current on assignments. She guarded it along with her cell phone; without them, she'd lose important lifelines.

MONDAY, SHE'D BEEN CALLED OUT of Advisory to Ms. Gillis' office, where she met Connie Sage, a local college student studying to become a deaf education teacher. Connie attended night school to complete her degree, still more than a year away.

Connie possessed excellent credentials. She'd learned sign as a child because her parents were deaf. Having the opportunity to sign at the high school provided bonus credits in her advanced deaf language class. It also allowed her to quit her day job of cleaning houses. True, house cleaning paid more than being an interpreter, but the experience and the added time working in the deaf community made up for any lost income. Plus, Connie was comfortable being in the high school. She'd graduated less than 4 years before, so she remained in tune with kids that age.

When she met Meg, she knew she'd fallen into a great job. *What a bright, shy, yet happy young woman. She treats me like a friend instead of an interfering interpreter.*

As Connie met Meg's teachers, she'd handed each one a list of accommodations to help her help Meg. The teachers appeared impressed by Connie's professionalism. Best of all, Meg realized *she'd* been given a fantastic, new lifeline.

Connie also had a list of procedures for her. At first, Meg was taken aback but after thinking about everything, she realized working with Louise had made her lazy. Connie suggested she speak up when she had questions, continue to check assignments daily, and advocate for herself.

During their first week together, Meg was elated when Connie used low signals, held close to her body, and chose to sit off to the side up front rather than stand and *perform* like Louise had done. She wore long-sleeved dark blouses to contrast with her ivory-toned skin. She kept her nails short with no polish, and she wore no jewelry to distract from her signing.

With Connie's full-time assistance, Meg did better on English assignments and circled in on appreciating History class. Plus, Eli's interest in history provided a fun, personal perspective, making the topics more interesting when they studied together.

Other advantages with Connie included her focus remaining exclusively on Meg. Even though she was young and cute, she never flirted with guys or engaged the girls as chatty friends, plus she suggested students wait and text Meg after school unless they needed to talk about classroom assignments.

Early November marked the midpoint of the first semester and Meg's chance to show she could handle attending a large city high school. Already, it felt like years instead of three months since they'd moved to Seattle as midterms slammed in, forcing her to spend every moment prepping for each two-hour testing ordeal.

In first period, Advanced Math, she finished her final test problem as Connie tapped her hand and pointed to the clock. With ten minutes left, she closed the stapled pages and set them in the teacher's test tray. As she exited the room, she wore her elation at finishing the test with a wide smile. Having longer than their regular class time erased the rush-rush feeling. Even if the teachers bulked up their test questions to push students to cover more material, the extra time eased every school-day tension.

During their thirty-minute break, Meg headed to the locker to exchange textbooks before rushing off to her next test. Connie followed her into the Physics classroom, seated herself at the side of the room, and took out a personal book to read during the test. This room, like the math classroom, held a tension similar to a rough piece of sandpaper rubbing against her skin. The usual joking around was absent. Faces looked pale. Bodies slumped. Cells phones lay collected at the teacher's desk. Students cleared their desks of all materials except a pencil and the class textbook.

Today's physics midterm consisted of a series true and false, short answer, an open-book review of terms, and an essay. A few early questions stopped Meg; she hated true-false items. She often saw many possibilities instead of black and white truths. After doing the short answer questions next, she moved to the open book challenges.

Meg finished her essay as Connie tapped her arm indicating five minutes left. She nodded, scanned her test pages, then followed the stream of classmates depositing tests on the teacher's desk while collecting their cell phones. In the hall, she lip-read snatches of conversation as students stopped to chat. "...hard but I nailed the essay", "I hate true and false", "...think I passed", "I'm starving". Funny how she agreed with every comment she intercepted, especially the one about being hungry.

The cafeteria was jammed with students eating, talking, and studying. Meg's goal of fitting in remained a work in progress. She still didn't have a group, so she sat at an empty corner table with her back to the rest of the students in the room.

From day one, she'd seen herself as pigeon-holed, as *different*. True, she had a different way of communicating, but signing and reading lips gave her reasonable connections, even advantages over other students. Her English bio brought her more notice and acceptance; still, today, she ate alone and spent the rest of her lunch break reviewing for a test in CTE.

Connie left to work on her own assignments. She was expected to write a dozen or more observations every week, mostly about how Meg functioned as the only deaf student in the school. She'd signed to Meg before she left, "If all deaf students worked as hard as you do, interpreters would have a much easier time. It's a joy working with you and watching how each week you take on more responsibility for your learning."

Meg stared at her. *If she really believes that, then I need to show her just how much more I can do. She makes me want to be better than she believes I can be.*

Day two. Testing. Round two included English and History tests with a PE conditioning skills competency test mashed in between. Not a bad way to release testing anxiety.

The extra day to prep for her English exam proved vital. Mr. Vance shared three possible topics he'd consider for their test. By a blind draw, he selected the theme she'd prayed for. While she smiled to herself, others looked pained by the selection. She wrote with confidence and finished in time to reread her paper, checking for writing errors as well as faulty reasoning. Ms. Gillis should be proud of her progress.

Meg took her seat in History class and inhaled deeply several times. Mr. Oberlander was so serious about American history she imagined most every student in the class, except Eli, joined her in feeling overwhelmed. Maybe others also questioned the value of rehashing what happened one or two hundred or more years ago. Much as Eli tried to convince her of its importance, she hadn't made the jump to loving it. However, it was fun watching him try to sway her opinion.

Mr. Oberlander announced the essay topic. Meg watched Eli out of the corner of her eye. He winked. He'd helped her prepare, and he'd nailed the details she needed to focus on to do well on the exam. She closed her eyes to focus herself, then started writing.

Exhausted but relieved, Meg stashed her books in her locker and headed home. Earlier in the day, rain had passed through the area, leaving a mixture of cool air and clearing skies for her walk home. Perfect for thinking and reviewing what she'd written on her tests. At times like these, she missed her small, private deaf school. Those kids, like these, debriefed after tests and laughed about odd bits of nothing. Here, however, she was on her own. She could count her friends on one hand—actually, on two fingers: Kelsey and Eli.

The family's move into a big, bustling city with tall buildings had advantages and disadvantages. Views of Puget Sound and the mountains inspired her, but also hemmed her in. She missed the wide-open, wintry prairie, the barren orchards, the wheat fields with traces of snow, and Gran's farm. Maybe, someday, they could drive back to see how it looked and talk with the people who'd bought the farm. Maybe.

The private school had less than one hundred students, grades two through ten. Sherman Harrison had over a thousand. Both schools had fees, but with Mom as the receptionist, Meg enjoyed a reduced tuition. Here, money went out in clumps of hundreds of dollars, especially if she wanted to participate in activities. She really needed a job.

If they didn't need to purchase a car, their finances would hold. Fortunately, buses covered most places they wanted or needed to go. Why had their dad walked away and not made any attempt to call them or text them to see how they managed without him still bothered her. She held onto Mom's unflagging determination and confidence that their lives would work out fine on their own, but she still missed him.

19

WHEN SCHEDULES RETURNED TO NORMAL, everyone sighed in relief. Walking to class with Eli returned as a constant. Kelsey's friends gave Eli the evil eye, but he persisted in befriending Meg despite demeaning 'in group' comments she observed clearly aimed his direction.

Meg felt the snub, but with Eli as an ally, everything changed. He'd learned a few basic signs and they'd developed a silly secret sign, QT, short for c-u-t-i-e and meaning, 'you're my special friend'. They'd flash the two letters to each other whenever they passed in the hallways. Meg started each text to Eli with 'QT', while Eli used it as his sign off to her. They promised they'd keep it their secret, even from their best friends.

During today's lunch time together, Eli nervously tapped his phone. Meg studied his face before she checked out what he'd sent.

Eli: **What's the smile for, QT?**

Meg: **QT. Glad to see you here for lunch.**

Eli laughed: **I'm excited you're going to the homecoming dance with me after the game tonight, QT.**

Meg: **QT. Really?**

He nodded. **Wait for me in the gym. I'll get there as soon as I can. QT**

Meg: **QT. Good luck in the game**

Eli's forehead crease deepened. He smiled at her.

Eli: **I like you a lot. Later? QT**

Meg nodded, then stood to toss her trash away. Stepping away from Eli gave her a chance to slow her racing heart and realize her first real date, a planned date, was coming up tonight. She floated to PE class, where she met up with Connie after she'd suited up.

"What's happening?" Connie signed. "You have a funny look on your face."

"Tonight's homecoming. Eli's taking me."

"Is it a dress-up dance?"

"No. Now I won't have to stand alone."

Connie grinned, then settled in to signing today's class directions.

Kelsey and Meg shot baskets after school even though the alley felt windy and contained piles of leaves. Once back inside the apartment, Meg pulled out her phone.

Meg: **I'm excited for homecoming with Eli.**

Kelsey: **A real date?**

Meg: **Maybe**

Mom and Toby attended the homecoming game. The Fishermen played well but were outscored by their opponent 21-20, which dampened the mood in the stands, but the crowd still sent the Fishermen to the dressing room with a standing ovation. Mom and Toby headed home as Meg turned toward the school cafeteria to wait for Eli.

She stood in the shadows near the entry, watching the students file in as pairs, groups and singles. Her hands dripped with sweat; she ran them down the sides of her dressy jeans and straightened her scoop necked sweater. Kelsey was right. Others dressed as casually as she had. For once she'd fit in, if people looked her direction.

She checked her phone: 9:30. No message from Eli. When she looked up, she saw him entering the gym with his team-mates, stopping to receive pats on the back for their winning season even though the homecoming game ended in a loss.

She watched the in-crowd girls hug him and flirt as he continued to search the room. Was he looking for her? Maybe.

Eli spotted her and brushed aside girls who encircled him. His smile broadened as he reached her and signed 'QT'.

Meg signed back. Then, unsure what to do next, she dropped her hands to her sides. Eli took one hand and led her away from the wall to dance.

The pulsing beat of the music rose through the floor and into Meg's body. Dancers waved their arms, twisting in frantic jerks. Eli moved more deliberately, holding her hands loosely while staring into her eyes with a seriousness she'd not seen from him before. It made her squirm, but she almost liked it.

After two more songs and seeing the dance area emptying, they sat down with a snack. His friends came by and spoke with him, giving her a cursory once-over but making no attempt to speak with her.

By 11:00 the dance dribbled to an end. Eli escorted her to his car and opened the door for her. She slid in, noticing he'd patched the worn interior. It reminded her of her dad's car. *Dad seldom drove me anywhere in his car. Why was that? Did he resent me for being deaf? Did he blame me or Mom for my getting sick? Probably. Mom got blamed for most every problem.*

Eli tapped her arm and pointed. She'd been so preoccupied thinking about her dad she didn't realize they'd stopped in front of her apartment. She started to open the car door as Eli jumped out and finished opening it for her.

Standing at the hall door to 6C, Meg felt uneasy. Eli held her hand and stared at her. "Thanks for meeting me at the dance, QT."

She nodded and looked to the floor. When she looked up, he leaned forward and kissed her cheek, inches from her mouth, then backed away and scurried down the stairs.

Meg used her key and found her mom sitting at the kitchen table, sewing the hem of a skirt. She looked up. "Have fun?"

She nodded. "Night."

The next morning, Kelsey appeared at their apartment door, carrying her basketball. She and Meg headed out to shoot hoops. Meg knew Kelsey wanted to know about the dance, but she made her ask her questions: "Did you like the dance? Do you like Eli? Does he like you?"

Meg nodded and shot the ball over to Kelsey who turned, shot, and made a basket. When they tired, they went into Kelsey's apartment and drank huge glasses of water.

Kelsey grabbed her cell phone and continued the inquisition.

Kelsey: **So, are you and Eli a couple?**

Meg: **Maybe. Saw you with Parker. You two a couple?**

Kelsey: **Could be. He's hot. So is Eli. Any kissing?**

Meg: **A little.**

Kelsey: **And?**

Meg shrugged: **The rest is private.**

She felt sure Kelsey wanted more details, but her evening with Eli was only for herself. She knew Kelsey would share whatever she learned about them with her group. Did it matter? Maybe. For now, she wanted to keep their relationship private, especially since dating was a new part of her life, one she wanted to treasure for as long as it lasted.

20

THE FOLLOWING WEEK MEG RECEIVED her grade sheet. Even with Connie's help she'd faltered on some tests and failed to complete enough extra assignments to boost her grades. She scanned it and felt a wave of disappointment in herself.

**Sherman Harrison High School -
Mid-Term Grade Report**

Name: Meg Appens
Student Number 417632-2018 Midterm: Fall - 2018

Subject	Grade + %	Comments
1.Math	A- 95%	strong student
2 English	C- 70%	need make-ups
3 Science	C- 73%	missed test + 2 labs
4 PE	C- 73%	good skills
5 CTE	B 82%	OK
6 History	D- 60%	failing
Grade Average	75%	

True, Louise Feld was partly to blame, but they are my classes, my grades, and my responsibility. If I don't improve them, I'll never be allowed to tryout for basketball.

Now she had an appointment with Ms. Gillis to try to explain what had gone wrong. She hated to disappoint her after all she'd done to support her: answering so many questions, finding Connie, and providing a computer for home use. What could she say to Ms. Gillis to keep her support after such a poor showing?

Ms. Gillis slid a copy of her grade sheet in front of Meg and frowned. "This is a mixed start. What's happening?"

Meg shrugged.

"If I may," Connie said and signed, "Not all of this is Meg's fault. We've met with the teachers. She has until December first for retakes. Meg's a hard worker. I know she can pull up her grades."

Ms. Gillis: **I hope so. We take learning seriously.**

Meg: **I'll work harder. I want to play basketball.**

Ms. Gillis: **Dec. 1 is too late. Team tryouts begin Nov. 26.**

Turn everything in before Thanksgiving. Understand?

Meg: **Yes.**

Ms. Gillis: **Classroom success is our primary goal. Let me know how I can help.**

Meg: **Thank you.**

Once they left the counseling office, Meg stopped to sign. "I don't know if I can get everything made up in time. I keep slipping backward."

"I'll help you all I can. Do you want to meet at your place after school or at the public library?"

Meg grimaced. "Both."

THEY MET AFTERSCHOOL ON THE days Ms. Iris could watch

Toby. Having Connie's help made all the difference, especially in history. Mr. Oberlander's consistently vague directions frustrated her. He directed her to his online site, saying "Do what you can or come in during my afterschool hours. I hope you prove me wrong about your effort."

Back at home, Meg spoke with Kelsey and gained more insight into her missing assignments.

Kelsey: **Most teachers change late assignments to pass/ fail unless you convince them otherwise. To play basketball, you need letter grades. Tell them that.**

Talking with the teachers was embarrassing once again, but Meg scheduled time with her English, science, and history teachers, who agreed to consider letter grades if she completed and turned in quality work before Thanksgiving break.

Kelsey kept tabs on Meg's progress for a selfish reason: she knew the basketball team needed her skills. They'd had a losing season the last two years with the twins playing.

Kelsey: **Those girls are as helpful as a broom with no bristles. We need Y-O-U so get busy!**

MEG SPENT EVERY FREE MINUTE on schoolwork. Toby sensed she was on a mission, so he didn't bug her to play cards or race cars or explore the neighborhood. Mom noticed her increased focus and didn't assign her any additional tasks in the apartment.

Connie spent her free time, including weekends, helping Meg. Obviously, it wasn't mere ego pushing Meg. Her determination to earn a sports scholarship and attend college remained her long range focus. Connie used neon chart paper and made her two small banners: You're smart! You can do this! She hung one in Meg's locker and the other in her bedroom.

Toby joined in the push by making Meg his version of a supportive banner. He drew a racetrack with her name on the side of a leading car. His sign read, "Win the race!"

Before the Thanksgiving break, Meg dutifully made the rounds to her teachers to record her current status before reporting to Ms. Gillis after school. Once again, Connie attended the meeting. Together she and Meg watched Ms. Gillis study the updated grade sheet.

Sherman Harrison High School -
Mid-Term Grade Report Update

Name: Meg Appens Student Number 417632-2018
Midterm: Fall - 2018

Subject	Grade + %	Comments
1 Math	95% A	OK
2 English	70% C	need make-ups
3 Science	73% C	-2 labs
4 PE	80% B	OK
5 CTE	86% B	OK
6 History	70% C-	-1

Adjusted Grade Average   B-

Ms. Gillis: **To play, you needed to get rid of your D. You've raised several grades. Now don't let them slip again.**

Meg nodded and inhaled deeply: **I'll try.**

Ms. Gillis: **We'll be watching your grades closely. If they drop, you'll be unable to participate in sports.**

Meg: **I understand.**

Ms. Gillis stood and reached out her hand. "Good Luck. You have a prize in Connie."

"I agree."

Connie smiled as they left the counseling office. She stopped to text with Meg in the hallway.

Connie: **You've done a great job. I'll continue to help you, but you must stay on top of things. Check assignments daily. Make a calendar to show due dates.**

Meg: **I will. I'll be more responsible. Promise.**

Connie: **Good luck!**

WITHIN A WEEK'S TIME, MEG received her official grades, which she shared with her mom. Her family and Connie celebrated with a dinner of her favorite foods: juicy hamburgers with the works, potato salad, and double chocolate brownies. Things at school appeared to be getting better, brighter.

THEN THERE WAS CONNIE AND Zach, who'd accidently met near the sixth-floor landing. Connie struggled with a large cardboard box heading down the stairs. She missed the edge of a step, falling forward against Zach, who was heading up the stairs to visit the Appens family.

He grabbed her and helped her right the box, bending to pick up the clothing scattered down the stairs. He stared up at her. "Are you okay?"

"I'm fine, thanks."

"Let me carry the box for you. Are you heading to your car?"

Connie closed the lid of the box. "Yes. I'm taking this to the shelter near my apartment. The family I was visiting doesn't have a car and... well... Thanks."

Once Zach learned Connie was Meg's interpreter, his visits to Seattle increased with the hope of finding her there. Mom and Meg watched them together and raised their eyebrows. Zach deserved someone special like Connie in his life.

Their friendship grew quickly. Together, they'd take Meg and Toby to various sights around Seattle on weekends, ending with Connie and Zach going out afterward.

Mom observed how Connie looked at Zach, much the same way Meg looked at Eli. Toby called them looking with 'mushy eyes' like the television teen shows Meg watched. He often headed into the bedroom to play with his cars, hoping Zach still had time to stick his head in the room, come in, and play with him when Connie was around.

Zach didn't disappoint, but his time with Toby shrank when Connie waited nearby.

21

BETWEEN MIDTERMS AND THANKSGIVING, MEG and Toby visited Stan's Market to taste and judge dozens of fruits and veggies, looking for new flavors they liked. It soon became a game. Stan selected a free sample then watched for their reactions. Meg liked most everything. Toby tried them all and swallowed at least one bite of each offered food, but he rejected half or more for a variety of reasons: too sour, too salty, too slimy, too plain, or too icky.

One afternoon Stan had his nephew Jun ask Meg if she wanted a job stocking shelves. She'd work two hours on weekend mornings. "Stan will pay you ten dollars and send you home with a bag of fresh food."

Meg smiled. "I'd like that. When do I start?"

Stan bowed slightly. "Please. This weekend." He pointed to an apron. "Wear this. Look official."

MOM AGREED MEG COULD WORK for Stan since she'd be home to supervise Toby. Knowing she'd bring home a bag of groceries from Stan's gave Toby the incentive to give her a huge hug along with a list of suggestions to ask Stan to place in the food bag and the warning, "Don't bring home yucky, slimy things."

Meg tallied her potential earnings. If she worked most weekends the rest of the school year, she'd make at least two hundred dollars. It wasn't much, but it would show Mom she was determined to help pay for her school and sports fees.

WORKING FOR STAN, SHE ARRIVED before the store opened to dust shelves, unpack boxes, and remove old or wilted items from his crates of fresh produce. She also swept the store and sidewalk and righted his signs.

Stan had a steady flow of early morning shoppers Meg got to know by face. Most didn't speak English and didn't know she was deaf, but they often smiled. Meg enjoyed watching them banter with Stan.

As the days grew closer to Thanksgiving, Meg and Toby made a list of Asian food they wanted Mom to add to their Thanksgiving dinner, including long green beans and sweet buns filled with taro. Stan suggested others. She ended up bringing home bok choy and Chinese cabbage, then used the public library to learn how to incorporate them into their holiday feast, now expanded to include Connie and Ms. Iris.

THE PREDICTED STORM BEGAN EARLY Thanksgiving Day. The small kitchen counter held a finished pumpkin pie. Sweet potatoes and green bean casserole awaited their turn in the oven *after* the turkey was close to being finished. Toby's dreaded brussels sprouts sat in a pan on the stove next to a steamer ready to be filled with Asian veggies and a large pot for potatoes. The meal promised to be festive and plentiful.

Zach and Toby played cards on the floor beside the couch where Ms. Iris sat talking with Della and Connie, who were looking through Meg's scrapbooks. Suddenly, the lights flickered and went out. The oven went dark. Neighborhood lights were out as well. Fog and heavy clouds darkened the gray morning, leaving the apartment feeling like evening instead of noon.

Meg jumped up, feeling the room close in around her. She grabbed the large kitchen flashlight while Toby ran to their bedroom and brought out two more.

Mom lit candles as heavy rain slapped against the building and wind shook the thin windowpanes. It reminded Meg of riding through the car wash where water surged against the car again and again. But this was no car wash. This was their Thanksgiving, her second most favorite family time together.

They settled into the semi-darkness as Toby held a flashlight under his chin and lit his face like a scary monster.

"Want to hear a scary story?" Connie asked.

"Yes!" Toby sat on the arm of the cozy chair where Connie sat and shined light on her hands and face.

Candlelight cast an eerie glow throughout the rest of the room as she shared the story of One-Eyed Bill, the Mysterious Dog of Old Hook Road.

Everyone watched and listened, enjoying the funny and scary story Connie also signed for Meg's benefit.

Meg watched Zach's eyes follow Connie's every move. His smile reminded her of Eli's as he came into the homecoming dance.

Toby wiggled with excitement as the story ended. "I like scary stories and candles and the flashlights. It's like Halloween, but what about dinner? We can't cook anything."

"Today we'll be pioneers," Mom said. "We'll make a different kind of feast if the power doesn't come back on. Luckily, you just ate snacks, so we have time to plan."

AFTER ANOTHER TWO HOURS OF candles and flashlights, the day hadn't brightened, and the power remained off. The leaves still clinging to the trees fluttered furiously as the trees bent in the howling wind. Papers that earlier blew in mini tornadoes now whirled and pressed in rain-soaked clumps against the sides of buildings. People passing on the street below fought against their umbrellas turning inside out.

Meg hated unexpected darkness; she'd retreated to rest on her bed to watch what little daylight shown in. Hordes of butterflies rose through her body and gathered in her chest. The absence of light caused her to breathe in gasps. Night never bothered her, but unexpected darkness made her uneasy, fearful an unknown person or being might arise at any moment.

The entire neighborhood and beyond remained dark, increasing her feeling of isolation, ramping up her uneasiness. *This must be how it feels to be blind. Being deaf, I still have a world of colors and shapes. Being blind would be harder. But, if I were blind, I'd never worry about the darkness. Right now, I wish the lights would come on.*

As she leaned closer to the window, she knelt in a wet spot on her quilt. She jumped up, aimed her flashlight down, and saw a thin stream of rainwater leaking in from the bottom sill of the window frame. She ran to the kitchen, grabbed a small bowl to catch the water and told everyone what had happened.

Toby raced into the room. He turned his flashlight toward the window. "Cool. It's raining in our bedroom!"

"Not cool, Toby," Zach said. "Della, call the super. He needs to come fix this."

"He and Kelsey are away for the day. Looks like we're on our own for now."

Meg and her mom pulled the damp quilt off the bed and hung it in the shower. By the time they returned, the bowl had filled with water. Zach hurried into the bedroom with the large pot intended for the potatoes, now repurposed to collect the constant dribble of water.

Ms. Iris appeared in the doorway. "Toby, go get all the bubble gum you have. My Erv used to solve problems like this in our apartment. These ancient window frames with their thin glass need to be replaced. That's why your electric bill is bound to be excessive this winter. If you have enough gum and we chew it to make it soft, we can plug the hole until the super can fix it properly."

Toby gave everyone his bubble gum leftover from Halloween. They stood in the bedroom chewing and laughing. Zach molded the chewed pieces together and stuffed the sticky blob into the crack. Within a minute, the water stopped dripping into the room. Everyone waited and watched for a long minute. Seeing no leaks, they nodded their approval of the bubble gum fix and returned to the living room to resume their candle-lit evening.

Zach and Connie pulled Meg's bed away from the wall, then stayed behind to watch over and replace the pot if future drips occurred. She noticed their heads together, talking, laughing, and maybe more.

Four o'clock and still no power. Two hours ago, they'd carried food containers that wouldn't fit into their refrigerator into Ms. Iris's. Now everyone was starving. Ms. Iris and Mom merged what foods they had to make sandwiches. They added the crackers and cheese Connie brought with Iris's grapes, and apples, then served Oreos cookies and pumpking pier for dessert.

"This is fun," Toby said between bites. "It's my first Thanksgiving picnic!"

Zach ruffled his hair, "Hopefully, this will also be your last. I was so counting on having hot turkey, gravy, mashed potatoes, and brussels sprouts."

"Me too, except for brussels sprouts. Can I..., may I have another sandwich, please? This is a fun Thanksgiving!"

Five thirty. Darkness arrived outside. Mom walked Ms. Iris back to her apartment and helped her get situated in the darkness. Zach and Toby, tired of cards, put them away, leaving space for Connie to sit with Zach at the table to talk privately. Meg couldn't help but notice how interested they appeared to be just sitting at the table with their hands touching.

Meg sat, watching the darkness settle in second by second. Suddenly, she shouted: "Zach! Zach! I see flashing!"

He hurried to the window shouting. "It's coming from the same building I saw before. Someone is signaling."

Toby pushed between Zach and Meg. "What does it say, Uncle Zach?"

Zach studied the flashes for a moment. "It's Morse Code. It's maybe a list of names." Zach began reading: "I, S, O, N, M, O, N, R, O, E, J, Q, A, D"

"Is More's Code what we saw last time?" Toby asked. "How do you see words? Everything runs together. Can you write down what it says?"

Zach laughed. "It's pronounced more- ess. It's named after Samuel Morse who invented it in the 1830s. Remember, we talked about this. Morse Code is a signaling system using flashes of light or using a telegraph key. Watch how the flashes have spaces between them. Each set of flashes makes a letter of the alphabet or a number or even a whole word. It a bit like sign language."

"Cool! Can you teach me how to read the flashes?"

"Sure, Toby. Get a piece of paper and a pencil...and bring the large flashlight. You can be a code detective. I'll tell you all the letters I can. Write them down. We'll figure out the words later."

"Isn't the Morse Code a bit out of date?" Connie asked. "Don't we use satellites and other, faster ways to communicate?"

"Yes," Zach answered, "but the code is still used at sea with flags, or it can be done with telegraph keys or light flashes like these when power is cutoff."

Toby rushed back to the window to write the letters Zach told him: "Y, L, E, R, P, O, L, K, T, A, Y."

"Wait, Uncle Zach. I can't write fast. Besides, I can't see any words. It's just a pile of letters."

"Just keep writing. We'll figure it out later."

As Zach, Connie, and Meg bent over the letters Toby had copied down, the power came back on. Candles extinguished, flashlights put away, and the city lights blinking in the window, their memorable, candle lit Thanksgiving Day picnic ended.

After a bedtime story for Toby, Zach and Connie left. The apartment returned to its normal pace, except for Meg, who continued to wonder about Connie and Zach *and* the strange signals they'd all witnessed.

IT WAS TEN O'CLOCK THE next morning when Mom answered a knock on the door. Kelsey's dad entered, carrying his toolbox. He dug out the gum and patched the leak. "The gum was a clever idea, Ms. Appens."

"It was Ms. Iris who thought of it."

"This old building has more problems than I can keep up with. Let me know if you need anything else."

Della presented him with a list. He read it and shook his head. "Some of these are doable; some are not what we agreed to when I rented you the apartment as is."

Della crossed her arms. "Please circle the items on the list you *do* plan to take care of."

He circled several items and abruptly left the apartment. Della shook her head, retaped the list inside a kitchen cupboard, and returned to wiping the already-wiped kitchen counter.

Meg lipread their conversation. *Now I get it. Lack of money is why we live here.* Then, sensing her mom's frustration, Meg backed away to the bedroom to work on Monday's assignments until it was time to head to work in Stan's store.

22

BASKETBALL TRYOUTS BEGAN TUESDAY. COACH Pauls' sign-up only listed returning players and the two girls with limited skills who tried out every year. Last year, he needed them to round out his team, but try as they did, they failed to score a single point. He knew the tall girl he'd seen in Ms. Young's PE class hadn't signed up. Maybe if he found her, he could interest her in trying out. It was worth a shot even though Coach Young hadn't mentioned her. Maybe she didn't have any ball skills. Maybe height was all she had going for her.

Monday at the end of the day, Coach Pauls stood in the main hallway, looking for her. Ah, there she was. She stood close to six-feet tall. He followed her through the crush of students into the locker hallway and watched her. She wasn't in a hurry like most of the kids, pushing and shoving their way to freedom.

As the locker area cleared, he shouted, "Hello? Miss? Hello!"

She kept fiddling with things in her locker as if she didn't hear him.

He hurried closer and tapped her on the shoulder. "Excuse me."

Meg turned, expecting Eli. She gasped.

"I'm Coach Pauls. I want to talk to you about trying out for basketball."

She frowned. He didn't move his lips enough for her to understand what he wanted. Plus, his moustache interfered with his words.

"Please." She held up her hand as she fumbled through her pocket, then handed him a small card.

He pulled back for a second, then accepted the card:

My name is Meg Appens. I'm deaf. Please write a note, text me, or speak slowly.

(My interpreter is Connie Sage)

Thank you.

HE NODDED AND SPOKE SLOWLY. "If you've ever played basketball, please come to the gym after school tomorrow for tryouts."

She smiled. "I plan to sign up before I leave today."

He nodded. "Good. Hand me your phone. I'll put in the team information number."

When he finished, Meg nodded and watched him walk away. Kelsey was right. Coach acted anxious; he needed her height. If he'd waited a few minutes, he'd have seen her name on his list.

All the way home, she pictured herself running up and down the court, passing, prepping for a layup, scoring. She barely felt the street beneath her feet. She was wanted.

After dinner she hurried to Kelsey's apartment to tell her

about talking with Coach Pauls.

Kelsey: **I told you he'd be interested. Why didn't you sign-up earlier?**

Meg: **Got busy. Don't worry. I'll be there.**

Kelsey: **Meet outside the gym locker room at 3:15. Don't be late. Tryouts last to 5:00. Wear your best gym shoes.**

Meg: **You mean my only ones! Thanks!**

3:10. STILL NO SIGN OF Kelsey. Meg double-checked the bulletin board inside the locker room.

Girls JV and Varsity Basketball Tryouts

DECEMER 2

3:30 - 5:00

Late Arrivals will not be allowed to tryout

Final Team Selections posted Wednesday, afterschool

She couldn't wait any longer if she wanted to have time to warm-up. She entered, found an empty locker, changed, slapped a hot pink lock onto the latch, and headed into the gym.

The scent of sweaty sports socks along with the sight of single shoes, rumpled shirts, and sweaters littered the space below the opened section of gym bleachers. Once beyond them, she noticed the two empty ball carts. A sea of balls flew toward the hoops. She felt the floor vibrate as girls passed her, running in pairs from center court, passing balls back and forth, and taking shots.

Just then a ball flew in her direction. She caught it and threw it back to a tall girl, who nodded and turned to make a three-point shot. *Looks like I have competition.*

Kelsey ran up and tapped her shoulder. "Hey! Sorry. Had to get a signature from my math teacher. Might need you to tutor me."

Meg nodded. "No balls. Let's run laps."

They circled the edges of the gym until Kelsey grabbed a stray ball. The girl who'd lost control nodded and gestured to them. Kelsey tapped her shoulder. "Marti will share with us."

The girls dribbled and passed until suddenly everyone stopped and moved to the open section of bleachers. Two coaches waited until everyone settled.

Coach Pauls spoke to the group. "Welcome to JV and varsity tryouts. We see a lot of familiar faces, but each of you must tryout each season. If you're new or not yet a junior, you'll need to prove yourself as a JV, but all varsity positions are open. Any questions?"

Meg tried to decipher the conversation between students and the coaches but couldn't. She should have asked Connie to stay. Too late now.

Kelsey grabbed her hand. "Later."

Meg caught her intent and nodded.

"Let's get started," Coach Young, the girls PE teacher, held up her clipboard. "Step forward as I call you name."

Kelsey nudged Meg. "Go! She called your name."

Meg approached Coach Young. "Meg Appens A-p-p-e-n-s."

Coach Young nodded distractedly without looking up. "Got it. Next?"

Kelsey raised a thumbs up.

Coach Young blew her whistle to silence side conversations as she double-checked names. "As I read off your names, form two lines."

Girls moved into their lines.

Coach held the clipboard covering her mouth, making it impossible for Meg to know which line she needed to join. Kelsey nudged her and jerked her head to one side. Meg hurried to join that line.

The girls in her line laughed and shook their heads at Meg's slowness to join their line. As she stood there, she read one girl's lips: "The new player must be deaf. If she's that slow, she'll never make the team."

She watched those around her laugh. She felt her face heat up and her insides tighten as she stood in line, praying Kelsey could guide her through tryouts. Last week, Kelsey suggested she go in with Connie and talk with the coaches. But Meg hoped to fit in based on her skills, without receiving special considerations or being denied a chance to tryout if they knew she was deaf. Was her stubbornness about to interfere with her trying out? Maybe, but she'd talk with them when or if she was considered for a team.

As it turned out, Kelsey faced her from the other line. She mouthed, "sorry." Meg replied with a shrug.

Running suicide laps, dribbling, passing, making flying lay-ups, and free throw shooting filled the tryout time. Sweat ran down Meg's body as she reached deep to pull up every ounce of energy. Her confidence grew as she was able to key-off the movements around her and not make many obvious errors.

Once the girls settled on the bleachers, Coach Young reminded them to check the bulletin board daily. Next, she read off the names of girls they wanted to speak with after they dressed. Kelsey nudged her. Maybe she *should* have spoken with the coach ahead of time. Now it might be too late.

She took her time showering and dressing. Kelsey gave her a hug. "You did great. Now you have a chance to talk with the coaches. I'll wait for you outside."

As Meg was combing out her ponytail and securing it, she turned to watch the girls talking among themselves. "Appen's flies in her lay-ups. She's got such long arms we should call her Meg the Ape. Too bad she can't follow directions better. Glad we won't need to compete with her for a spot."

Meg turned away before anyone saw the tears filling her eyes. *Evidently some of the girls don't know I'm deaf. Doubt it changes their continuing rude comments. I see girls who are in my classes. Why didn't any of them stand up for me? Do they really think I look like an ape? Maybe trying out is a bad idea.*

Meg sat, waiting her turn to speak with the coaches. Her earlier exuberance disappeared, replaced by dread while sitting on a bench. She checked her cell phone: 5:20. What would she say to the coaches?

When her turn arrived, she entered the office and sat on the chair facing both coaches. Coach Pauls smoothed down his moustache and took out his cell phone. He remembered she was deaf.

Coach Pauls: **Where did you play basketball last year? What positions?**

Meg: **Yakima school for deaf students. I played forward, guard and center.**

Coach Pauls: **Kelsey tells us you read lips.**

Surprise caught inside Meg. *So, Kelsey shared her situation. That could be good or bad.* She nodded and looked down to her hands.

Coach Young: **Nice to see you, Meg. Did you bring your interpreter?**

Meg: **No, but she'll come to practices if I make the team.**

Coach Young: **We'll start you on JV to learn our procedures, see how or if this will work. We'll need to find a quick way to let you know the plays. For now, welcome to JV!**

Meg: **Thank you.**

She judged their conversation was over, so she stood and left the office feeling satisfied. Making the preliminary cut made her want to jump up and down.

Coach Pauls followed her out of his office and signaled to Kelsey to come inside. Meg waited for her to come out. She returned with a smirk on her face. Her fingers busy on her cell phone.

Kelsey: **Congrats. Pauls said to bring Connie tomorrow to practice. Let's go. I'll buy you a soda, and we can talk."**

Meg smiled as Kelsey playfully pulled her to her feet.

ONCE THEY SETTLED INTO THE cafe, Meg texted her mom and Ms. Iris to tell them she'd be later than expected. She needed this time with Kelsey to learn more basketball details.

Meg: **I need Connie at practices.**

Kelsey: **You do. Coach Young gives detailed directions. I remember how frustrated she made me. I can't imagine how you'll feel. Let me type out the plays I remember. I doubt she's changed their numbers - too much work.**

Meg: **I'll take all the help I can get.**

Their route home took them along a busy street. The early

evening sidewalks remained crowded with shoppers and last minute delivery trucks double parked and emitting strong exhaust fumes. Meg thought of the wide-open spaces across the mountains, where sidewalks didn't exist. The gritty big city air took time to adjust to, especially since it flavored everything she ate.

Back home she found Toby settled in, finishing his homework in Ms. Iris's apartment. She'd fed him and, from the amount of chocolate on his face, he'd munched more than one of her fabulous oatmeal chocolate chip cookies. Toby loved Ms. Iris. Still, it was too bad Gran wasn't here to watch over him. Sadly, their mom needed her two jobs to make ends meet. *Why do some dads disappoint their families and vanish like wheat chaff on a windy day? Why did mine really leave?*

With Toby tucked in bed, Meg sat down to her homework. *Blah! I'm so tired, so buried in homework. I need to find more energy to keep up my grades and play basketball. I need Connie's support at practices and games but I can't ask her to stay and not get paid for her time. Wish money didn't always control what we can or cannot do. Maybe trying out was a bad idea.*

As she closed her math book, the apartment door opened. Her mother looked exhausted but still managed to share a hug. She signed. "How were tryouts?"

Meg did a brief unenthusiastic happy dance. "I'm on JV. "

"Congrats, Honey. Then why do you look sad?"

"I never thought about asking Connie to stay for practices and games. She'll need to be paid. I know we can't afford to pay her."

Mom yawned as she sat down at the kitchen table. "Once the coaches see how talented you are, they'll find a way to cover her time, or we will. Now, head to bed. We'll talk more in the morning. Love you."

154

23

THE NEXT EVENING MEG LET herself into the apartment. She tossed her book bag on the floor and dropped into the overstuffed chair by the window. She closed her eyes and waited for the tension and tiredness running through her body to drop away.

Toby was still across the hall with Ms. Iris. She should pick him up, but she needed a minute alone. Tears streamed down her face. *I've done my best, watched for signals, participated in the drills, made about 85 % of my shots, and 90% of free throws. That should be enough for the team to accept me, but it's not. Maybe a short nap will help improve my mood.*

She yawned and stretched as Toby burst in and hopped onto her lap. His hands flew as he started sharing his day. "Guess what I did today?" He rummaged through his backpack and produced two rumpled drawings of her shooting baskets. "I want you to hang these up. Ones for your locker."

Ms. Iris stood in the doorway. "He's so excited we came over and let ourselves in, hoping you'd gotten home when we weren't looking,"

Meg hugged Toby and signed, "These are great!"

"You're shooting 3-pointers!"

"Thanks. Hang one on the fridge for Mom to see, okay?"

Ms. Iris waved and left as Mom came in the door, wearing a look of expectation.

"How was your first practice? Are the girls friendly?"

Meg waggled her hand side to side.

Mom sat down at the table and signed, "Be patient. Think about the girls who didn't make either squad."

"You're right. But I worry about talking with Connie. If she comes to practices, it adds two hours each day. Then there are the games as well. I need her, but I can't expect her to *give* me her time."

"There's no point in worrying about it. Talk with her. See what she says."

THE NEXT AFTERNOON, CONNIE ATTENDED practice. Earlier in the day, Meg asked her about coming to practices after school. Connie shared, "I'll ask to use my hours with you at practices and games as my class project. I can write how you adapt to the team and how they adapt to you. I'm certain it will work out."

But Meg worried she was keeping Connie from her evening class homework. Fingers crossed, she hoped it would work out. If so they'd both win.

Meg focused on actively watching the other JV players moves. When she felt unsure of one of Coach Young's plays, she picked a slow responding girl and watched her adjust her movements. It helped. Fewer balls bounced off her side and back, and she made fewer wrong moves.

Once they'd include her in their passes and let her make long shots, she'd prove her worth. She scolded herself about her expectation of automatically making varsity. She knew she needed to prove herself on JV and not be a show-off like

Rayanne. That girl thought she owned the boards like Sue Bird, but she didn't come close to any players on Meg's old Yakima team. Responding accurately to more plays was the key to improving her value to the team.

As practice ended, Coach shared their ratings and percentages aloud. Some players fist bumped; others looked away. Meg received a strong shooting rating, but her team skills during dribbling and passing dropped below yesterday's accuracy. Was she nervous, tired, or missing too many incoming plays?

Back in the locker room, she wished the girls mumbled like Coach Pauls. It would be easier if she didn't lip read their insults and sarcastic comments, but she wanted and needed to know what they thought about her, even though knowing hurt.

"Did you see ape-y Meg? one girl asked. "She thinks she's a great shooter."

"Well, she is," another replied. "I can't make 3-point shots like those. Can you?

Reading the remark, she frowned. *They act like deafness is contagious. As long as they ignore me, I'll be a benchwarmer.*

The first girl spoke again. "I hope Coach sees she'll be a burden to the team. Whoever heard of a deaf girl playing team basketball?"

Lipreading that comment sent anger rocketing through Meg. She almost gave away her awareness to the comments by turning toward the girl to let her know she *had* played on a team. Her deaf team used the same practice routines: hours of conditioning, shooting, running, passing and receiving the ball.

Meg shook her head and looked to see if anyone noticed

her reaction. Nope. They'd moved on to talk about the cute guys in their classes they might want to pursue as boyfriends.

At dinner Meg swirled her fork through her lasagna. *I'm glad Kelsey made varsity. She belongs there. If they ever give me a chance, it will probably be as a last-chance sub. I wish there was a way I could prove myself sooner.*

Mom waved and signed "Are you okay?"

Meg reached over to tickle Toby before she signed, "Right now, Toby owes me a rematch at Go Fish."

Toby waved his hands in silent applause, got up from the table, and returned with the Go Fish cards. He signed, "The loser does dishes the rest of the week."

The end of week one practices, Connie handed Meg a cupcake at lunch.

"What's this for?"

Connie signed, "A Celebration. I've spoken with both coaches. They'll allow me to sit behind them so I can listen to what they share. They suggested I ask Kelsey to teach me their play calls so I can signal to you. But we may also need other signals."

Meg's signing raced out of her hands at breakneck speed. "Fantastic! When can you start? Does Kelsey know? Is that cheating? What other signals?"

"Slow down. It's not cheating. I'll call Kelsey tonight. We need extra signs for spur of the moment plays coach calls in."

Kelsey willingly worked with Connie on the plays most often called in. Erasing last year's play numbers and systems. and replacing them with new ones worried Meg. She needed to watch Connie, keep an eye on coach, and stay alert to team movements, all while playing her position. Connie also worked out a special signal. She raised her arms, shaking small pom poms. Once she had Meg's attention, she signed the play number. After days of dizzying practice watching so many different things, Meg's response and reaction to team plays increased dramatically. If she ever played in a real game, their system could improve her value to the team.

24

ONCE ZACH MET CONNIE, THEY became fixtures in the apartment. Toby thought it was great. Meg enjoyed getting to know Connie away from school and appreciated her extra time attending practices. She'd successfully turned the basketball time with Meg into her class project, which represented one-third of her final class before she began practice teaching. Her instructor was impressed with her ingenuity and dedication to helping Meg beyond the school day.

Connie laughed. "She's suggesting my practice teaching placement might be working with you until both of us graduate. How would that be for you?"

Meg laughed and smiled and hugged her, then wiped tears of relief from her eyes.

ONE CHILLY DECEMBER WEEKEND CONNIE couldn't come over, but Zach still came. He spent the afternoon playing with Toby and promised to cook the family a dinner using Thai Curry, his new favorite spice. Unfortunately, he needed to survive teasing and the grimaced faces of Toby and Meg about over-seasoning of the meal. His penalty: buying pizza and living through the complaining until their cheese pizza dinner arrived.

Once it became dark, Toby began his nightly vigil at the window, hoping to see the flashing lights. When he wasn't watching, he played with the flashlight, holding it beneath his chin to create a fierce monster face.

"Toby." Zach said quietly. "It's starting. Grab the notebook and a pencil."

Toby raced around the apartment to find his pencil. He opened the notebook as they began decoding messages.

Zach read off, " I, S, O, N, something, O, N… This person is on the top floor of the tallest building and is signaling names." He held up the paper for Della, Meg and Toby to read.

Toby took the paper from Zach. "Do you know what this says?"

"Not yet. For now, let's keep writing down what we catch. This coder is fast."

Toby persisted. "How do you know those signals say anything?"

"I recognize the 'i-s-o-n' as the ending of a word. When I was thirteen, I had a ham radio. I learned to look for clues like word endings and patterns of letters."

Della grinned. "I remember your ham radio. I'd just graduated from high school when Dad brought it home. You two worked every night learning the Morse Code. Didn't you finally get your best signal when you moved up the hill to our dilapidated hayloft?"

"Yeah. We'd go up there and send messages. Once we talked with a guy from Alaska and another time a woman from England."

"Wow! That's crazy," Toby said. "How could you talk to someone so far away with a flashlight?"

"We didn't. We sent our messages using radio waves. We

tapped out the Morse Code one letter at a time and .... Come here and look. Watch the flashing."

They all stood at the window, watching as Zach signed, "Remember, Morse Code uses a special combination of lines, called dashes, and quick dots to represent letters and numbers. This code sender uses long and short flashes. Toby, Write this down: A, N, T, H something, something E, S, G, R."

"Why is he sending that?" Toby asked.

"I don't know. Maybe the code sender has a friend in another building, and they signal each other."

"Can you teach me the More's Code?"

"Sure, but it's called the Mor-ess Code." He turned to Meg and signed. "Maybe you'd like to learn it as well. It's a lot like sign language since it uses shortcuts. You might learn something interesting."

Meg wrinkled up her nose as she signed, "Not sure I have time for anything extra. Schoolwork and basketball keep me too busy already."

Toby frowned. "Come on, Meg. It'll be fun. Maybe the person is from far away."

Meg shook her head and crossed her arms.

Toby recorded the letters as fast as he could. When the flashing stopped, he asked, "Can we signal back to the person?"

"I don't see why not. What do you want to say?"

"How about, Hello. Can we be friends?"

Zach slowly flashed letter after letter. "Sent. Now we'll wait. If any message comes back, you need to record the letters like coders do."

"Am I really a coder?"

"Yes. Starting this minute."

Zach and Toby received a short message back: Yes. Then

the coder continued sending rapid flashes over the next few minutes. Zach sent one last message asking the coder's tag or name. •— —• •—• —•— — came back. It spelled PRY. Another message followed: — — • •

Zach explained, "Flashing GE is short for good evening, or good night. PRY is signing off."

Toby was so excited he couldn't fall asleep. He pestered Meg, signing to her, asking if the coder was still sending.

She signed back, "I didn't look. I need to finish my schoolwork, and you need to go to sleep."

"But this is fun. When I grow up and I'm in the Army like Zach, I want to be a code person." He kept flashing — — • • on the ceiling until Mom came in and took away the flashlight.

ON ZACH'S NEXT VISIT, TOBY wanted to learn more shortcut signals. Zach made a list, then suggested they each needed a coder handle.

"What's a handle?"

"It's the name you use when you signal someone," Zach explained. "Your mystery friend's handle is PRY; maybe initials. Think up what you want to be called. Keep it short." He looked at Meg. "You, too. It might come in handy."

Toby thought and thought. "How about TCODER short for Toby Coder?"

"Sounds good."

They selected their handles: ZW4 for Zach, TCODER for Toby and MA1 for Meg.

When Mom sent Toby for his bath, Zach sat with Meg at the kitchen table and shared his book on the Morse Code. He signed, "Toby can record the signals, but you'll need to help with the spacing between words." He stood and went to the window. "Let's see if our secret coder is still watching."

Zach began: ZW4 to PRY.

The flashes came back quickly but faintly as if the flashlight battery was running low. Meg studied the flashes but couldn't see the spaces between letters, let alone distinguish any words from the recorded signals.

When Toby emerged from his bath, Zach spoke each letter to Toby, who wrote down as many as he could.

Zach's hands flew with a response then waited.

PRY: MU_T_ _ARNFROM_ _ _STKS

"Does this really spell something?" Toby asked.

"Yes, but we're missing letters. The way we've recorded it's gibberish."

Toby squinted up toward Zach. "What's gibber-some-thing?"

"It means something doesn't make any sense."

Toby asked, "Can we signal back?"

"Sure, bud."

Meg and Zach had pulled out their phones to text their ideas back and forth.

Zach: **Say hello.**

Meg: **Ask PRY to slow down.**

Zach: **Good! Ask for short words.**

Zach sent a brief message. Meg and Toby sat beside him, waiting for returning flashes. After twenty minutes, they gave up and closed the shade.

"That's it for tonight, buddy. Let's make a list of short questions to ask PRY the next time I'm here."

25

BASKETBALL SEASON STARTED SOON, TURNING every practice into a minor scrimmage and setting up new plays. Meg ignored the slights and played her position well, keeping an eye on Connie's signaling, silently hoping her JV teammates would send her the ball when she had clear shots. The subtle elbow and shoves told her any chance at being an integral part of the JV team remained difficult.

Since Eli also played basketball and the guys used the main school court on alternate days, they seldom saw each other after school. Meeting at the flagpole each morning, walking to classes, and sharing their lunch break was the extent of their time together. Meg enjoyed every moment they shared. Was she falling in serious 'like' for Eli? Maybe.

Weekends, instead of meeting up to study together, she attended his varsity home games. The Fishermen once again maintained their scoring strength, continuing to be the district team to beat. Aftergame meet-ups at the local ice cream shops provided another chance to see and be seen with Eli.

As an uninvited part of the sports in-crowd, she kept on the periphery of the elite table group conversations even though Eli pulled her in next to him. She read lips and smiled blankly as conversations sped non-stop around the table, preventing her from joining in. She felt invisible except for Eli holding her hand under the table.

The two weeks before winter break every teacher assigned enough homework to overload the strongest students. Projects would be due mid-January when the semester ended. Now was not a good time to get behind, but she kept the bedroom curtain open until Toby's bedtime so he could watch for flashes from their room. In January, if schoolwork slowed, ha, ha, maybe she'd have time to learn to signal and ask PRY questions.

Zach arrived Friday night and stayed over to Sunday evening, allowing time for them to sit with the living area window shade raised high to watch for flashes. When a short message flashed, Zach high-fived Meg and Toby. "The person said hello and asked who we are."

ZW4: 3 F R I E N D S

PRY: G R E A T P R Y H E R E L E T S T A L K

Zach introduced them to PRY and signed "PRY wants to know what we want to talk about."

Toby suggested "Why PRY uses the code."

Meg signed, "How about a riddle?"

Toby cheered. "Ask Why the chicken crossed the road."

Zach laughed. "You got it. Toby."

PRY: F U N N Y T O G E T T O O T H E R S I D E

Toby looked surprised. "PRY's really smart. Let's try another."

Zach and Toby asked several jokes and got back good answers as well as silly guesses.

Toby enjoyed writing down jokes, riddles, and short questions to send to PRY. With all their communications recorded in their coding notebook, Toby kept it tucked under his pillow beside his flashlight to be ready at a moment's notice.

He dragged Meg or Mom to the library to check out books on how to signal the code, then wanted to buy his own copy. Every night, he practiced short messages on the ceiling until Mom came to tuck him in. On weekends when Zach stayed over and stretched out overnight on the floor, the coding sessions never lasted long enough to suit Toby. His visits happened less seldom as Zach's Army group engaged in more weekend maneuvers.

One Sunday evening, Zach and Toby sent their message asking for shorter words and slower flashing.

PRY: Y E S B O T H

Through trial and lots of errors, they learned PRY was flashing POTUS, meaning the presidents of the United States.

Zach sent Toby's question: Why?

PRY: H I S T O R Y

ZW4: S E N D A G A I N

PRY: W A S H I N G T O N A D A M S J E F F E R S O N M A D I S O N

MA1: F I R S T 4

PRY: Y E S !

MA1: F A V O R I T E ?

PRY: J E F F E R S O N

TCODER: G E

PRY: G E

Toby looked disappointed. "I thought we'd be doing jokes."

Zach laughed. "We can and we will. Just make them short. While I am gone, maybe ask about math."

Toby frowned. "Nah. Sounds like school. Can't I do something fun?"

Zach thought a minute. "How about asking about PRY's favorite things?"

Toby shrugged. "I guess."

Zach showed Toby how to plan for communicating with PRY. "Write out your short question. Below each letter, draw the dots and dashes that represent each letter. Remember to leave spaces between the letters and longer spaces between sentences. As you get faster, you can share more complicated messages. For now, do easy, easy words. Meg can help you with spelling."

As December moved closer to winter break, Meg and Kelsey continued to work together.

Meg: **This load of tasks hitting at once makes me crazy. How can we do massive assignments and still play well?**

Kelsey: **Persevere. Donkey basketball is coming.**

Meg: **Donkey?????**

Kelsey: **You'll see.**

The last Thursday before winter break, the gym filled to the rafters with enthusiastic teachers, students, parents, and families anxious to watch the teachers play the students. The game was all in fun with proceeds supporting school basketball.

Teachers wore outrageous outfits with wonky hats and were given a ten-point lead before the game began. Varsity players wore their team uniforms, doing their best to quash the teachers within the first ten minutes. The audience laughed and cheered for both sides. The cheer team and the school band provided entertainment between the ten-minute quarters, giving the teacher-players a chance to catch their breaths. The final score: Varsity boys 38, Teachers 12.

Meg watched Eli play, noticing his great hook shot and how effortlessly he stole the ball. By the time the varsity girls took the court, the teachers spent most of the time between plays bent over, resting. The final score was Varsity girls 20, Teachers 11. Meg enjoyed watching. *It must be fun to play against the teachers. Maybe next year I'll have a chance.*

After the game, Eli skipped the team meetup at the ice cream shop in favor of joining Meg and her family at their apartment for dessert and an extra chance to be with Meg before winter break.

Toby, Eli, and Meg played Go Fish before Toby headed to bed, leaving Meg and Eli to play Hearts. Mom headed across the hall to visit Ms. Iris.

Eli slowed down the game by holding Meg's hand, making it hard for them to lay down cards. Later as they watched a Monty Python film playing on late-night television, the physical contact became more serious, spreading to arms wrapped around each other's shoulders and heads nestled together. The captioning appeared too briefly to catch the humor, but Meg watched Eli laugh and enjoyed the warmth of his company.

When Meg walked him downstairs to say goodnight, Eli stopped at the entry, pulled her close, kissed her forehead and cheek, then stepped back to text to her.

Eli: **Thank you for inviting me over. I'll miss you. Maybe we'll see each other over the break. QT**

Meg: **QT Call me. Meet me at the library to study?**

Eli: **Why? It's winter break! Let's go to the harbor or**

something, NOT homework. QT

Meg: QT We have finals in Jan. I need to do well so I can play ball.

Eli: You'll be fine. Think of where you'd like to go with me. I'll fill the tank so we drive to Tacoma or Olympia or somewhere you've never been. QT

Meg: QT Drive to the ocean?

Eli: Too far. Let's save it for next summer. QT

Meg dropped her chin and felt her face flame with heat. *I think that means he expects to keep seeing me. Guess we're dating for real.*

He planted another kiss on her forehead, then slid down to kiss her lips.

Meg's eyes flew open as Eli backed away and disappeared out the door. She slowly headed upstairs, touching her lips. Her inside felt warm and fuzzy. She smiled. *We're definitely dating.*

THE GRAY MONDAY MORNING LIGHT slid in around the pull shade. Meg stretched and checked the clock: 8:30 She sat up with a start. She'd overslept. She never overslept. Why didn't Mom wake her up? She'd be late for school. Even Toby was still asleep. What was happening? Meg raced into the kitchen. No Mom. Where…*Oh. Winter break starts today.* She relaxed and saw a note leaning against the salt and pepper shakers on the kitchen table:

> *Enjoy sleeping in. Could you and Toby please locate the Christmas decorations and hang up a few to brighten the apartment?*

Ms. Iris is home if you want to leave him with her to do anything with friends. Text any change in plans, etc. XOX

Meg stretched and yawned. She took out bowls for their instant oatmeal, set out brown sugar, and heated water. Then she tiptoed back into the bedroom and carried her clothes to the bathroom to get dressed.

When she stepped back into the bedroom, she noticed Toby's bed held an empty pile of blankets. She found him sitting on her bed looking out the window. Maybe she should take him to the Variety store or to see Stan after breakfast. They'd not been to the stores together for a couple of weeks. Basketball practices, homework, and days of heavy rainfall had interrupted their looking around.

She checked the sky: grey clouds. A good day to let Toby wander the neighborhood shops. She owed him.

Drat! She stopped. She'd promised Stan she'd work extra days for him. She hadn't set which days yet; they'd need to stop in and get her schedule. But, today had to be kept as Toby's day to wander.

THE NEIGHBORHOOD MERCHANTS LOVED TOBY. He always said hello and investigated their new merchandise, telling them what he liked. Since Meg now worked at Stan's, he'd had fewer chances to drop in and sample the unusual fruits and veggies. So, after they ate, cleaned up their dishes, and located the Christmas box, they headed to Stan's Mini Market.

"Ah! Toby!" Stan greeted him with a wave. "How are you? Come to taste my winter fruits?"

Toby waved and started looking around. He picked up little, orange-shaped orbs. "Are these baby oranges?"

"Yes. Mandarin oranges. You taste."

Toby took one and handed Meg the peels. He carefully separated the sections and popped one into his mouth. "This tastes better than a regular orange, and I can peel it myself!" He looked at Meg and signed. "Can we buy some?"

Meg handed him money. After he paid Stan, they continued to wander around the store. Stan signaled to Meg. She hurried his direction. "You come, 8:30 tomorrow? Unpack my boxes? Many more holiday things to put out."

"I'll be here."

Stan nodded and stepped away to help an early customer.

THE VARIETY STORE WINDOW DECORATION included shiny red items: firecrackers, shiny swags, dolls in red kimonos, and boxed candies. Kim Han, the owner, greeted Meg and Toby with a wave, then turned back to reading his Asian newspaper. The entire shop looked festive with items appropriate for Christmas he'd keep available through the end of January for various Lunar New Year celebrations. Toby wandered from aisle to aisle, looking at trinkets, sniffing incense packets, and asking questions Meg couldn't answer.

After more browsing, Toby bought two red paper lanterns before they moved on to the neighborhood park, where he played on the swings and the slide until a wintry rain began. They raced back to the apartment to hang their holiday decorations, after which Toby wrote his Christmas letter and wish list, asking for a loop-the-loop racecar track, the Battleship™ game, and a larger, more powerful flashlight.

THE NEXT MORNING, MEG REPORTED for duty at Stan's. She unpacked boxes of canned veggies and placed them on the appropriate shelves. She also dusted the showcase filled with Asian knickknacks that seldom ever left the case to be fondled by prospective buyers. Two hours later, she headed home, picked up Toby from Ms. Iris, and let him investigate the fresh produce Stan sent with her.

When Mom arrived, Toby shared his latest least favorite vegetable: bean sprouts. Mom declared him a food critic. He immediately rushed to his bedside crate, pulled up a notebook he used for drawing, and created a new section: Toby's New, Good, or Icky Foods. Bean sprouts made the first entry on the icky side.

26

THE FOLLOWING DAY WHEN MEG returned from Stan's, she and Toby hung the last of their holiday decorations. She felt her phone vibrate: a text arrived.

Eli: **Can I come over? QT**

Meg: **QT Yes. When?**

Eli: **Now QT**

How strange. He said he'd be gone during winter break, staying at a cabin and going skiing. Must have changed his plans. She really liked Eli. He didn't shout at her or distract her with wild hand motions. He often held her hand as they walked in the hallways between classes. Twice he'd kissed her, making her knees fluid as melting butter.

Now she hurried into the bedroom, combed her hair, put on a nice sweater, then sat in the rocker, waiting for him to arrive.

He arrived draped in cold air and the scent of winter. His smile made her feel liked and important. With cell phone uses limited at school, most students shied away from speaking with her, not certain what to say or even where to stand to talk to her. Not Eli. He walked up to her, tapped her shoulder, and waited for her to turn to face him.

However, things hadn't started out that way. In November, before they'd started to become a couple, he'd almost scared her beyond her ability to ever forgive him.

It was after school. Meg was walking down the main hallway and turned the corner, heading toward the gym along the dimly lit hallway. Suddenly, the hair on the back of her neck bristled; someone stood close behind her. She inhaled slowly but kept moving, gradually increasing her pace. The dim light aggravated the feeling she was being followed, reminding her of another time when a man came up behind her, grabbed her sports bag, then her. That time things didn't end well.

With so many students milling around in the halls, nothing bad could happen to her at Sherman Harrison, could it?

Someone tapped her shoulder. When she turned around, no one was standing close enough to tap her. Danger leaped into her mind. Why was someone playing mean tricks? She walked faster.

Suddenly, an arm grabbed her around the waist. A bolt of fear shot through her. She screamed and put her hands over her face. The arm dropped away. Students around her stopped and stared. Meg raced through the gym door, crying.

Once inside, her breathing slowed. She started to relax. There'd be no repeat of the attack years ago; no one throwing her to the ground. Or might there be? She stayed where she was, semi-hidden, frozen against the wall behind the door that lead to the locker room, waiting for her heartbeat to slow.

The gym door slowly opened. Meg quietly removed her backpack and clutched it to her chest, ready to protect herself or swing it at the person entering the gym.

A hand snaked around the edge of the door. Meg lifted her backpack above her head. Then she saw Eli's face. He looked bewildered. "Why are you crying?"

"Years ago, a stranger grabbed me."

Eli reached his hand out to her. "I'm sorry. I didn't know. Forgive me."

Meg pulled away. "Why did you sneak up on me?"

"I wanted to surprise you."

Meg's mouth pulled tight. Her eyebrows drew together as she took out her phone to text him.

Eli watched her face without looking at his phone even when it buzzed.

Meg: **You scared me. Don't ever do that to a deaf person. A strange man scared me once by coming up behind me. He hurt me, but I got away.**

Eli looked at his phone and nodded. He spread his hands wide and shrugged as he backed out of the gym.

Meg stood motionless for several minutes, trying to decide what to do next: find Eli and talk it out, stay after school and shoot hoops with Kelsey, or head home. Hoops won. The activity would help soak up the adrenalin racing through her body and give her time to decide what to do next.

Kelsey saw her jumpiness, but Meg refused to share anything as they shot baskets. On the bus home, both were too exhausted to text.

As Meg climbed the stairs to her family apartment, she stopped. Eli sat on the floor beside the door. His faint smile softened her anxiety.

He stood. "I'm sorry. Forgive me?"

Meg wiggled her hand side to side.

He reached for her hand, then stopped and pulled back before touching hers. "I wasn't thinking."

She shrugged and tried to smile. "I know. Want to come in?"

Eli shook his head. "Just wanted to make sure you're okay. See you tomorrow." He turned and hurried down the stairs, leaving Meg standing at the apartment door, wondering what tomorrow would be like. Would the encounter alter their relationship? If so, how?

THE NEXT DAY, ELI STOOD at the main entrance to the school, watching Meg approach. He shifted nervously from foot to foot as she stopped in front of him.

"Hi, Eli."

"Hi. Are we still friends?"

"Yes."

He pulled out his phone.

Eli: **If I promise to not scare you again, will you still be my special friend? My QT?**

"Yes," she said.

Eli reached for her hand. "Walk you to class?"

She nodded.

Eli took a deep breath and reached for her backpack to carry it for her. His thoughtfulness sent a shimmer through her heart. He stopped, took her hand loosely, and pressed it against his chest until he felt her relax. Only then did they continue down the hall.

Meg watched his eyes crinkle with caring when they stopped in the doorway to exchange hand squeezes.

He turned to face her. "Meet me after class?"

Meg nodded and entered the room ahead of him, enjoying her personal silence amid a classroom of animated, chattering students. It had been unfair of her to freak out and not explain, but the terror she felt in the dusky hallway brought back another, long-ago dark hallway. Maybe soon she'd be able to deal with darkened spaces, just not yet.

True to his word, from then on, Eli approached her from the front or tapped her shoulder and waited for her to turn to face him before he stepped close.

27

ELI TOOK THE STEPS TWO at a time to Meg's family apartment. He had great news. He pushed the button Zach had installed beside the door to 6C. It lit a bulb mounted inside the apartment near the door, letting Meg know when someone waited outside.

When she opened the door, her smile warmed him. He cared about and admired her far beyond her ability to help him through math class. He might in fact be falling in strong 'like' with her. Today's news might reinforce their blossoming relationship if she said 'yes'.

He entered the apartment and saw Toby standing on the counter, hanging a string of Christmas cards along the upper edge of the kitchen cabinets. He immediately went to help him.

Meg watched them laugh as they stretched out the cord. Eli acted like he cared about her entire family. He always spoke with her mom, played with Toby, and brought small gifts to the family. Today it was a bag of his mom's homemade Christmas fudge with peppermint bits. Toby eyed them before asking Meg how many he could have.

"One now. One after dinner."

Toby's lips pouted, but he took one, and bit in. "This is

real-ly good. Thanks, Eli. Your mom makes good candy!"

"You're welcome, kid. Maybe we can shoot hoops if it stops raining."

Satisfied, Toby headed off to play in the bedroom as Meg and Eli moved to sit together on the couch, holding hands.

"I'm glad you came over."

Eli took out his phone.

Eli: **I have news. Can your family come with my family to the mountains? We can ski together. QT**

"What?"

Eli: **We rented a huge cabin. My parents said I could invite your family. Please say you can come! QT**

A trip to the mountains sounded wonderful, but would Mom agree? She took out her phone.

Meg: **QT Where? How many days?**

Eli: **Stevens Pass. The week after Christmas. QT**

Meg: **QT I'll ask.**

Eli: **Good! I need to go. Buying a tree today. Can you come along to help me find a tree? QT**

Meg shook her head. "I can't. Sorry."

He kissed her cheek and texted before stepping toward the door.

Eli: **Text me when you find out if you can come to the mountains. QT**

MOM AND MEG SIGNED A conversation about the mountains after Toby was asleep. No reason to get his hopes up with so many details to consider.

"Make a list, honey. I'll check about getting days off."

The next morning, she sat with her mom, considering the details on her list.

Why Go	*Why Stay Home*
Time with Eli	*Zach coming*
Meet his family	*Work at Stan's – shoe $ $*
Fun/break from routine	*Take care of Toby*
Fun in mountains	*Extra BB practice time*
Sled and tube	*No app so we can chat*
Problems Going	*Problems Staying Home*
Meet Eli's family	*Alone most days*
They don't sign	*Entertain Toby every day*
Mom must work	*Eli/Kelsey gone*
No snow clothes	*Not meet Eli's family*
No cell service???	

MAKING THE LIST MADE THINGS clear, especially since Mom discovered she couldn't get the time off. Meg also learned there'd be sketchy cell service, limiting her chances to text or talk with Eli and his family.

Meg: **QT Can't go to mountains. Thanks for asking. Have fun!**

Eli: **I'll miss you. QT**

As SOON AS SHE SENT her message, she wished she could take it back, but reality determined their decision. Writing notes to talk with Eli's family would be tedious. From her lip-reading conversations at school, she knew strangers found her talking voice annoying; some people called it muffled, making her embarrassed in front of strangers.

Disappointment escaped in a steady stream of tears running down her face. *I'll miss him more than he'll miss me.*

He'll be skiing and playing in the snow. Even our short trip to visit Aunt Zinna's family is a no-go. I can pick up extra hours at Stan's Market for shoe money if Ms. Iris can watch Toby. Why is money so often the reason for our decisions? It's not fair!

MEG AND ELI MET AND exchanged gifts the afternoon of December twenty-third. They sat together holding hands on the apartment couch, watching Toby create a blanket-pile car racetrack on the floor in front of them. She gave Eli a book of math puzzles. He fastened a silver locket around her neck with a mini photo of them taken at the homecoming dance.

"I'll miss you," Eli signed and laughed at how clumsily his hands moved.

Meg signed. "Me too."

HALF AN HOUR AFTER ELI left, Zach arrived in a burst of energy. "Surprise!"

Toby raced to hug him. "I didn't know you'd come today."

"Della wanted to surprise you. Can you grab my sleeping bag before I drop it? Watch out for my backpack and my cot!"

Toby grabbed whatever Zach handed to him, including a large bag of wrapped gifts. "Wow! Some of these are for me! Can I open one early?"

Zach ruffled is hair. "Got to wait, kid. But one thing's for sure. We'll have lots of evenings to watch for flashes and send messages to PRY."

28

HAVING ZACH AT THE APARTMENT during the Christmas season felt squishy. Luckily, he was an early riser; otherwise, they'd have had a hard time moving around the living area with him stretched out on his cot next to the kitchen table.

Christmas Eve, they enjoyed a family favorite meal of hearty vegetable soup and fresh bread before they each opened one gift. Mom enjoyed finding a new sauce pot to replace her dented one used every day for fixing hot cereal. Meg opened a box filled with school and art supplies. Zach blushed when he opened a grooming kit. Toby told him, "It's so Connie won't be kissing your scratchy face."

Toby chose a big box, thinking it might be a racetrack. Zach had wrapped two pair of socks in a large box filled with wooden slats, saying "Use these as a track until you get a real racetrack when you're older."

His face momentarily showed his disappointment, but he quickly dashed off to use the slats, after tossing the socks under the tree.

CHRISTMAS DAY, THE FOURSOME ENJOYED a morning of opening presents. The star gifts included Mom's new winter coat, Toby's 'for real' racetrack, and Meg's new court shoes. Zach handed his sister an envelope with two coupons: brunch at their favorite restaurant and tickets to an ice hockey game for four guests. The rest of the day, they played games, including Toby's new Battleship™, and racing cars on his 'for real' track, before sitting down to a festive dinner and watching a holiday movie.

Zach's presence renewed the feeling of family celebrations with him visiting at Gran's farm. Meg wondered how much longer she'd feel lonely without Gran. Sleeping beneath the quilt she'd made, seeing her smiling face in the photo on the table, and looking through photo albums remained their last connection. She held onto them like a lifeline, especially during holidays. She also missed Eli, but in a different way; she'd see him once school resumed after winter break.

Each drizzly day, she, Toby, and Zach scoured the neighborhood and downtown Seattle, investigating new places. They wandered through shops with seventy-five percent off sales, looking at a myriad of items they'd never want or need, including fancy tire rims, massage chairs and a gigantic, movable cabinet on wheels. They ate at food trucks parked along the waterfront before they explored the sea-inspired shops, and free admission day at the Seattle Aquarium.

On dry days, they took buses to city and county parks to wander trails, scout for wildlife, and learn more about the area. The troll under the Fremont Bridge ranked among their favorite stops, along with the Government Locks. Toby became fascinated with the gum wall in Pike Place Market, vowing to chew a pack of gum and save it to add to the wall whenever they revisited the market.

Each afternoon, they returned to the apartment, filled with laughter and stories they shared with Mom when she returned from work. In the evenings, they watched for the flashing lights, ready to return messages to PRY. Their coding and decoding skills grew stronger as Toby's code notebook pages slowly filled with their messaging.

THE AFTERNOON ZACH LEFT FELT as sad as the day they'd left Yakima last August. Toby hugged him and cried; Meg barely held back her tears. "Come back soon," she signed, knowing he'd return whenever he could.

Zach hugged everyone as he stepped back. "Take care of each other and keep reading the flashes."

"We will," Toby signed. "Meg promises to help me."

Zach's energy and his love of them meant a lot. Their adventures helped Meg forget missing Kelsey and Eli. They'd return in a few days along with her normal school life, which included her beloved basketball, an activity she treasured every moment she spent on the practice court.

CONNIE WASN'T BACK FROM VISITING her family in Oregon, but Ms. Iris had returned from her granddaughter's home with exciting stories she shared when she watched Toby, allowing Meg to help Stan with his inventory. The tiny backroom in his shop was stacked to the ceiling with dusty boxes that looked to never have been opened. She discovered a dozen boxes with paper fans imprinted with Happy 2016, mouse-nibbled boxes of green tea and cartons of incense burners. Stan's nephew, Jun, selected sale items, rearranged shelves to display them, recycled empty cardboard boxes, and made a trip to the dump with unsellable items.

Meg helped Stan make sale signs since her English was stronger than his. They both left out adjectives, but she was learning to slip them in to meet the guidelines in her English classes. She realized she was *almost* excited to get back to history class, since it meant spending homework sessions with Eli.

Midday on New Year's Eve Day while Meg was playing cards with Toby, her phone vibrated.

Eli: **May I come over? QT**

Meg: **QT Yes.**

Eli: **When?**

Meg: **QT Any time**

Eli: **Open your door. QT**

Meg jumped up and flew to the door. When she looked through the fisheye, she saw Eli's grin. She nervously undid the locks and opened the door.

Eli stared at her and signed, "Hi"

She returned the sign as she let him into the apartment. He hugged her and then handed her a small cooler. "This is for you."

Meg grimaced as she set it on the table.

"Look inside."

Just then Toby burst across the room and grabbed Eli's hand. "Play with me."

Eli pulled Toby to a stop. "In a minute. Wait here. Watch Meg open the cooler."

Meg lifted the lid as if she expected a wild beast to jump out. What she saw inside made her laugh and quickly close the lid.

Toby grabbed the cooler and peered inside. "Cool! Thanks Eli!" He signed to Meg," Can we take it outside right now?

Meg nodded. "Grab our coats. Let's go."

They hurried to the alley, opened the cooler, and began making snowballs with the fluffy snow from the cooler. It was a small pile but enough for a brief snowball fight before they gathered as much as they could to make a tiny snowman. Toby carefully set their creation in the cooler, carried it back to the apartment, and saved it in the freezer before he hurried away to play with his racetrack.

Meg and Eli sat holding hands on the couch.

"I missed you," Meg said as she looked down at their connected hands.

"Ditto. I'm glad to be back."

ELI STAYED FOR NEW YEAR'S Eve dinner and shared his adventure aloud while Meg's mom signed the details to her. "I loved the snow and the skiing, but the cabin was strange; they called it rustic. It had a huge open space, a loft and four bedrooms. We fed the potbelly stove all day and all night to keep warm. The bad part…there was no sink, no indoor bathroom, and no electricity. We used candles and lanterns for light. I was glad we brought heavy sleeping bags because the cabin got icy cold at night.

"I felt like a pioneer. We heated our food on the potbelly stove and ate our meals inside at a wooden picnic table. When we came back from skiing, we ate, played board games, and read, then went to bed early. It was fun, but I'm glad to be home."

"Was the skiing fun?" Mom asked.

Eli's face lit up. "Amazing. I skied all day, every day and

some evenings until the slopes closed. I love night skiing when it snows. You'd have loved seeing the mountains and trees covered with snow. It almost made up for the rustic cabin."

Toby asked, "Did you have snowball fights?"

"Nope. When we go up for a day this winter, maybe all of you will come along. We'll make teams for a proper snowball fight."

Their evening was spent playing board games, eating snacks, and waiting for midnight fireworks. The entire Appens family and Eli joined Kelsey and her dad on the roof of the apartment building to watch late night displays set off from the top of the Space Needle and from along Elliott Bay. Kelsey handed out party horns, challenging them to blow as long as possible. Meg blew hard, feeling the vibrations move through her horn, suddenly wishing she could hear why everyone laughed so hard. Being deaf in times like this made her realize how much she missed during the noisy celebrating of the new year.

The group ended their rooftop viewing by twelve-thirty. When they headed down the stairs, Eli pulled Meg aside and kissed her. Every ounce of her body thrummed as he kissed her a second and third time. If this was a sign of what lay ahead, it might be her best year ever.

As Meg got ready for bed, she rehashed Eli's description of their mountain trip. A day trip sounded like fun, but it was probably a good thing she'd stayed home. Sounded like she'd have spent most of the trip alone in the lodge or freezing in the cabin, except for times she might have snuggled with Eli.

Once she climbed under her covers, she let her mind wander, remembering their kisses on the roof. They felt different from the ones they shared earlier in December. Had something changed or was she imagining or hoping they were becoming a real couple? She exhaled slowly, fluffed her pillow, and drifted off to sleep.

While they all slept, PRY, their Morse Code friend sent hours of unread messages, lasting until sunrise.

29

NEW YEAR'S DAY AFTERNOON, AS Meg cleared away dinner dishes, Kelsey arrived, filled with fresh energy and wearing new clothes. The texting began as soon as they sat down on the couch.

Kelsey: **Get your shoes?**

Meg: **Christmas. Wish I was on varsity.**

Kelsey: **JV will be OK. Lots can happen. Varsity may need a swing player. It could be you.**

Meg: **JV is better than varsity bench warmer.**

Kelsey: **Shop, then hoops tomorrow? Saint Vinnie's got new stuff.**

Meg: **At Stan's til 2:00.**

Kelsey: **Great. After then. Only 3 days then back to SHHS.**

When Kelsey headed downstairs, Meg frowned. She hoped 2019 meant Kelsey's friends would tolerate her, even if she played JV. She'd know soon.

TOBY SAT ON THE FLOOR in front of the television, playing

with his racetrack. The sound was turned up as he watched a large building collapse, creating a gigantic cloud of dust as it crumbled to the ground. The reporters' excited voices filled the apartment.

"That was amazing, Carl! Now we're about to experience that again!

"As we step into the new year let's not forget the building event of the season, or rather the first take down of the century: the implosion just south of Jackson. It promises to be the biggest demolition of a Seattle building in nearly sixty years.

"It happened in the same area of Seattle, to make room for our first, major professional sports facility the...."

Mom called out to Toby as she set a cheese crusted tuna casserole on the table. "Toby, turn off the TV, get Meg, and come to dinner."

30

AN ICY WIND FLOWING ACROSS Elliott Bay chilled Meg to the bone. She buried her face in the tall collar of her jacket and wished she was back in bed, staying warm and cozy or that today was still the weekend instead an early morning school day. The highlight today would be resuming her rituals with Eli: him waiting for her, walking her to classes, eating lunch together, and meeting briefly after school before their basketball practices.

The first day back in school resembled the beginning of the school year, with students greeting each other and checking out each other's fashion updates. Guys hovered around girls with renewed interest, while the girls acted shy, probably fake shyness, as they headed into the last three weeks of their first semester.

Assignments wound down with fresh reminders to finish their projects, study for upcoming exams, and turn in all late assignments, 'because half credit is better than no credit at all'. *Must be a standard speech every teacher gives. As if we didn't realize what was at stake.*

Mr. Oberlander's assigned history project in lieu of a test was due the day before mid-term exams began. He'd suspended the last section of answering unit questions, explaining they'd be expected to incorporate the answers to those questions into their project, share important suggested readings, and discuss notable people. He called it 'History in Action'. It accounted for fifty percent of their grade, which left many students shaking their heads with dismay if they'd not started working on it before the break. It demanded more detailed, more intense work than studying for a final. The outline of their project was due this week.

Meg talked with Connie about her idea to expand and embellish her earlier project. Was that a risk? Maybe, but it could help her understand history and might improve her grade if she could incorporate the unit questions effectively.

By the end of their talking about the project, Connie smiled. "I think it's a good idea if you double-check that you've added enough info from your outside reading."

ALL THE BASKETBALL TEAMS EXPERIENCED great starts. Her JV basketball practices plus games twice a week, as well as Eli's on other days, limited their time together. Her JV basketball continued to be difficult. She missed some of Coach Young's shouted play calls, and her habit of keying off other players didn't always work. The early personal slams of teammates calling her Ape Appens and ignoring her when she had a clear shot continued. Caught between lip reading their taunts and ignoring their slights, she continued to miss ball assignments. Even though she'd made multiple game-saving plays, Coach Young seldom played her. Meg's main job settled into blocking opponents and passing the ball to teammates. *Some team sport! Only when you're respected. Even with Connie's signaling in plays, it's not enough to make varsity.*

Kelsey's games landed on different days at different

schools, providing less time for them to connect. She was fast becoming a star player, with mentions in the school news and local sports section of the daily papers. Meg was excited about her success and a little envious of her increasing chances of being noticed and garnering a college sports scholarship.

IN THE CLASSROOM, CONNIE REMAINED a life saver. Meg's continued difficulty with abstract ideas, especially in history, depressed her. She struggled through chapters and lectures filled with lists of dates and places about long dead Americans at war with each other and fighting over land. Connie patiently broke down concepts by asking Meg questions about her personal life experiences and struggles, sharing how they related to events or moments in history.

"History follows a logical sequence just like your life does, Meg. Events have consequences. The same with countries across decades and centuries. Look at the events you read about. Ask yourself, did the event cause the country to grow or change or rebel? How do events in your life change you? Look for the cause and review the effect to help you understand how events in history affect change, good or bad."

WEEKS PASSED. GAMES WERE PLAYED. Projects turned in. Tests were predicably difficult. Halls felt unusually empty as the semester slid to an end. Thank heaven for an early release day following the end of the testing week. It gave the teachers a chance to finalize current classes and prep for the new semester. It gave Meg an extra day at Stan's Market, which also introduced her to her first ugly encounter with a customer.

Meg saw the woman in the market most every week. She was picky about what she bought, handling, squeezing, and examining every single tomato, apple, and orange, looking for imperfections she could show Stan and argue about how much he should discount them for her.

Stan was busy with a delivery person, so Meg walked over to assist the woman. "May I help you?"

The woman looked up. Her eyes narrowed. She wore a snarl on her face. "Do you know this apple is blemished?"

Meg nodded. She picked up another apple and offered it to the woman. "This is a better one."

"I don't want to talk to you. You speak funny. Get Stan. I want to complain how rude you are to me."

Meg nodded and stepped over to where Stan stood with the delivery person. She waited for them to finish talking then she pointed to the woman. "She wants to speak to you. She says I am rude to her."

Stan stared at Meg and shook his head toward the customer she'd pointed out. "I'll talk with her. You forget her. I know who is rude person."

Meg watched Stan approach the woman as she busied herself away from their conversation. Her brief humiliation melted away as she hung onto Stan's compliment. It surprised her. She knew he appreciated her hard work, and now he appeared to be standing up for her. She walked outside to reorganize the produce displayed in the open crates. The woman passed her, shook her head, and hurried down the street.

The following week, Meg met Connie in the school library. Her face was serious; her body looked intense. Something was wrong.

Connie handed her the first semester grade sheet and waited. Meg looked at each class grade. Math A, English C,

Science B-, PE B-, CTE B, and History D. All classes except History showed improvement. Had she failed her History project?

Meg's heart sank. The D meant she might not be allowed to play basketball. "What can I do?" she signed to Connie.

Connie signed, "I made an appointment with Mr. Oberlander for 2:50."

Meg checked her phone. "In 5 minutes?"

Connie nodded and started walking. Meg hurried after her. This meeting meant she'd be late for basketball practice.

As they entered the room, Mr. Oberlander sat at a table with two chairs facing him. A folder lay on the table.

Meg and Connie sat down.

He slid the folder across the table. When Meg looked up, he spoke to her through Connie's signing. "You still have late assignments from early in the first semester."

"Part of the problem was her first interpreter," Connie explained.

"I remember, but all assignments are part of the semester grade. She's done better since then, mostly B-'s and C's on assignments. Depth is still missing in her answers. Her project was acceptable, but overall, she's still falling short."

Meg felt like a bystander as their conversation speed along with Connie signing while also ignoring her. She looked away, too embarrassed to follow their conversation.

When Connie finally turned, Meg didn't like the look on her face. Her face was more serious than she'd ever noticed.

Connie signed, "He doesn't usually allow students to make up assignments after one month of being late, but I've asked him to allow you to take an oral test on some missing assignments and to let you explain your project. I'll relay the questions and your answers. Understand?"

Meg nodded

"You'll have the rest of this week to prepare. The talk will be after school Friday."

Meg nodded, said thank you, and looked down to her hands, folded in her lap.

Mr. Oberlander handed Connie and Meg each a copy of the assignments to be addressed and the possible topics he'd ask her to explain. "I will select one, two, or three and ask about a dozen questions. You will need to explain yourself using valid details on the missing assignments and your project, got it?"

Another nod

Meg and Connie entered a small conference room to talk.

Tears streamed down Meg's face, blurring the questions on the list. She signed: "How can I reread the book and be ready by Friday? What about basketball practice and JV games? "

She signed, "You may go to practices. He'll call Coach Young and okay it with her, but no games until after Friday, assuming you have positive results."

Meg closed her eyes, taking deep breaths to calm herself. When she opened her eyes she signed, "Thank you."

"I'll help you study. We'll go the public library after school, or I'll come to your apartment."

Relief spread through Meg as she signed. "When can we start?"

"Tonight, after practice."

CONNIE WORKED WITH MEG EACH night in the public library until closing. Ms. Iris watched Toby until she returned home to reread the texts and then discuss each chapter's questions and how they related to her project. By Friday afternoon, she'd prepared for questions about her early assignments and added depth to her project. Now she dragged herself to face Mr. Oberlander. Only the remote chance she improved her grade kept hope of continuing to play basketball alive

Mr. Oberlander invited Connie and Meg into his office. Once they started, Meg relaxed and answered his questions, providing as many details as she could related to the early years of the republic, the organization of the US Government, Manifest Destiny, and early settlers. From the look on Mr. Oberlander's face, she thought she was doing well until he asked, "What do we learn from studying history?"

That was *her* question all along. Could she answer it? If she wanted a chance to play basketball, she had to pull herself together and give him her strongest response.

Meg signed, "When I first started classes here, I asked myself that question. It took me all semester to figure out an answer. Our problems come from people putting their rights above others and making decisions without listening to each other. We keep making the same mistakes, just with different people and in different ways.

"In our class, you talked about all the different sides of Manifest Destiny. The government saw it as expanding the country. The Native Americans, the Mexican government, and the settlers had conflicting views. Each had valid issues. Should I talk about them?"

Mr. Oberlander nodded.

Meg continued signing her ideas, ending with, "Being deaf, I listen in a different way. I read expressions as people speak or sign to me. I really believe words can hurt all of us, even kings and presidents. If we stop to listen and consider what we're saying and how it affects others, we can make things better for each other.

"When I watch the news, I see we are still not cooperating like we should. We're still not taking responsibility for our actions. We need to watch and listen to each other, so we'll stop repeating our mistakes. I'm trying to change myself, from judging others before I get to know them. Everyone needs to care enough to listen to others. We need to look at problems and decide what changes we can accept that will improve all of our lives."

Meg gave examples from her life experiences, tying them to world challenges, as Connie taught her. When she finished, her face felt as if it was on fire. Had she been too honest? Could she truly change like she'd just suggested?

She watched Mr. Oberlander's face. He was usually hard to read, but this afternoon, she clearly saw his reaction.

Connie signed his comments, but Meg also made an effort to watch his lips beneath his twitchy moustache for clues.

"You've done a fair job answering my early questions. Now the question about why we need to learn from history: I don't agree with everything you said, but I appreciate your honesty. You still need more details to support your ideas, Miss Appens. However, I've changed your grade to a C-."

Meg nearly cried. She'd passed. Basketball and the fringe benefits from playing returned to her life. Thanks to Connie, her own extra effort, and Mr. Oberlander's willingness to let her express herself and listen to her views, she'd proven she could think more deeply than she realized.

31

ANOTHER MORNING OF ICY WIND off Elliott Bay made Meg shudder. The highlight of the day would be Eli, waiting for her before first period. But, even warm thoughts of him couldn't chase away the icy cold impact of being the lone deaf person in the school.

Meg's new semester schedule remained mostly the same, even first lunch; only one change: she now took Human Physiology instead of PE. Luckily, Connie continued with her exuberance intact. More students knew Meg needed to sit up front, so when she entered the new classroom, one student gave up his front row seat. She hated being the person to displace others, but appreciated his consideration.

The impressively detailed physiology book covered the body's cells and organ functions as well as how they worked together. The charts and graphs fascinated her. Maybe it would help her understand her body in action, especially while playing basketball. If she paid attention and studied diligently, it could point to a career as a sports trainer or a physical therapist, careers where her deafness might be less of a limiting factor. For now, her goal would be to carry the monstrously heavy text to class every day and use her special seating to her advantage.

The early slam of being labeled 'Ape' permeated the JV team. Ignoring the insult became more difficult each day, especially since Coach Young didn't appear to notice, or maybe she didn't care. Meg's main team assignment remained blocking opponents and passing the ball to whichever teammate looked her direction. She tired of being almost invisible, wishing they'd more actively let her help win games.

With Connie's help signing in plays and her own love of basketball, she continued putting on her face of false confidence. Maybe she needed another approach to gaining a scholarship, but what could it be? Without financial help, her future receded like the outgoing tide without a reciprocal high tide waiting to offer a positive outcome.

Mr. Oberlander's latest history project came due the last week of May, with their first draft due by spring break. Once again, he suspended their answering the text questions and replaced it by asking them to integrate all chapter questions and their answers to their new topic, US Imperialism. He spent class time sharing important readings from notable people, suggesting independent reading and materials about the era. Meg observed a collective shaking of heads from her classmates. This class felt more advanced, more like a college class. His justification: if you don't learn to read and analyze, how will you ever become a critical thinker?

The project plus a brief final exam accounted for sixty percent of their semester grade with ten percent based on class attendance and thirty percent based on participation in small groups.

Without Connie, the small group sessions would have created an unsurmountable challenge. Her quick signing and vocalizing of Meg's comments allowed her to participate in her small group in a timely, active manner. Those sessions interested her, as did what her groupmates had to say. Slowly, she found herself speaking up more and more and noticed her groupmates listening to her ideas without judgement.

In addition to staying up late to finish class assignments, basketball practices consumed every ounce of energy she could hang onto. Games should have been the cause of her tiredness; instead, she experienced long moments of warming the bench. True, their season was progressing well, but she itched to help make game-enhancing plays she knew she could provide.

SINCE WINTER BREAK, TOBY'S TIME with Zach made him more proficient in recording the words flashed in Morse Code. He'd race through his homework to spend more time as what Zach called being a Junior Ham, connecting with the unseen, unknown person signaling from the nearby tall building. With Zach's and Meg's help, he mastered sending simple messages. The receiving and decoding messages still presented a challenge. Meg smiled at the thought of Toby with his notebook constantly at his side. The Morse Code became his obsession, second only to his loop-the-loop racetrack.

Meg's frustration over selecting her semester project in history turned to a solid idea the evening Toby handed her his Morse Code notebook and asked, "What does this mean?"

She stared at the roughly recorded letters, looking for a way to separate them into discernible words beginning with, M E R I _ A I S _ _ A T _ O N. As Toby recorded more letters, she realized the message referred to America's involvement in world wars. She asked Toby to send back a simple message: Why Important?

Brief messages came back over the next hour. Toby faithfully wrote down every letter he could. Night after night, Meg asked short questions, feeling a conversation and a kinship developing with PRY.

One morning, she raced up to Connie, who was busy copying down class information for her. She signed, "I found a great focus for my history project. Can we meet after school today?"

Connie grimaced. "What about basketball practice?"

"There's a special teachers' meeting. Practice is cancelled. Meet me at the public library?"

Connie nodded. "I'll be there."

Meg felt a heavy weight lift away. With Connie's and PRY's help, she hoped she'd create an acceptable history project; maybe get a B or even an A.

Over the next few days and evenings, Meg wrote out her ideas on her computer. She spent time thinking about how today and what happened in the past related to her life. The value of looking back through history started to make sense.

Mr. Oberlander shared, "In one week's time, each of you will have 2 minutes to explain your plan before I ask any questions. I want to be certain everyone has chosen a broad enough view before going any further into projects. Remember, this replaces our unit tests, so be thorough."

Meg could feel the collective groan circle through the classroom as students turned to one another with rolled eyes and head shakes.

SHARING OF PROJECTS STARTED THIS week. Student after student stepped forward to share their ideas. Meg's hands dripped with sweat when she stepped forward to share her topic. She shifted her weight from foot to foot then started. "My project is how Manifest Destiny and American Imperialism are alike. Both are about controlling land and natural resources. Both are about a determination to gain physical land and increase power."

Mr. Oberlander squinted and tipped his head. "Who told you this?"

Meg signed and Connie translated, "I have friends who showed me a few comparisons, but I found most of the connections myself."

Mr. Oberlander tapped his pen and bit his lip. "Keep gathering proof. Permission to continue is granted."

Surprised, Meg blinked, nodded, and sat down. Each student so far had faced at least half a dozen questions. Was he writing her off or did he think she'd created a strong project? She definitely needed to ask.

After class she got her answer. "This is an excellent project idea. Be sure to show the comparisons clearly. I'm anxious to see how this goes. You've been paying close attention in class. Nice work."

32

HISTORY JUMPED AHEAD THROUGH A long list of wars, often called 'conflicts', with a surprising connection to the unknown coder. During Zach's next visit, Meg shared the conversations about how the coded exchanges with PRY related to history class.

Zach signed, "Might be a good time for you to begin to code yourself."

"I don't have time. Classes, homework, and basketball take up every minute."

Zach grinned. "And Eli? You seem to have time for him."

Meg flushed. "We're helping each other study. He's good at history, and I'm good at math." She paused. "We also shoot hoops with Kelsey and..." Another pause

"And what, Meg?"

"I like him. He's kind. He's helped me get my assignments while Connie's been out with the flu."

"I see. Sounds like a great partnership."

"It is. He comes over to study on the days I watch Toby."

"Does he know about PRY?"

"A little, but mostly we study."

Zach let the conversation drop and went to help Toby with more signaling shortcuts. From the log they'd been keeping, they'd only learned PRY was a retired college teacher who taught history and enjoyed their time communicating. It appeared PRY carefully guarded his or her privacy but became excited and more engaged when the conversations turned to history.

LATE IN JANUARY, MR. VANCE handed out their second mid-term English project directions and rubric. "This term we'll write about people we know. Pick a favorite relative who's had a strong influence on you. Persuade us of their influence on your life. Make sure you can sustain a paper for more than two pages.

"For this paper, we will share your overview, not read the entire paper aloud. Check my listing online of assignments for more details. You'll need to turn in your rough notes, your preliminary writing by the end of February for full credit. Read through the guidelines. Tomorrow, I'll answer questions. I'll need your essay subject by the end of the week. Now, on to discussing the skills behind writing to persuade others."

Meg noticed a collective restlessness around her as students reacted to the paper with relief. She certainly did. She thought about who she'd choose: Mom, Zach, even Toby inspired her. But the more she thought about it, the more she leaned toward writing about Gran. She could use some of her earlier ideas, the ones she'd written that ended with her 'F'. This time she'd be more focused, even though the project promised to be bittersweet.

At home that evening, Meg pulled out the scrapbook she and Mom created about Gran after she'd died. They'd collected old photos of Gran as a child. a teen, a young mother, and as the grandmother Meg knew and loved.

Her mom reminded her a lot of Gran. Even though she was her mother-in-law, they both had slender frames, were of medium height, and shared a similar look of fierce determination in their eyes. Both women wore their dark hair long or in a loose bun, and expressed themselves through their quiet countenance. Would Mom eventually have the same beautiful white hair as her mother-in-law? Meg hoped she would; it looked so distinguished on Gran, a farmer's wife who never graduated from high school, a woman who was as smart as her own mother. However, Della had enjoyed the opportunity to attend community college classes and become a sought-after bookkeeper before she married Hal, Gran's youngest son.

Meg slid her fingers over her father's picture with her mother on their wedding day. *They look so happy. Was mom truthful when she said their breakup had nothing to do with me being deaf? What went so wrong he walked away from us? Why couldn't Gran or Mom stop him from leaving?*

Page after page, Meg saw Gran's life unfold in the photos beneath her fingers. When she came to Gran holding her as a baby and the photos of them in the porch swing, tears threatened. *I miss you so much, but lately I feel I'm losing my memories of you.*

Meg closed the album and stared unseeing into space. After dinner, she pulled out the album again and told Mom about the English paper and missing Gran.

"Writing about her is a wonderful idea, Meg, but even if you don't write about her, you won't forget her. You can still talk to her. I do, almost every day."

"You do? Really?"

"Really. When her face starts to fade, I pull out this album and look at her. I can still hear her voice and her laugh. I know that will also fade, but we can each carve out a special place in our hearts to keep her with us always."

Meg's tears matched her mom's. "What if I can't remember her except when I look at pictures of her?"

Mom patted Meg's hand. "When you sit down to write, I have no doubt images and the days you spent with Gran will come flooding back. Then we'll have a new page for the album and your story about her for you and especially for Toby as he grows up."

Meg took the album to the kitchen table and thumbed through the pages, looking for inspiration on where to begin her project. She settled on the two of them sitting in the porch swing. A perfect photo for her cover page. Now for a title.

Title ideas floated around in Meg's head, but nothing felt right until she looked at the photo again: the porch swing. Perfect.

WHEN MEG GOT BACK HER first draft, comments covered her paper: too short, tedious, needs lots more details, watch your tense changes, talk about why she's a favorite relative, give us more info about your relationship with her, needs to be longer than two pages for full credit. Rough draft points: 30/50

Ouch! She'd need to get busy fast. If she didn't there'd be no point in thinking about basketball. She set to work, running through stories about Gran to elevate her paper and bring Gran to life. She couldn't remember her voice, but she did remember her win-win solutions for most of the problems Meg brought to her.

Gran's Porch Swing by Megan Appens

I remember Grandmother Appens as a wonderful

woman who loved me very much. Her full name was Adele Marie Easton. She grew up in eastern Washington, where she met and married Barney Appens when she was seventeen. They were orchardists, raised corn and wheat, and had a large garden to help feed their family.

In the early years, as autumn ended, I helped rake leaves into piles and jumped in them while Gran stood nearby, laughing. She brought out cups of homemade apple cider for us to share. We'd sit in the porch swing, talking, singing, and laughing. That's also where she read stories to me. I loved hearing her voice.

In the winter, I made snowmen with her and helped shovel the snow off the front sidewalk. I also carried in wood to keep the kitchen trash burner going. In all my photos and remembrances of Gran we're laughing and smiling.

After I became deaf at five years old, she treated me the same way she did everyone: with total kindness, patience, and love. She learned to sign so she could continue to talk with me and sign stories to me.

Gran always had time to sit with me in that porch swing. I never remember a time when she was too busy to help me with a task or tackle a problem. For example, when I had trouble with a young girl coming into my fourth-grade class, Gran sat with me, helping me go from mad to creating a plan. The little girl had stolen my book and run away with it. I'd chased her but couldn't catch her. Gran suggested a different solution. "Why don't you bring her cookies?"

"Why?" I signed.

"Obviously, the girl needed the book or why would she steal it? Take her cookies and tell her you miss having the book, but if she needs it, she can keep it.

Or tell her you'll read it to her if she gives it back."

I thought about it for a while, then agreed to try Gran's idea.

In school the next day, I handed the little girl a small bag of Gran's oatmeal cookies. The little girl looked at me and signed, "Why are you giving me cookies?"

"I always eat Gran's cookies when I read. What page are you on?"

The little girl's lips curled down into a frown. "I can't read."

I told her, "I'll read it to you during lunchtime if you want."

The little girl looked at me, nodded, and ran to get the book from her desk. After that day, I signed the words in many books to the little girl and other kids. My rules were that I'd keep the books safe for all of them to look at, and I promised they could borrow them and read them whenever our teacher allowed.

One of my other favorite times with Gran was watching her make quilts. She often used a sewing machine, but she preferred to sew quilts by hand. Her fingers made intricate stitches so small they looked like machine stitches. Each seam matched every other perfectly.

Next, she added decorative feather stitches making each quilt a colorful work of art.

Every family member was given one or more handsewn quilt. Mine is a crazy quilt made from remnants of my outgrown clothes. It covers my bed as a constant reminder of her love and caring and the wonderful times sitting together on her porch swing

Gran's daily examples provided a lasting influence on my life. Telling the truth, trusting myself and others to do the right thing, honesty, hard work, accepting myself, and appreciating my family are values I learned from her. I treasure each one and do my best to honor them and her every day.

Gran died suddenly last spring. No one could have predicted her death since she had been a strong, determined woman. Now, I worry I'll forget her. Even though I think about her most every day, I can't remember her voice since I was only five when I became deaf. I wish I could have held her voice in my head, but it's gone. My mother says Gran will always be with me. I hope so. She is my favorite person after my mother and my brother Toby. I'll always carry her love in my heart.

She turned in her project, early and proudly, knowing she'd honored Gran. Hopefully, Mr. Vance would find it acceptable, and she'd be able to embellish her final draft enough to earn a passing grade, no, a good grade, an A or a B.

33

CONNIE AND MEG STOOD IN Coach Pauls' office after school, waiting for him to appear. He sat down and nervously shuffled a stack of papers before he spoke. Meg suspected he planned to break the news she was no longer needed on JV. She braced herself, hoping she could hold back any embarrassing tears.

"I've asked you both here because we're thinking of using Meg as a replacement for Lettie Chambers on varsity. She broke a bone in her foot over the weekend and will be unable to play for several weeks, maybe the rest of the season."

Meg nodded. She'd read coach's lips and confirmed the news through Connie's signing.

Coach continued: "Can you learn the varsity plays over the next week?"

Meg stared, unable to move, but finally nodded.

Coach smiled. "Good. I'll see you at practice in a few minutes. Do you have questions?"

Connie spoke up, signing as she spoke. "I read an article last week about a deaf basketball player. His coach started using sign language to send in defensive plays. I was wondering if you might consider using a few signs with your team?"

Coach Pauls frowned as Meg expected.

Connie continued, "The team actually embraced the tactic and scored sixteen percent more points after they adopted signed-in plays."

Coach Pauls answered with a curt nod. "Let me think about it." He stood and looked at Meg. "Better get changed. Practice begins in ten minutes."

Meg hurried to the locker room and found Kelsey tying her laces. "Meg?"

Meg danced around, waving her arms, "I'm replacing Lettie."

Kelsey rushed to Meg and hugged her. "Great! Get dressed fast! Coach doesn't tolerate late arrivals."

Meg held her arm. "Don't tell the team I read lips."

Kelsey frowned but nodded. "OK. Come on!"

COACH PAULS RAN PRACTICES SIMILARLY to Coach Young. The team moved as though on autopilot, having come up through JV. In fact, May Evers, the team captain, led warm-ups, allowing Coach Pauls to watch their movements and shout out suggestions. Connie quickly signed each to Meg.

The team accepted Meg as a stand-in but didn't engage with her except during ball drills and running practice plays. She'd not expected anything more, knowing she'd need to prove herself, which she intended to do once she had time to learn the new plays.

Kelsey treated her with the same disregard she did every day at school. However, back at the apartment, things changed. They spent free time together out back, shooting and practicing Coach Pauls' unique plays. Meg watched

Kelsey intently, wishing she signed so learning plays would come faster. Since that was not the case, maybe Connie would remain their intermediary.

At this point in the season, the team's win rate was above sixty percent. With six weeks left in the regular season, they hoped to gain a spot in district playoffs, go on to regionals, and maybe the state tournament. Lettie, their best guard, sat on the bleachers, watching Meg's every move but making no offer to coach or speak with her. Meg was on her own, but she knew she'd be a strong replacement player if given the opportunity to prove herself.

School. Practice. Games. Homework. Eat and sleep. Repeat. Much to Toby's sadness, Meg no longer had time to work at Stan's, so she no longer brought home a bag of produce. While the pace was exhausting, Meg loved the potential opportunity to play varsity ball. She was holding her own, assisting on important plays, and gradually winning over the team.

The only brief shift in Meg's focus came on Valentine's Day. The senior class sold and delivered pink carnations to students during their last period. Meg sent one to Eli, Connie, and Kelsey with a brief note reading, "Thank you for being there for me. Meg"

In return she received a carnation from Kelsey and Connie; none from Eli. Disappointed, she walked home and trudged up the stairs. Her heart fluttered when she found a bouquet of red roses waiting outside her apartment door. The attached card read: You are a dozen times more important to me than anyone else, QT. Eli

She smiled and felt a rush of happiness spread through her body. He did care.

MORE THAN TWO WEEKS PASSED. It appeared Coach didn't see the value in using sign language. Until... Connie signed a set of plays he shared during a half-time talk.

He'd noticed Connie's quick gestures and Meg's nod. He followed another and another quick exchange before the team returned to the court for the second half of a neck and neck game with a rival team that always bested them. When today's game ended in a 44-43 squeaker, but a win, Coach pulled Connie aside. "Tell me about your signals to Meg."

"Am I doing something against the rules?"

"No. I just wondered what your signs mean."

"I send in a message or the play number so Meg knows your next move."

"It's so quick."

"Meg's a smart player. She watches and ...."

"How do you know my plays? "

"I've studied them. It's my job to be Meg's ears for all school classes. I'm staying for basketball because Meg's a great kid. I want her to have an even chance to play."

Coach scrunched up his mouth and nodded. "Thanks, Connie."

DURING THE NEXT WEEK'S PRACTICE, Coach watched the exchanges between Meg and Connie more closely. Once on the court, Meg responded to all the adjustments on her position during a scrimmage. He also noticed the times Meg was free and how the team ignored her in favor of a more seasoned player, often resulting in a failed shot because the seasoned player stood out of position to score.

After practice one afternoon, Coach met with Connie again. "Can you teach the entire team one or two plays using sign?"

"Of course. Choose the plays you want signed."

Coach's self-consciousness was obvious, but he practiced the hand signs with Connie's guidance.

AND SO IT BEGAN. COACH had Connie teach the numbers of two defensive strategies in sign. He'd yell to get their attention then he'd sign a play number.

At first, the team looked skeptical. Some ignored the signing and missed plays. Meg read both Connie's signals and Coach's signing. He was getting the hang of it but being a novice signer, he moved his lips as he moved his hands, as if it took both to share a message.

Having Coach send in signed plays wasn't noticed by the other team. As more and more Sherman Harrison players followed the signed directions, the team experienced greater defensive success. The next games, they scored additional points. Meg noticed another change: teammates began including her, allowing her to handle the ball and shoot. She often garnered needed points.

The following week, Coach added two more signed plays and saw immediate results. Scores continued to rise during games where they'd previously come away losing. They won one game 48 - 47 in overtime. In their next game, they pulled to within one point against their nemeses, a 4-A team losing 50-49, an unexpectedly close game for their 3-A ranking. Game after game, they gained momentum. Coach Pauls' excitement and pride grew.

Week after week, their acceptance of Meg increased. But now, Lettie looked ready to return to the team. How would her return affect Meg's playing time? Would she even remain a swing player?

34

ONE CHILLY, MARCH WEEKEND MORNING, Zach arrived with a large bag of *Dream Creame Knots* and a box for Toby. "I've come to give Toby a very, very belated birthday gift and to watch my niece play ball."

Toby rushed to take the box from Zach's hands, tore off the paper, and gasped. A set of binoculars appeared on the box cover. "Is this really what's inside? Just for me?"

Zach laughed, "You *can* share it, if you wish. Open it."

Toby and Zach attached the leather carry cord, and Toby began looking around the apartment using the binocs. "Wow! Everything is huge." He turned them on Zach. "Those medals on your uniform looks huge! Mom, you have loose hairs stuck on your collar."

Mom swatted them away. Everyone laughed.

Toby surveyed the kitchen, looked out the window, and read signs too far away to read without the binoculars. "This is super. Thanks, Zach! Here. Take a look."

Zach ruffled Toby's hair as he took hold the binoculars. "I hear you are becoming a great decoder of those flashes. Now you can watch them up close, maybe discover more exactly where they're coming from."

"I'll get my notebook and show you my notes. I get messages almost every night. Can you help me figure out more words?"

Zach thumbed through the notebook, then handed it back to Toby. "Nice work. You could take my job away with this. Have you noticed any patterns?"

"Meg has. She says the messages are dates of battles, names of generals, and ideas to help on her project. Maybe you worked for some of the generals."

Zach signed, "Let me see their names." He broke out laughing and reached over to ruffle Toby's hair once again. "These are famous generals from the last hundred years. Only a couple of them are alive, and they are very old men."

"Older than you or Mom?"

"Yes. Way older." Zach shook his head and chuckled.

Meg shared, "I used some of the information in my interim history paper. Earned a 'B.'"

Zach gave her a silent applause, then signed, "Sounds like you're making a great connection with PRY. Any idea why he or she is flashing words and numbers?"

Toby and Meg shook their heads.

Zach grinned. "Maybe you should ask, Toby."

THE FAMILY SNACKED ON DONUTS and listened to Zach talk about his latest assignment. Then he signed, "So Meg. What time is the game today?"

"Five-thirty. It's the district championship. We're one step closer to the state tourney."

"Guess I picked a great time to come watch."

"I hope I get to play."

"I thought you played all the time."

"Lettie's back this week."

Zach looked surprised. "But she broke her foot."

"Only a hairline fracture. She's learned the new plays as well as the sign language plays."

"I hope you get to play. I'd love to see you in action."

Meg nodded and silently hoped Lettie would not retake her position as a guard, but not because she didn't like her. She was okay, a bit snippy, but okay. Meg, however, wanted the position for herself.

Kelsey wanted Meg out there too. "You are as good as Lettie and you're a better team player. Lettie's a ball hog."

The Sherman Harrison gym filled to capacity to decide the team heading to the next round of the state championship series. Thirty-two teams from across the state had started the process. Sixteen remained, each wanting to advance as one of four teams heading to the state finals with hopes of becoming state champs and earning bragging rights. This year, both the boys' and girls' teams from Sherman Harrison remained in contention.

The girls' game played out as a shooting contest with scores staying within five points of each other. As the game wound down, both Meg and Lettie played. The teams continued to trade scores as the minutes ticked closer and closer to the end of the game. Coach shouted and sent in sign language plays at a dizzying pace. The latest one called for Lettie to pass the ball, but she ignored the call, went in for a lay-up, and missed. The Fishermen were down one point. The score: 48-47.

Their opponents, the Gulls, raced down court, stopped, and shot. Score: 50-47. The Gull fans went wild.

The Fishermen responded with a quick break and a pass, but it bounced off the rim. No basket.

The Gulls pressed down the court, went in for a lay-up, but missed. Meg grabbed the rebound, raced down the court, and was fouled. She made her two free throws. Score: 50-49. Fans for both sides jumped to their feet, shouting encouragements to their teams.

As the Gulls moved down the court, they lost control of the ball. Meg recovered it and passed it to Kelsey, who dribbled the ball just past the mid court line and threw a long shot with three seconds to go. The klaxon sounded as the ball cleared the rim with a whoosh. Fishermen pulled out a win 51-50 and headed to the next round of championship games, their first visit in four years.

Sherman Harrison fans jumped up and down and stomped their feet, shaking the bleachers with their excitement. They stayed around to celebrate as the pep band danced around the court while the exhilarated students blasted out the school fight song.

Back in the dressing room, Coach Pauls congratulated the team. "Well done, ladies. Your teamwork was the key to our win. Our upcoming practices will need to stay focused. Before state, we'll add another signed play or two. Thanks to Meg and Connie, our secret weapon may be making a difference."

MEG'S FAMILY MET AND CELEBRATED the win at the local ice cream shop. Kelsey and her team friends had already arrived and sat at a large, round table. The ice cream shop buzzed with excitement as more and more Sherman Harrison fans crowded inside.

Most rushed to the team table to pat the team members on

the back. Meg watched, wondering if they'd stop by her family's table; none did. She inhaled deeply and looked back at Toby, who stood beside their table, imitating a player tossing the ball to the hoop, shouting, "He stops, he shoots, he scores! The crowd goes crazy!"

Lettie pushed back from the team table and headed to the Appens table. Meg looked up at Lettie's snarly face. "Why didn't you throw me the ball? I could have made a three-pointer. You're lucky they fouled you. We could have lost the game because of you."

Players seated at the team table watched the conversation. Several girls walked over. Kelsey arrived first.

"Don't listen to Lettie. She's just jealous." Kelsey turned to Lettie. "Why aren't you glad we won the game? Basketball is a team sport. It takes the support of all five of us to score every point."

Lettie stood nose to nose with Kelsey. "I'd expect you to take her side."

Kelsey waved her hand in the air and pointed to the girls who'd joined her at the Appens table. "Looks like other team members support Meg."

Meg looked from one face to another, feeling nervous as the center of so much conversation. She stood abruptly. "Please be happy we won."

Lettie glared at her. "I'm going to the coach. You're deaf. You don't belong on our team."

Another team member chimed in, "Let her go, Meg. You did the right thing."

Meg watched Lettie back away and hurriedly leave the ice cream shop. She looked to her mother, who signed what had been said. Meg scanned her teammates faces. They looked at her with kindness. Several patted her on the back before they returned to the team table or headed out the door after Lettie.

Back home, Meg stood in the shower, letting the steady stream of hot water cascade over her, hiding her tears. *Lettie was so angry. I don't understand why. Did she think I was being a ball hog like she is? The team supported me. Did they do it because of Kelsey, or did they think I did the right thing? I dread our next practice.*

SHHS halls buzzed with conversations about both teams' successes. The increased scheduling of tournament practices zapped Meg's reserve energy, causing her to collapse into bed earlier than usual, but still feeling exhausted the following morning. Her pile of assignments took second place in her mind. *Will I stay on varsity after Lettie talks with the coach? I've seen nothing that means he plans to bench me permanently. He's just added more sign language plays. Lately, many of my teammates are using sign language greetings in the hallways. I might be getting closer to being accepted for myself.*

35

AS THE STATE BASKETBALL TOURNAMENT moved closer, basketball fever took over the school. The boys' chances of winning the state championship remained high. The girls' hopes grew stronger as they returned to contention for the first time in nearly half a decade.

Practices wore Meg down. Homework suffered. Her time with Eli all but vanished. Luckily for Toby, Ms. Iris had time for him, providing a steady place to finish homework and play with the other kids she watched. Mom remained deeply buried in tax season, causing their leisurely family dinners to disappear, replaced by hurried meals and quick goodnight kisses and tucking in.

Toby took solace in using every spare moment after dusk to record and signal to PRY. One night he interrupted Meg's homework and signed, "I think PRY is mad. I send messages but it's been a long time since I've gotten any messages. Can we call Zach and ask him to come over and help me?"

Meg signed, "Zach can't come whenever you have a question. He's coming for the basketball tournament. Until then, record any messages you receive."

"Can you look through my notebook?"

"I will once I get caught up on my schoolwork. Now, go

play or send messages. It's half an hour till your bedtime."

Toby didn't care what PRY sent, as long as messages kept coming. The fact PRY called him Funny Kid made him excited. He liked having a coding friend. But he began to wonder if PRY was tired of his silly messages.

After Meg finished her homework, she picked up Toby's notebook. She looked at his entries. His skills improved daily, allowing him to capture more words from PRY's messages, especially about Meg's history project. She should include those pages of info from PRY in her final copy. Maybe it would impress Mr. Oberlander. Luckily Mr. Vance found Gran's Porch acceptable with instructions to "go deeper and expand your persuasive comments" 35/50. Your showing stronger writing.

Toby was right about a change in messaging. It had been days, no weeks since PRY sent anything. Maybe he or she moved or lost interest in their endless questions. Once the tournament ended, she'd spend more time learning to code and try to uncover why things changed.

SATURDAY EVENING, MOM SAT ON the couch, mending the knees of Toby's favorite jeans. She'd turned to the local news with the subtitles locked on so Meg could read the news if she wandered into the area.

Meg stopped when the screen showed photos of their neighborhood and the newly fenced off area.

"That's right, Bill. Seattle's second implosion is just days away. The sports venue will grow once again with the addition of a parking tower, velodrome, and swim complex, making Seattle a sports destination for national and international events.

Here's the 1960s implosion footage to give viewers an
idea of what to expect as we set the countdown clock."

MEG WATCHED THE FOOTAGE SHOWING the Kingdome's
collapse in a gigantic cloud of dust. Toby applauded and began
rushing around, mimicking the explosion with wild gestures.

Mom noticed Meg's interest and signed, "Well, there goes
our neighborhood. At least my jobs have stayed in the area. I
was afraid they'd move out of town. It won't be long before this
entire area will be hit by wrecking balls to make way for pricey
apartments and condos."

"What will we do?

"By then, hopefully you'll be in college, leaving Toby and
me to find a new place."

Meg nodded, thinking about making it to college. *Hopefully Mom's right about everything. All the more reason to keep
my grades up to grab a sports scholarship. Me and every other
girl on the team.*

Meg turned her attention back to the closed captioning of
the television news.

"Moving on to local sports, here's Fred Manning.
What's the word on the state high school basketball
championships, Fred?"

"Well, Marty, we're moving closer to both the boys'
and girls' state championship games. We're lucky this
year that both will be in the Puget Sound basin. Our
boys are playing in the Tacoma Dome, and the girl
are on Mercer Island. With both SHHS teams in the
mix, it should be exciting for our viewers. Tickets are
still available but going fast, so grab your seat soon.

We'll have more news and team details in the eleven o'clock hour. Back to you, Marty."

"In other news…"

Mom turned off the television and called, "Toby! Come finish your book report. Toby?"

No reply.

"Toby?" She found him in the bedroom, signaling with his flashlight. "I know you like being a coder, but you've not finished your book report."

"Just a few more minutes." he said without looking away from his binoculars. "I'm waiting for stuff for Meg, but PRY isn't answering. I have to keep signaling."

Mom reached for the binoculars. "No. It's getting close to time to go to bed."

36

THE FIRST DAY OF THE women's championship arrived with clouds and rain, typical for late March in the Pacific Northwest. Meg was up early with jitters racing through her at breakneck speed. Pacing the apartment didn't help.

When she looked back into the bedroom, Toby lay sprawled crosswise, his typical position, with his covers spilling onto the floor. She wished she could sleep in; maybe the day would go faster if she had.

She checked the clock: 7:30. She could get homework started but didn't think she could concentrate. The game tonight demanded she play her best for the team and be seen by college basketball scouts who attend championship games.

The neighborhood was abuzz about the impending buildings to be taken down. She should take Toby to view the huge city block now a fenced-off area. He'd love to see them before they crashed to the ground. Neighbors were warned to stay away during the implosion because of the massive cloud of dust and debris. It was expected to match the one produced in the 1960s. Television stations broadcasted the history of the project, as well as film of the Kingdome folding into itself over and over and over. This morning was the last chance to see the area; the implosion, previously scheduled to take place on

Monday, had been moved to late this afternoon because of the forecasts of incoming bad weather predicted to begin by Sunday evening.

Already, several nearby small buildings, including her mom's second job building, had been dismantled, leaving vast spaces of exposed dirt, concrete, and blacktop, providing a true picture of how vast an area the city block covered. Before bedtime tonight, the tall apartment buildings would be reduced to a massive pile of rubble, if the clear weather held.

Meg's game didn't start until eight-thirty. She'd need to be ready by four o'clock, to catch a ride with Kelsey and her father and board the team bus leaving at four-thirty.

The plan was for Mom to return from her weekend job, pick up Toby from Ms. Iris, then meet Zach and Connie for a quick dinner before heading to Mercer Island. They needed to arrive early if they hoped to grab good seats for the Sherman Harrison game.

After breakfast with Toby, she played cars with him; then they walked over to the fences around the area where the buildings would be imploded. Hundreds of people stood looking into the vast empty space where offices and business had recently served their neighborhood. Now the tall brick apartments, the last structures standing in the way of completing Seattle's gigantic sporting complex, had a date with demolition.

They continued their walk through the neighborhood with a short stop at Stan's Market, followed by heading home to fix their lunches. Three more hours to fill before leaving for the big game.

Math homework completed. Physics text read. English

mid-term project... so much writing yet to be done. She delayed that task by doing a load of family laundry.

With no sign of Kelsey in her basement apartment, she read more history while she waited to toss their clothes into the dryers.

3:00. Clothes dried, sorted, and put away. Maybe she'd check Toby's Morse Code notebook for the most recent code messages from PRY. Scanning it more thoroughly than she had previously, she noticed weeks with no entries. Had Toby mentioned that to her? She found him building mountains with their covers on the floor of the bedroom piled next to his racetrack. She signed, "Toby, why are there no new messages in your code notebook?"

Toby shrugged and looked up. "PRY stopped sending messages. I think PRY moved."

"Why are the last words scribbled out?"

Toby looked at them and shrugged. "PRY sent those so fast I couldn't keep up. Now, I don't have anyone to signal." Toby turned back to playing with his cars.

Meg took the notebook to the kitchen table and scanned what Toby recorded. It didn't make sense. She called Toby to the table and pointed to the last page of letters in his code notebook and began signing. "Tell me about these. They look different. There are no history words or lists or questions. This is just a pile of letters."

Toby shrugged. "I've been telling you the messages stopped."

Meg closed the book. "If PRY is gone, we can look through this tomorrow. It's almost time for me to leave, so start to clean up. I hope Ms. Iris gets back in time to watch you until Mom comes to pick you up."

Toby signed, "She will. I can hardly wait to see that old building come down tonight."

"You'll miss it 'cuz you'll be at dinner and then my game."

"Can't I stay home and watch it?"

"You're not old enough to stay alone."

"But I did last week."

Meg felt her patience wearing thin. "It was fifteen minutes. You'd be alone more than four hours."

"I'm no baby."

"I know, but you can see it tomorrow on TV."

Toby put on his fake-y sulk, took the binoculars, and sat at the window, more to ignore Meg than to decode any incoming signals.

THE CLOCK CONTINUED TO MOVE as if in slow motion while Meg's insides jittered like riding on a bumpy road in a car with no shocks. Heavy clouds gathered, dimming the daylight. It was still too soon for Meg to leave for the game. Toby set aside the games he'd been playing on Meg's cell phone so they could play checkers to pass the time.

3:45. Meg's butterflies did laps throughout her body. As she straightened her bedcovers and adjusted the curtain. The cloud cover dipped to near the tall buildings to be imploded.

Meg saw faint flashes. "Toby! Bring your binoculars. Hurry! I see flashing"

Toby joined Meg at the window. He trained his binoculars on the tall apartment building. He tugged Meg's sleeve. "It's S-O-S! It's coming from PRY's building!"

"Send a message. Ask if it's PRY."

Toby sent the message and waited. Shortly a message came back. Toby began writing: ...17SOS817SOS817SOS

Toby's eyes grew wide. He began signing fast. "I think PRY's in trouble."

"Where's my phone?"

Toby shrugged.

"Find it, now!"

Toby grabbed the bedcovers and shook them. The phone fell onto the floor.

Meg grabbed it, then turned to Toby. "It's dead. You forgot to charge it after playing your games."

"Sorry."

Meg looked around the apartment and grabbed the flashlight Toby held. "I'm taking your flashlight. Find another and signal to PRY that we got the message."

"OK."

She signed, "Wait here for Mom to pick you up. Don't answer the door unless it's Mom or Zach or Ms. Iris, understand?"

"What do I tell Kelsey if she comes?"

"Tell her to go without me."

"But Meg..."

"Do as I say. Understand?"

Toby nodded to Meg's back as she hurried out. She waited outside the apartment until she was sure Toby had time to lock the door. Then she raced down the stairs and started toward the fenced-in buildings.

The clouds hung low, stealing the afternoon light. Rain threatened to start early. She crossed against traffic lights and raced between cars, causing drivers to slam on their brakes. Her concern for PRY overshadowed any possible caution.

As she approached the fences, she stopped and looked up. The flashing had come from inside the fence. What could she do to help PRY?

37

A 10-FEET HIGH CYCLONE FENCE topped with razor wire surrounded 2 buildings including PRY's building, and the rest of the recently leveled block. Signs posted every few feet read: Keep Out... Danger... Stay Back 100 feet.

Meg searched the fence for a way get inside. The sections were tightly bound and padlocked.

A guard raced toward her, frantically waving his arms. She ran away from him, searching section after section, looking for any loose space between sections.

One area had a small gap. She slammed against the fence, forcing a space large enough to squeeze through and slipped inside.

The guard ran her direction, waving his arms.

She crossed the open space and raced into the doorless entry of the tallest building.

Even with all the windows removed, the interior was dark as a moonless night in a forest. Meg flipped on Toby's flashlight. A opening near the entry must had been an elevator. It had no door. When she flashed light inside, she saw a deep, empty hole.

The stairs around to the left were still intact. She started up, two steps at a time. Her heart raced as she reached the second floor, then the third, fourth, and fifth. Toby's message suggested PRY was on the eighth floor, apartment 817.

Debris filled the stairways, but she raced over and round it. A side ache slowed her. She felt as if her lungs might explode, so she stopped and bent forward to catch her breath.

Knowing the implosion was scheduled for late afternoon, she forced herself to resume moving. The police or a guard would soon find her.

Eighth floor.

She turned the flashlight's beam to read apartment numbers. Turn right to apartments 820 through 850. The wrong way. Seeing 801 – 819, she turned left, racing over more debris piles and passing rooms with no doors. She hurried on until she came to 817; the only apartment with an intact door.

She turned the handle. Locked.

Meg slammed her body against the door over and over, then raised her leg and kicked the handle until it gave way. She raced inside, down the entry hall, flashing her light from side to side, following a faint light ahead of her.

Entering a barren area backed by a wall of windows with the glass removed, she stopped and gasped.

A frail man sat in a wheelchair, his legs and shoulders bound with duct tape. He held a flashlight in front of his face with prayer-like hands.

When he saw Meg, he dropped his hands and the flash-light. It rolled across the floor.

Meg directed her flashlight onto his face. His lips said, "Help me."

Finding a small loose end around PRY's ankles, she tugged at it, then yanked and yanked until it gave way. Next, she unbound his body from the wheelchair.

His face showed a combination of fear and relief as Meg laid her flashlight on his lap, picked him up, and began running down the hall toward the stairs.

Down, down, down, Meg cautiously hurried, one-step at a time, over the debris with the light from the flashlight bobbing across the walls and stairs. PRY was as light as Toby, but how long could she continue without stopping to rest?

This wasn't like the times she toted Toby around the apartment on her back. He held onto her as they played capture. PRY's arms hung useless, making him unable to grab hold of Meg.

On the fifth floor Meg stumbled, dropped the flashlight, and almost dropped PRY. The flashlight bounced down the stairs in front of them.

Meg gasped and slowed her pace, knowing from her race up the stairs, many held piles of building debris. At this slower pace, she felt PRY's weight. Her arms vibrated with weakness. How long could she continue even one more flight?

A series of lights appeared below, moving closer and closer to Meg and PRY. Were people coming to help, or was it someone intent on harming them? Should she stop and hide or keep working her way down the stairs?

The stairs shook as a handful of police and firefighters wearing headlamps rounded the turn on the stairs just below Meg. She stopped when their flashlights blinded her. They reached out to take PRY from her arms.

She saw their lips moving but couldn't make out what they said in the dim light, so she made no attempt to speak or sign.

Hands reached out to steady her and escort her down the stairs. They were the only way she remained upright.

OUTSIDE THE BUILDING THE AREA was flooded with flashing red, blue, and white emergency lights, turning the area as bright as noon. Her escort guided her through the crowd of emergency personnel to an aid car parked next to the fences. The aid workers covered her with a blanket, took her blood pressure, and handed her a bottle of water. They talked to her, but she felt too exhausted to read their lips. She leaned back against the open door where she sat on the back of the aid car.

That's when she noticed the second aid car loading PRY inside. The doors closed; the aid car turned on its sirens and lights and drove away.

A policeman approached Meg and sat beside her. She knew he was asking her questions, but she didn't answer. He patted her arm as she read his lips: "Rest a little longer. I'll be back in a few minutes."

Meg sat still for a couple of minutes, then looked around. No one stood nearby. She made a sudden decision.

She slipped off the back of the aid car and hurriedly made her way to the opening where the emergency vehicles exited.

Once there, she raced across the street and into an alley, where she squeezed behind a dumpster to rest and hide. She exhaled slowly but kept watch until she was certain no one followed her.

Maybe she'd gotten away, and she'd not have to explain why she broke all kinds of laws and ignored the warning signs posted everywhere. At least PRY was safe. Hopefully he'd recover.

Why would anyone want to harm a frail, retired history teacher? Why was he bound into his wheelchair? Will the people who tried to harm him come looking for me, thinking I know something? I need to make sure no one finds me or tries to harm my family.

MEG STAYED SAFELY BEHIND THE dumpster for what felt like hours. The rainstorm started in earnest and continued to pelt the area. Still, no one moved her direction. The implosion was due any minute. Would she be safe where she'd hidden?

Minutes went by. Nothing happened. They must have delayed the detonation. Maybe it was safe to go home now, before anyone found her and took her to the police station to question her. She rushed past people who, despite the downpour, had gathered to watch the flurry of activity. Across two streets and down one block she slowed to a walk.

Back at her apartment building, she trudged up the stairs, still wearing the aid car blanket. She had no key, so she knocked in case Toby was still home. No answer. She slid down the wall too exhausted to move.

A hand shook her shoulder. She woke with a start. Zach squatted next to her. "Are you okay? he signed.

Meg nodded as tears streamed down her face.

Zach unlocked the door and led Meg inside, where she collapsed on the couch.

He signed, "Toby said something about PRY being in trouble but he didn't know where you were."

Meg nodded. "I tried to help him."

"Why didn't you answer my text?"

"My phone's dead. Why are you here?"

"Your mom sent me to look for you after Kelsey's dad asked why you didn't take a ride with them."

Meg shook her head and let tears freely flow down her face. "Is there time to go to the game?"

Zach checked his watch. "Of course, but you'll be too late to play."

Meg exhaled deeply and nodded. "I know, but I need to

be there."

Zach watched her stand and sway before she rolled her shoulders and shook out her arms and legs. "I need a shower. I'll hurry."

Zach nodded.

As Meg went into the bathroom, he called his sister to report on Meg. "Yes, Della, She's fine. I guess she went to help PRY.... No. I don't know what happened, but Meg is a dirty mess.... I did try, but she isn't sharing any details....Yes.... I know.... But she wants to come to the game anyway.... We'll be there as soon as she gets out of the shower.... Right. Bye."

MEG EMERGED FROM THE BEDROOM wearing her team uniform and street shoes. She grabbed her jacket from the coat tree as Zach opened then locked the door behind them.

Meg slowly made her way down the stairs, using the hand-rail and listing forward. Zach noticed but didn't stop her or ask any questions. She'd tell them what happened when she was ready.

A shiver of fear ran through him. *Had Meg done something foolish? What if she'd been hurt in her hurry to help PRY? What if she'd gotten more injuries than the scrapes and scratches showing on her arms and legs?*

WHEN THEY ARRIVED AT THE game venue, they saw the SHHS girls warming up. The scoreboard showed it was the end of the first half. SHHS was behind seven points.

Meg watched Zach look around the SHHS section. She saw where her Mom, Toby, and Connie sat. They returned Zach's and her wave.

He turned to Meg and signed, "Can I do anything for you

before I take my seat?"

She shook her head and signed. "Please tell them I'm fine. I'll explain everything after the game."

Zach hugged her and made his way around the court to join the others.

Meg sat in the bleachers behind the team's seating area. Fellow teammates turned toward her. She watched them out of the corner of her eyes and made no attempt to meet their gazes. *Maybe I shouldn't have come. Maybe I shouldn't have left the aid car. Maybe I should have told the police what happened, but I don't know what really happened to PRY.*

Kelsey turned from team warmups and gave Meg a strange, questioning look. Meg shrugged and looked away. How could she ever explain what happened even to Kelsey the only person who might understand? What about Coach? He hadn't seen her yet.

Coach noticed Meg when the team returned to sit down to wait for the start of the second half. He glared at her briefly before he turned his focus to the court. By the time the referee blew his whistle, all eyes returned to the start of the second half. Meg sat, alone amid a huge crowd, temporarily forgotten.

The game ended with a loss for SHHS 53-46. Meg felt their let down. She stood and followed the team off the court. When they turned into the team locker room, she stopped outside the entrance. Entering would be a bad decision. No one would want to see her. All her hard work to be an active part of the team ended this evening. Once she'd calmed herself, she'd head out of the arena to wait for her family.

38

MEG THOUGHT ABOUT PRY AND his rescue. Had she been foolish to think she could handle things by herself? She'd put Toby in jeopardy by leaving him alone. She'd broken into an area marked Keep Out. She'd run away from a guard and the police. Maybe she could have tried to make the guard understand, but would he believe her? Probably not. PRY would most likely have died if the implosion had taken place on time. Then she'd have had to live, knowing she'd let him die.

Someone tugged Meg's arm. Kelsey stood beside her, breathless. "Coach wants you to join us."

The team sat on the locker room benches, wiping away tears as well as sweat while they guzzled from their water bottles. Coach stood by a white board; he watched Meg and Kelsey enter the room. All eyes followed his gaze, then dropped away with looks of disgust. Coach's eyes followed Meg until she sat on a bench behind the team.

Meg felt heat rise through her body like a furnace set on high. She dropped her gaze to her hands, glad she couldn't hear what she imagined was being said.

WHEN THE TEAM HEADED INTO the showers, Meg remained seated, not certain what to do next. Coach had already left the locker room without stopping to speak with her.

As she exited, Zach, Connie, Mom, and Toby stood waiting for her inside the exit near the locker rooms.

Meg stepped into her mother's arms, letting her tears flow before they walked to Zach's car for the ride back to the apartment.

On the drive, she learned about what happened before the incident. After her family and Connie shared an early dinner, they'd headed into the arena. Mom felt a strange need to locate Meg and sent Zach back to the apartment to check if Meg was there. When he later showed up at the tournament with Meg, everyone felt relieved. Zach reported on her battered condition but shared she explained she'd not been attacked, and her scrapes were minor.

Now, back in the apartment, they waited for her to share what had happened.

Everything came out in bursts of signing. When Kelsey came by to pick her up, Toby told her Meg had gone. Mom was furious about Toby being left alone when she arrived home to pick him up. Gratefully he'd gone to stay with Ms. Iris.

Meg cried as she learned each new bit about their concerns. By the time she finished explaining, everyone, even Toby was in tears. Questions began flying. She answered most of them, especially about PRY, then signed, "He was a tiny, frail man with white hair. For some reason someone left him taped to his wheelchair in his old apartment. Toby's decoding his SOS and the apartment numbers saved his life. I hope he'll be okay. I left the area before anyone could try to talk with me."

Mom asked. "Why did you leave?"

Meg looked away before she answered. "I knew you'd wonder where I was, and I worried about Toby. No one would ever believe me about the signals. They'd have arrested me for trespassing. How could I ever explain what had happened?"

Kelsey, who'd come in earlier when Meg was explaining, gave her a hug as she got up to leave. Meg stopped her. "Please don't tell anyone about this. Please?"

Kelsey nodded and let herself out.

Zach put his arm around Meg and gave her a gentle squeeze. "You should tell the police, but let's wait until tomorrow. If it's okay, sis, I'll spend the night on your lovely, hard floor after I take Connie home."

Mom nodded. "First, let's celebrate all being together and PRY being rescued. Anyone ready for a scoop of ice cream and fudge sauce?"

Meg watched them eat their dessert and felt an immense exhaustion overpower her. She headed to her bedroom space and crashed. The next thing she knew it was ten o'clock Sunday morning, and her mom was shaking her shoulder.

"The police are here. They want to speak with you."

39

THE NEXT DAYS UNFOLDED WITH a series of unusual circumstances.

Day 1- Sunday

Just before ten, Mom checked through the fisheye before answering the door. Three police officers stood with their ID extended. She opened the door slowly.

"Ms. Appens?"

"Yes." She grabbed the collar of her sweater and stepped back.

"May we speak with Megan Appens regarding her whereabouts early yesterday evening."

"Of course. Come in."

The police were seated around the kitchen table when Meg entered the living area. They stood when she approached the table.

A young female police officer spoke. "Meg Appens?"

Meg nodded.

"I'm Officer Frost. We need to ask you a few questions about your whereabouts early yesterday evening."

Meg nodded and signed to her mom, "It's okay. I can do this." Her mom nodded and explained Meg's deafness to the police officers and offered to interpret for them.

The officers stopped her. "Ma'am, we'll need to take Ms. Appens statement, but we'll use our interpreter. I'll call ahead to the precinct. Everything needs to be on the record."

"May we ask Meg's interpreter to attend as well?"

"Yes, but in a non-official capacity. One of us will remain here with your family and Meg until we have an interpreter confirmed. Might be an hour."

Mom called Connie and arranged for Zach to stay with Toby. Then she and Meg rode in a police car to the station. Connie joined them there after showing her credentials and explaining how she worked with Meg at the high school.

"All well and good, Ms., but we'll be using our own interpreter. He's on his way in. Be here shortly."

The group sat together in silence in an interrogation room, waiting. Meg's hands became sticky with sweat as the hands of the clock seemed to move slower than normal. Her chest tightened with a sudden, deep pressure as the police interpreter entered.

"This is Mr. Danon. He'll share aloud what we ask and how Meg responds. As her parent, do you accept this arrangement, Ms. Appens?"

"Yes," Della answered.

Meg was asked to explain everything that had happened over the past few months. Luckily, Toby handed Meg his code book as she left so she could show the officers what had transpired and when.

When asked, "Why did you leave the scene?" Meg signed,

"I knew I'd be in trouble for entering the property, but I had to help PRY. I had no identification and I'm deaf, so I ran away. I had to get to the basketball tournament. My family and my interpreter were there, waiting for me."

Mom interrupted. "Let me explain. I guess we should have contacted you last night. We'd planned to contact you this morning after Meg woke up. She was so stressed we didn't think a few hours would make any difference. How did you find Meg?"

"Not your concern, Ma'am. Now, we have a few more questions."

The questioning went on for another hour. They couched the same questions in different ways, as if trying to catch Meg in a lie. She wasn't certain if she was in trouble or not; it certainly felt like it. By the time they'd returned home, she, her mother, and Connie were exhausted.

Kelsey sat on the front stairs when they returned. The girls stared at each other.

"What's happened? Is everyone okay?"

"We're fine."

Kelsey whipped out her phone and texted: **Can you talk?**

Meg signed with Mom and then texted Kelsey: **Meet on the roof?**

After they settled into the lean-to, Meg texted the details of what had happened at the police station. Kelsey stared at her phone, then at Meg and then back to her long, long texts.

Kelsey: **You okay? Is PRY okay? Have you told Coach yet?**

Meg: **The police asked me to not tell anyone, so please**

keep this a secret. PLS!

Kelsey: **Promise. This is like a spy TV show.**

Meg: **I know. I'm tired and stressed. Can we sit and not talk?**

The girls sat in silence. Meg felt herself falling asleep and did nothing to stop her drowsiness. When she woke up, Kelsey was watching her.

"How long did I sleep?"

"About an hour."

Meg stood and stretched before her fingers raced across her cell phone screen.

Meg: **I need to go. Thanks for listening. Remember- DO NOT TELL ANYONE.**

Kelsey held up a mock scout's honor signal and locked the doors behind them as they returned to the apartment stairway.

MOM TURNED ON THE LOCAL midday news at noon to hear what if anything was reported about what had happened. When the report began, Meg sat with her quilt from Gran wrapped around her, waiting to know what was shared with the media.

"In a twist on last night's expected implosion in downtown Seattle, there has been an unexplained delay, but may be weather-related. Local officials report the implosion intended to make way for the new sports complex has been postponed until at least next weekend. A spokesperson said details will be made available soon. We'll keep you posted as updates become available."

"In other news around the city, we turn to sports and results of last night girls' basketball tournament. It appears...."

Mom turned off the television and looked at Meg, huddled under her blanket. She moved to sit beside her. "Can I get you anything?"

Meg shook her head, untangled herself from the quilt, and went to rest on her bed.

She'd hoped the police would tell her that PRY, whatever his real name might be, was doing okay, but so far, they shared nothing. At least they hadn't charged her with a crime. It was as if nothing happened, as if it was a horrible nightmare.

Toby handed Meg his code book. "I thought you might want to keep this."

"Thanks, Toby, but you keep it. You did all the work. You saved PRY's life. You're a hero."

"I am?"

Meg sat up and hugged Toby. "Yes. I am so proud of you."

He raised his arms and pumped them up and down. Then he went back to playing with his cars on his bedspread.

Day 2- Monday

Spring break officially began. Mom called Stan's Market and made excuses for Meg's not coming to work, promising she'd return tomorrow at eight-thirty sharp to work the rest of spring break week.

Meg took the morning to clean her side of the room. Being busy calmed her. She half expected the police to reappear at their door. Texts from Connie and Zach startled her when they appeared on her phone. She jumped when Toby tapped her shoulder. Needing to get outside, she took Toby to the neighborhood park and let him play until he complained he was hungry. The rest of the afternoon, she rested on her bed and waited for a text from Eli. It never came. He must have heard about her no-show to the tournament by now. Why didn't he call?

Dinnertime was followed by watching the local evening news where nothing but a rehash of the postponed implosion was reported. Why was it still not explained?

Day 3 – Tuesday

Meg's day at Stan's kept her busy in the back room, unpacking boxes of spring merchandise and packing away the wintery items from his knick-knack shelves. She kept her cell phone on vibrate, waiting for Eli's call.

Toby rummaged through an unexpected bag of groceries from Stan's, trying every unusual fruit and vegetable. He pronounced the bok choy still a favorite, then sat down to make a list of what he'd like her to bring back next time.

Still no news on the implosion. Still no text from Eli. Maybe his family went to the mountains or the ocean for spring break.

Day 4 – Wednesday

More hours at Stan's. While she worked to refresh the produce in the sidewalk crates, a pair of girls from her basketball team headed her direction. When they spotted her, they crossed the street in the middle of the block and kept walking. A deep ache settled inside her chest. *So this is how it's going to be. How will I face anyone at school next week?*

A police car was parked in front of the apartment building.

Not a good sign. Why were they here? Did they have news of PRY? Was he feeling better?

Meg passed them coming down the stairway. Officer Frost smiled and nodded but didn't stop to speak.

Concern raced through Meg. She took the stairs two at a time to find out what, if anything, had been shared.

Mom signed, "They're still investigating the case, but the press was told this afternoon about Pat Okana's rescue. Since you are underage, your name will probably not be mentioned."

"So, PRY is Pat Okana? Is he feeling better? Can we visit him?"

Mom shook her head. "Mr. Okana is doing better, but he may not have visitors. He has a police officer stationed outside his room. We'll check later this week. Maybe you'll be allowed to visit, but I don't expect that will work out. At least he'll recover. That's all they shared."

Not knowing why PRY was left to die in the implosion bothered Meg. Maybe she'd never know why any of this happened.

She charged her phone. Still no texts from Eli. Maybe he'd be back on the weekend for the SAT test or he'd text her. She'd really like to see him and talk with him.

THE EVENING NEWS ANNOUNCED AN update on the implosion.

"In a stunning surprise, the police department reports an unnamed person was rescued from one of the buildings set to be imploded. Details are sketchy, but the individual is stable and is expected to make a full recovery."

"Jon, that sounds like a plot for a mystery. Keep us

posted. In other news around the region...."

Day 5 and 6 – Thursday and Friday

Meg finished out the weekdays at Stan's. With no further sightings of disgruntled high school students, she let out a sigh of relief. Hopefully, Monday, when school resumed, her basketball fiasco would be old news or no news at all. Wishful, fanciful, thinking.

Still no word from Eli.

Day 6 - Saturday

Meg entered the school cafeteria ten minutes before the SAT test was scheduled to begin. Her insides continued doing jumps and flips. Add on her inability to sleep last night, and she might be making a mistake taking the test today. But the money had been spent. If she had to retake it next year, she vowed to pay for it herself.

No students spoke to her, nodded, or looked her direction as she took a seat in the front row. *Looks like my no-show at the game has gotten around. I'm less than invisible. Maybe I should have brought Connie after all. No. I need to start doing things for myself and by myself.*

She scanned the room, thinking Eli might be there. He wasn't. *He must have changed his mind about taking the test today. Maybe he's waiting for summer to sit for it. Or maybe he's avoiding me. No, he wouldn't waste spent money just to avoid me.*

The proctor went over the rules and confiscated all the cellphones as he passed out the test packets. Meg caught most of his comments, except when he faced away from her. She started turning through pages, checking ahead to see what was covered and in what order. A hand slapped down on her test packet. "What are you doing.?"

"Looking to see what tests we have."

"That's cheating! I told everyone to wait for my signal to begin. Are you deaf?"

"Yes. I am." Meg handed the proctor her card. "Sorry. I missed that direction."

The proctor gave the signal to begin and began a continuous route through the rows of tables, watching students work, looking for cheat sheets, and students checking out neighboring students' test pages. After a few minutes, he sat down but popped up every few minutes to wander among the hundred students spread across the cafeteria. He paid special, close attention to her, which disturbed her concentration.

Meg breezed through the math section. During each five-minute break, she stood, stretched, and kept her eyes away from the other students.

She slowed on the English questions and hesitated over the writing section. The abstract questions continued to challenge her. She'd practiced with Connie over the past weeks and now trusted she'd give each one her best-educated effort.

By the end of the testing, she felt limp as a noodle, but she walked home the long way to clear her head and push down her frustration. Attempting to handle the testing independently was a huge mistake. She needed Connie with her to explain the directions so the proctor wouldn't be on her case through the entire test. At least she could retake the test if or when she failed it *this* time.

Day 8 - Sunday

Meg woke to Toby sitting beside her bed, staring at her. "What's wrong?"

"You were making strange sounds. Did you have a bad dream?"

"I don't remember." She stretched. "What time is it?"

"Ten o'clock. Kelsey's here."

Meg quickly threw off her covers, straightened them, and grabbed her clothes. Kelsey sat at the kitchen table, drinking a cup of cocoa with her mom.

"Hi, sleepyhead!"

Meg waved. "Back in a minute." She rushed to the bathroom to dress.

The girls moved up to the roof to sit in the sun while they texted.

Meg: **What have you heard about me?**

Kelsey: **Lots of rumors, nothing true.**

Meg: **Rumors are worse than facts.**

Kelsey: **Most people say you think you're better than the rest of the team. That you stayed home so the team would lose. To get even for not playing more. Dumb, huh?**

She stared at Kelsey and shook her head: **There is no way I can prove them wrong. The police won't let me talk about what happened.**

Kelsey: **I know. Sorry, Meg. Want to go with us to**

Alki? Toby can come too.

Meg: **I'll ask Mom.**

Spending Sunday at the beach, watching Toby splash around in the icy cold water, pleasure boats cruise by, and the ferries glide across Elliott Bay took her mind off the fiasco awaiting her tomorrow at school. *Maybe I should stay home, pretend I'm sick. No, I need to set a good example for Toby and face my problems. Besides, it's not going to change anytime soon, so I might as well get used to being shunned. If only Eli would call, I might have a second person on my side. Perhaps he's joined the people who think I'm all glow and no show.*

An entire week with no word from Eli convinced her he'd joined those who decided she was a flake or a snob or just plain mean. She desperately wanted to explain things to everyone, but still wasn't allowed. Hopefully, Kelsey had kept her promise. She'd know tomorrow when she returned to school. She gagged and swallowed down the bile that crept into her mouth.

All night, Meg tossed and turned, watching the hands of the clock slowly edge forward. She opened her eyes for the umpteenth time before sunrise. Not a great way to face a school full of angry or disappointed classmates. She got up, straightened her covers, and made a vow to herself: *I will not cry. I will not cry.* That's when her tears began.

40

Day 9-Monday

THE FRONT HALL WAS A sea of groups reconnecting after spring break. As she passed by the clutches of people, she felt eyes follow her. As she approached her locker, heads turned her direction. Then everyone turned their backs to her. The shunning began.

Looking through the mirror hanging inside her locker door, she noticed a few people giving her glares and making ugly or obscene hand gestures her direction. The only good thing about any of this, they must have thought she added value to the team. Otherwise, they'd have ignored her as usual.

In classes, she kept her focus on Connie and each teacher's discussion, regardless of how interested she was. Each class felt several hours long instead of ninety minutes. Connie offered to sit with her at lunch, but she shook her head and signed, "Thanks, but I need to be by myself."

After school she walked to the flagpole in case Eli might be there, waiting to speak with her. Half an hour later, when he was a no-show, she headed home. She fed Toby his snack then settled down to homework before starting dinner.

Kelsey texted her, but she didn't answer. She charged her

phone and waited to hear from Eli. He didn't call.

Day 10-Tuesday

In Advisory, Meg received a message.

Meet me after school in the coach's office.
Bring your interpreter.
Coach Pauls

She worried about what she might be able to tell him, but that concern faded when Kelsey contacted her.

Kelsey: **Eli is spreading a nasty rumor about you. Meet me at lunch outside at the farthest bench.**

Meg sat looking at her sandwich, unable to eat a bite until she heard what Kelsey had to share. It couldn't be any worse than what she was experiencing every minute of today before, during, and after classes.

Kelsey sat down and shook her head.

Kelsey: **Eli is telling everyone he dated you because he felt sorry for you. He says you did it! Sex.**

Meg's eyes widened. Her mouth dropped open. She couldn't breathe. When she looked around, students stared at her, pointing, laughing, then turning away. She grabbed up her backpack, rushed to the nearest bathroom, and closed the stall door. She braced herself against the stall wall breathing hard, fighting down tears and losing.

After a few minutes, she checked her phone. It was time for her next class, but she couldn't move. *How could he say such things? He knows they aren't true. All we've ever done was kiss a few times. How can I face anyone now? Is he doing this because of the basketball game? No. Then why? I thought he cared about me. How could he be so cruel?*

She stayed in the stall until she felt too weak to keep standing in the cramped space, then walked out the closest exit and headed home.

She got a text before she'd gotten more than a few blocks away.

Connie: **Are you OK? Remember: meeting coach after school.**

Meg: **See you then.**

For the rest of the afternoon, she wandered the neighborhood. When she found a pocket park, she sat on a bench to wait for the end of the school day. Meg reread her last texting conversation from Kelsey several times. A heaviness drained away her hope of finding support from anyone outside her family.

A new text arrived from Kelsey. Meg almost deleted it but stopped. She needed to know whatever she could about what Kelsey was hearing.

Kelsey: **People are bad-mouthing you. Wish I could tell them what you told me. I need to keep my friendship with the team and hear the chatter about any college recruiters who attended the tournament. A scholarship is the only way I can attend college.**

Meg hadn't replied. She checked the time and slowly walked back to school by crossing the open field she'd crossed on her first day at SHHS.

A few guys passed her as they cut across the field, heading home. Some faces showed pucker lips; some made sexual gestures. She kept her head down and entered a back door near the coach's office.

Connie stood in the hallway. She looked up when Meg approached, her expression questioning. All Meg could do was shake her head. The hurt running through her felt like a heavy weight pressing her toward the floor. She'd need to try to avoid everyone as much as possible and stop reading their lips to feel sane.

Seated in Coach Pauls' office, Meg waited for him to ask questions. Connie sat beside her, ready to sign what was said.

"I imagine you have a valid excuse for not letting us know you'd not make the game in time to play?"

Meg nodded and signed. "There was an emergency, and my cell phone battery was dead."

"Care to explain what happened?"

Meg looked at Connie, who shrugged. "I'm not sure what I'm allowed to tell you."

"Were you sick or injured?"

"No. I can't share what happened."

Coach looked bewildered. "Have your parents contact me. We need to get this straightened out. I can't have team players just decide to stay home."

"My mother… I'm not allowed to share what happened, yet. Neither is she. As soon as I have permission to tell you, I will. I'm sorry."

Coach stared at Meg. "This is unacceptable. Without an explanation, you won't be allowed to play next year. I thought you wanted to play."

Meg swallowed hard. "I do. I wanted to be there." She stood and walked out of the office. Connie caught up to her as she headed out the side door.

Connie signed, "Awkward. When can you tell him what

happened?"

"Maybe tomorrow. We need to go back down to the police station later today."

MEG AND MOM RETURNED TO the police station as soon as Meg got home. She didn't bother to share her conversation with the coach. There was nothing to tell.

Happily, they did learn Mr. Okana, Dr, Okana, had been released from the hospital and would be moving into an apartment with a caregiver. It appeared some of the details about the incident would be explained to the public via the news media very soon.

MEALTIME USUALLY MEANT SHARING STORIES and the day's happenings. Today, Meg didn't engage in conversation, leaving Toby to relate stories about his day at school and his chance to be president of his class for the following week. It included bringing in something special to share. He chose his Morse Code book and flashlight.

"Can I tell my class what happened to Meg?"

Mom shook her head. "You may tell them about signaling with your flashlight and about making a new friend. Meg's incident is still private, so don't mention it."

Toby nodded, but he was visibly disappointed about keeping the secret.

Mom reached out and patted his hand. "If you want, we can make a batch of cookies for you can take to school for the Friday's afterschool Film Special."

"How many in a batch," Toby asked.

Mom thought for a minute. "If you keep Meg's secret, we'll make twelve dozen."

"That's a lot." He stared into space, drawing his eyebrows together and scrunching up his nose. "I figure it's one hundred forty-four cookies. With frosting?"

Mom grinned. "With frosting."

"Cool! I'll keep the secret."

Day 11-Wednesday

The morning announcements ended with, "Tomorrow's special assembly will be held after second lunch. Afternoon classes will be shortened to sixty minutes. Bring your Fisherman's spirit!"

ANOTHER DAY OF BEING FRIENDLESS except for a brief smile from Kelsey when they passed in the cafeteria on her way to eat lunch with her group. *Minute by minute, our friendship is sliding back to just being outside school. Is she afraid she'll lose her place in her group if she befriends me, or is it because I've asked her to keep the secret? Maybe this is the way it will always be with her. I miss my old school more each day I'm here.*

Feeling alone in a school with over a thousand students didn't seem logical, but it was her reality. Thank heavens she had Connie to talk with when she had the energy to talk. She knew her mom was concerned about her, but what could she do beyond tell her mom she felt fine as she moved off to study, really to just to hide out behind the screen in her bedroom. All she wanted was sleep; one normal night's sleep.

41

Day 12 – Thursday

ROWS OF CHAIRS FACED THE student bleachers in the gym. The floor vibrated as the pep band played and students filed in. Meg hated all assemblies, and this one promised to be the worst yet. She felt the trembling of the bleachers as she climbed the steps. Since Connie was absent, she'd join the disenchanted students who sat in the back rows of the junior section, as far away from the assembly as possible.

When the boys' and girls' varsity basketball teams entered, the risers vibrated with foot stomps They waved to the students as they slowly filed in the rows of chairs up front. The assembly appeared to be to honor the teams. Not her concern anymore.

She looked for Eli. He sat next to his best friend and teammate, enjoying the applause and being seated in front of the student body.

Speakers, including the basketball coaches, took turns at the microphone. Students applauded. The pep band played. Trophies were handed out. Hopefully, the assembly would end soon. Meg watched the students around her to know when they could head back to classes. But they didn't move. They sat listening.

The principal continued to stand at the podium. Meg took the opportunity to review her history class notes until she felt the risers vibrate once again. She looked up and saw Officer Holton pushing Dr. Okana, in his wheelchair toward the microphone.

A strange trembling coursed through her as she watched Connie step forward to speak and sign, "Meg. Come down, please."

Students around Meg pushed her to walk down. Kelsey smiled and patted her arm as she passed. What was happening?

Meg stopped beside Connie. She looked at Captain Holton and Dr. Okana. Both nodded in her direction. Her mother, Toby, and Zach sat in the front row with Ms. Iris. All waved to her. Tears flooded her eyes.

Connie began to interpret the various speakers' words for Meg.

"Today we have a special pair of guests, Captain Holton of the Seattle Police Department and Dr. Pat Okana, a retired history professor from the University of Washington. They are here to share a story of courage and bravery by one of our students, Meg Appens."

Captain Holton rose and approached the microphone. "Meg rescued Dr. Okana from a very dangerous situation at great risk to her own safety. She ran into a condemned building that was about to be imploded. Thanks also to her young brother, Toby, who discovered the danger Dr. Okana was facing. His skilled use of Morse Code helped save Dr. Okana's life. Stand up, Toby."

Toby stood up, waved to Meg, and sat down. His face matched his red shirt.

Captain Holton continued. "Meg carried Dr. Okana down

eight flights of stairs to safety. Meg, please step forward."

He stopped speaking, opened a flat box, and took out a medallion. He carefully slid the ribbon over Meg's head. Students clapped politely.

Meg smiled and nodded as she reached out to accept his handshake.

He continued speaking. "The city of Seattle has awarded Meg Appens the Citizens Award for Bravery. It comes with a cash award of three thousand dollars. We sincerely appreciate Meg's courage to rescue Dr. Okana, a person experiencing grave personal danger." He handed her a large cardboard check like she'd seen television quiz show winners hold.

The students politely applauded again.

Dr. Okana spoke next. "Bravery exists across decades and centuries. It may be expressed in a cause or an attempt to do something unexpected in the face danger, fear, or difficulty. It means facing a situation where you are unsure if you have any support but know you *must* follow your heart.

"Bravery has many different faces: Lewis and Clark and Neil Armstrong, Beethoven and Stevie Wonder, Rosa Parks and Dr. Martin Luther King Jr., plus your fellow student Meg Appens. It's a combination of heart-filled courage, nerves of steel, and moxie, all unteachable forces of character.

"As a side point, I want you to know Meg not only showed great bravery, she forfeited playing in the finals of the state basketball tournament to rescue me from a life-threatening situation. Because of Meg's bravery, I'm here today to help honor her. Thank you from the bottom of my heart, Meg Appens. I owe you my life."

An audible gasp spread throughout the student body.

Suddenly, Coach Pauls, Coach Young, Mr. Oberlander, and

the rest of Meg's teachers were on their feet, clapping loudly. Within seconds, the entire student body followed suit, with a standing ovation that lasted a full three minutes. Meg wiped aside tears as students who had ignored her and even cursed her hours before joined in the recognition of her bravery.

Captain Holton again stepped to the podium as Dr. Okana was wheeled back to a place in front of the seated students and faculty. "We have one more award to present before we leave." He looked at the front row. "Toby Appens, please come forward."

The blush that had faded from Toby's face returned as he stood in front of Captain Holton. He reached for Meg's hand. She gently squeezed it.

"Toby, your sister would never have known that Dr. Okana was in trouble and run out to rescue him if you had not learned Morse Code and shared it with her. Instead of a celebration like this one today, we would be mourning the loss of a great educator and an outstanding member of our community." He opened the small box in his hand, lifted out a gold medallion on a black ribbon, and slipped it over Toby's head. "If you look closely at the dots and dashes carved into this medallion, Toby, you'll note that they spell 'hero' in Morse Code."

The assembled audience clapped for Toby. A few whistles could also be heard.

Captain Holton continued, "In addition, I have arranged a special surprise just for you, Toby. I've heard you have a race track you enjoy playing with. I happen to have a young friend who's an up-and-coming NASCAR driver who wants to meet you. He has offered you a chance to sit in his car and meet his crew. How does that sound?"

Toby enthusiastic nod accompanied a huge grin spreading across his face as he pulled Meg's hand to his heart.

Laughs and applause came again from the students and teachers.

Captain Holton raised his hand for quiet. "Meg and Toby are not just heroes. They are outstanding examples of what you young people can be. Often, when negative new reports fill the headlines, we forget that our youth can accomplish deeds of courage and honor — and many of them do. Meg and Toby, thank you for your contribution to the rescue of Dr. Okana. We are proud of both of you."

The principal dismissed the students to fourth period, then waved the press and reporters forward. Meg held the check and Toby held his medal as they stood with the principal and Captain Holton, behind Dr. Okana. Cameras flashed. The reporters spoke with the adults as Connie escorted Meg and Toby to their family. So much for keeping their names out of the paper.

Being hugged by her family and Ms. Iris brought more tears to her eyes. Toby grabbed her with a fierce hug around her waist and looked up with the widest smile she'd ever seen.

Connie tapped Meg's arm and signed, "You need to meet with the reporters before you head to class. Officer Holton will do most of the talking. They also want to speak briefly with Toby and your mother."

Finally, the story would be released. Her biggest hope was that her classmates would accept her for herself, at least for the rest of the week. Perhaps Coach Pauls and her teammates would even forgive her for missing the tournament game.

WHEN MEG ENTERED HUMAN PHYSIOLOGY class, the students

all stood and clapped. She felt her face heat up again as she nodded and sat down to get to work. The over-the-top attention rattled her and felt almost as uncomfortable as being ignored. The difference was how it made her feel inside. She'd gone from despair over the past few days to elation and embarrassment at being singled out for doing what needed to be done.

As Meg and Connie headed to History class, she was no longer invisible in the hallways. Students reached out to pat her arm. Some shouted to her; Connie translated what was said. Meg felt both giddy and awkward. Many of the same students who'd bad-mouthed and whispered behind her back just hours before appeared to be supportive. She wondered which side they'd stand for when no one was watching.

Eli sat in his usual seat and avoided looking her direction. She deeply felt his snub and forced herself to look away from where he sat.

Mr. Oberlander laid the tests packets aside and grinned. "Today, we'll skip the test. I'll save it for our next class session. Instead, we'll review and answer your questions. A special guest will be with us momentarily."

Just then, Dr. Okana and his caregiver rolled into the classroom. He bowed his head toward Meg as his wheelchair was positioned in front of the lectern.

Mr. Oberlander applauded. The students stood and joined him. "Class, please welcome, Dr. Okana. He was my mentor at the university. It's a privilege to have him with us today. I've asked him to explain how history is important to us in our daily lives. Dr. Okana."

Mr. Overlander looked toward Meg and grinned as he stepped aside.

Dr. Okana took the offered microphone, bowing his head toward Mr. Oberlander and Meg before he spoke.

When he finished, the class stood and clapped. Mr. Oberlander shook his hand. Dr. Okana bowed, then waved to the students as he was wheeled from the classroom.

Mr. Oberlander turned to the class. "Today, we learned of Meg's bravery. She's shown that trait most every day in this classroom. Yes, I know about your student snubs, insults, and mocking sign language you think you hide from us teachers.

"Meg works fluently through two languages while most of you work with one. Remember, bravery has many faces. Use the remaining class time to work in pairs to review for our test."

CONNIE SAT DOWN NEXT TO Meg when the classroom emptied. "I'm proud of how you handled everything today and all the days before this one. I enjoy working with you. Let me know if you need anything before classes tomorrow. Congrats on being recognized by the entire city and hopefully by more of your peers. You're an amazing young woman."

Meg gave Connie a hug, then gathered up her backpack and her giant check. As she turned on her phone, she saw one message: **Meet me at the flagpole.**

42

MEG STUDIED THE BRIEF MESSAGE, noticing he'd not added QT at the end. Something had definitely changed. She slowly gathered up her texts, put on her jacket, and walked toward the front exit.

After his avoiding her since the basketball tournament, Kelsey's telling her what he said, and her reinforcing what she saw by lip reading what he said about her when he thought she didn't see, what could Eli have to say to her? Did she even want to know?

She stood inside the front doors of the building, watching him talk with friends as they passed, laughing at whatever they said. She turned and headed for a side door and walked to the city bus stop in time to see the bus turning the corner and heading down the hill. The next bus would be thirty minutes. Did she want to stand and wait? Not really.

She started home, using streets one block off the main road in case Eli went looking for her. This week had been an emotional rollercoaster from being shunned and untouchable, to learning of Eli's lies about her, to being honored and patted on the back. She didn't relish being a hero; she just didn't want to be ignored. The walk home should have helped her reclaim a sense of calm. It didn't.

The route took her through blocks of residences, past small businesses, and along tree-lined streets where tree blossoms floated down like pink snow, covering the sidewalks with their delicate petals. *Dr. Okana was so frail and dependent in the dark building. Today he looked amazing; proud, strong, and independent, especially in Mr. Oberlander's class. If he can overcome his devastating situation, I can handle my situation as well.*

Maybe I rushed to make a place for myself at SHHS. Maybe I should have tried to make friends before I rushed to play basketball. Should I try out next year? Will the team accept me? If they do, will it be because they want and need me or because they feel sorry for my being deaf or because I was a hero for twenty minutes?

A light rain began; the wind picked up. She shook her head, held her giant check over her head, and lengthened her stride. Talking to herself had taken her close to home more quickly than she expected. Home: a strong word for their small apartment, but she felt the tensions of the day drop away until she turned the last corner.

Eli stood in front of her building, leaning against his car. He looked soaked.

He saw her before she had a chance to change course and avoid him.

He walked toward her. "I waited for you at the flagpole. Did you walk all the way home?"

Meg nodded and set down the cardboard check. "I needed to be alone to think."

"About us?"

Meg waggled her hand back and forth.

"May I come up and talk with you?"

Meg hesitated. Did she want to talk with him or not? She

saw the pleading look on his face. "Okay."

Eli sat on the couch; she took a kitchen chair facing him while drying her damp hair. Neither said anything for several moments. She felt a wall rising through their silence. She grit her teeth and whipped out her phone.

He texted: **How are you?**

Meg: **What do you want?**

Eli: **To see you.**

Meg: **Why?**

Eli: **I miss you.**

He reached for her hand. She pulled it away.

Meg: **What do you miss about me?**

Eli: **Everything. Sorry I avoided you. Had a lot on my mind.**

Meg didn't respond except to stare at him and clench her jaw and her fists.

Eli: **Talk to me. Please.**

He reached for her hand again, but she refused to unclench her fist or let him touch her hand. He pulled his hand back as though he'd burned it on a hot stove.

Eli: **What's wrong? What are you thinking?**

She glared at him and dipped her head to type her response.

Meg: **You don't want to know what I'm thinking.**

Eli: **Yes, I do.**

Meg: **Really? Did you lose your phone? forget where I live?**

Eli dropped his head. His hands lay still.

Meg walked to the window. The world along the street moved at its normal hustle bustle, but rapidly the sky darkened. Clouds tumbled north as heavy rain skittered along the streets. The buildings in the distance to be imploded remained intact but lay shrouded in low clouds. Why were they still standing? She didn't know, and now she didn't care.

She turned toward Eli, waiting for him to text something, anything. She stepped closer. He sat, staring up at her.

Meg: **Did you ever care about me?**

Eli: **Yes.**

Meg: **When?**

Eli: **Until Christmas break.**

Meg: **And after?**

Eli shrugged.

Meg: **If things changed, why did you still meet me at the library and the flagpole? Why did you walk me to class and kiss me and bring us snow to make snowballs? Why did you send me red roses on Valentines Day?**

Eli: **I don't know. I thought maybe I owed it to you.**

Meg: **Owed it to me? Why not just tell me the truth?**

Eli shrugged then texted: **It wasn't planned. Her family stayed in a cabin next to ours. She liked to ski — she was fun to be with. She lives in Tacoma.**

Meg stared at him, trembling, breathing in gasps. She moved to the window again to try to settle herself.

He followed and placed his hands on her shoulders. She shook his hands off, turned, and waited for him to say something, anything.

Eli: **I should have told you.**

Meg: **You think? So, if you had a new girlfriend all this time, why did you spread rumors about me at school?**

Eli: **It's a guy thing. Didn't mean anything.**

Meg: **Wrong! Telling everyone we had sex is not nothing!**

She inhaled deeply and began to pace the kitchen area. She stopped and turned to face him.

Meg: **I saw you talking with your friends. I was told you said I'm easy, that you got what you wanted from me, the poor little deaf girl.**

Eli: **What do you want me to say?**

Meg: **I think you've said more than enough. You chose to destroy my reputation, to look like the mighty conqueror to your oversexed jock buddies. It's time for you to set the record straight, unless you prefer I tell everyone there's no way I'd ever have sex with any of you immature loud mouths.**

He paled. Watching her eyes, he shoved his phone into his pocket and left the apartment without looking back.

Meg latched the door behind him, then braced herself against it before her expected tears began, before she felt loss and loneliness overtake her.

To her surprise, she felt neither loss nor loneliness. No tears flooded her eyes.

Maybe it was too soon to cry over Eli, considering all he'd shared and the pile of events she'd weathered over the past few days. Or maybe he wasn't worth one, single tear.

She reached for the quilt that lay across the back of the couch. Feeling Gran's touch with each hand-tied knot she fingered, she curled up and drifted off to sleep.

It was dusk when she woke. Mom stood looking down at her. She stretched as Toby made a beeline to hug her and playfully jumped on the cushions next to her.

Mom set down the bag of groceries and watched Meg's face as though trying to gauge her mood.

Meg blinked several times, stood, and stepped into their warming hugs. *I have my family, Connie, Ms. Gillis, Ms. Iris, and Stan who believe in me and support me. No one is luckier.*

Epilogue

SEATTLE BANNER - BYLINE MINA FOSTER

Implosion Rescheduled after Dramatic Rescue from Building

(Seattle, WA) Details on the delayed implosion of a block in the International District are now available. Will Darvent, the Seattle Police Department's Public Information Officer, held a press conference this morning and shared a dramatic series of events, including the kidnapping and rescue of retired history professor Dr. Pat Okana.

Two young men, Zeb Latterly and Brice Crosse, sons of local entrepreneurs, have been arrested and charged with criminal trespass as well as the kidnapping and attempted murder of Dr. Okana. They are being held on two million dollars bail each.

Dr. Okana, a valued resource after his retirement, acts as the clearing house for student degree submissions. He evaluates and sends projects to eDocDataCheck, a company licensed to check written submissions for their percentage of plagiarism.

Latterly and Crosse submitted their team project as an

original work product. The results e-DocuDataCheck showed it contained 80% plagiarized information. Results of 5% are considered common, with 20-25% borderline acceptable. Numbers greater than that are unacceptable and result in those projects being rejected.

Accused of kidnapping Dr. Okana, Latterly and Crosse allegedly tried to force him to record their level of plagiarism at 12%. He refused. The following week, pretending to be replacement caregivers, they allegedly picked him up from a medical appointment, took him to his former apartment located in the building to be imploded, carried him upstairs, secured him to his wheelchair and left him to perish in the implosion.

Dr. Okana used the flashlight in the pocket of his wheelchair to send an SOS via Morse Code. His distress signal was seen by a young boy, Toby Appens, who alerted his deaf teenage sister, Megan Appens, to check on Dr. Okana. She entered the secure area and raced up eight flights of stairs to find Dr. Okana bound in his wheelchair. After untying him, she carried him to safety at great peril to both their lives.

This past week, the Seattle Police Department presented Megan Appens with their Citizens Award for Bravery and a check for three thousand dollars. When asked how she'd spend the money, Miss Appens replied through her interpreter, "My family recently moved here from eastern Washington. I want my mom to use the money however is best for our family."

No court date has been set for the trial of Latterly and Crosse.

Every one of us is different in some way, but for those of us who are more different, we have to put more effort into convincing the less different that we can do the same things they can, just differently

Marlee Matlin

Sticks and Stones
Reader's Guide Questions

What are Meg's strengths? weaknesses?

What circumstances hold Meg and Kelsey together?

How well does Meg handle situations and awkward moments, times when she feels unsupported or uncomfortable?

How does Meg grow and change from when we meet her at the beginning of the story and eight months later as the story ends?

What advice would you give Meg to help her overcome her fear of dark places?
Ponders

Did you ever experienced a traumatic event or had to face something that took you far from your comfort zone? What inner strength did it take for you to handle it?

We hear a lot about belittling and bullying in schools. Do you have any experience in handling those issues? What skills were needed? How did they work?

Being in the minority or being different from others in social situations can be stressful. Where have you seen or heard the best ways to handle those instances?

ASL Alphabet

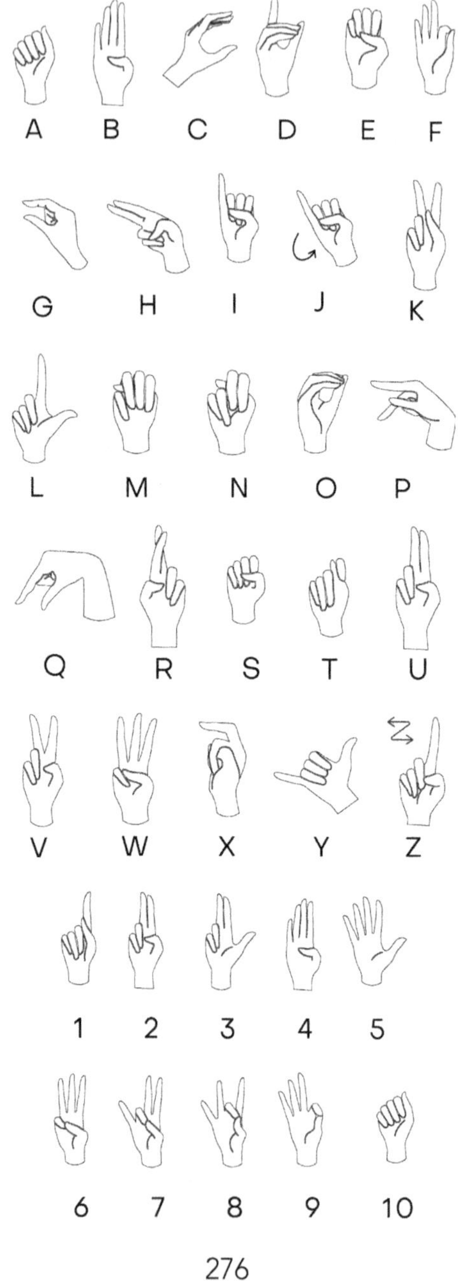

Morse Code

A	·—	N	—·	1	·————	
B	—···	O	———	2	··———	
C	—·—·	P	·——·	3	···——	
D	—··	Q	——·—	4	····—	
E	·	R	·—·	5	·····	
F	··—·	S	···	6	—····	
G	——·	T	—	7	——···	
H	····	U	··—	8	———··	
I	··	V	···—	9	————·	
J	·———	W	·——	0	—————	
K	—·—	X	—··—			
L	·—··	Y	—·——			
M	——	Z	——··			

84 Ribbons—A Dancer's Journey

"A pure coming-of-age tale with moments of quiet drama 84 Ribbons is about thriving despite the imperfections of life." YA Foresight, Foreword Reviews, Spring 2014. DanceSpirit Magazine's Pick of the Month, April 2014. "Any young dancer will find herself in Marta's story", Newbery Honor Author, Kirby Larson, Hattie Big Sky.

When the Music Stops—Dance On

Step into Marta's world in the multi-award-winning second book, Marta struggles to regain her ability to dance and support herself at the same time stepping into adulthood amid unexpected challenges. Will she find a deep well of strength to meet her life-changing situations head-on?

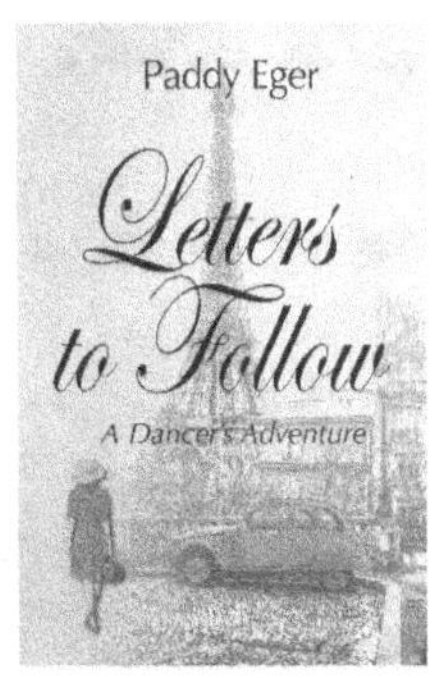

Letters to Follow—
A Dancer's Adventure

Dance, the central character, enters the stage with a tour jeté and then piroutette's gracefully through the life of Lynne Meadows. This third book in the series glides into Lynne's world with backward glances at the fortunes and falls that bring her to the commencement of an exciting and grueling adventure as a member of a dance troupe traveling in Europe during the summer of 1959.

Act 4—The Continuing Story of Lynne & Marta

The two young women embrace their changing lives. Lynne and Marta's friendship began when they joined the Intermountain Ballet Company as corps de ballet dancers. Across three stories they celebrated each other's successes and supported each other when heartache reaches into their careers and beyond. Will their relationship survive all that adult life throws their direction with hundreds of miles between them?

Tasman—An Innocent Convict's Struggle for Freedom

In 1850, sixteen year-old Irish lad, Ean McCloud, steps off the boat, his legs in iron shackles, and steps into serving a three-year sentence at the Port Arthur Penal Colony in Tasmania. Falsely convicted, he must now survive the brutal conditions, the backbreaking labor, and time in the silent prison—a place that breaks men's souls. Follow Ean's adventures as he seeks not only to survive but to escape!

About the Author

Paddy Eger is the multi-award-winning author of a four part ballet series: 84 Ribbons, When the Music Stops, Letters to Follow, and Act 4. These stories follow the two, young, professional dancers as they navigate the ballet company and dance opportunities as they step into independence and adulthood.

As a former dancer, Paddy shares her love of music and dance as well as choreography and travel through her young adult novels. "It's important to look at the struggles as well as the successes the characters experience so they are well-rounded and human."

Eger's historical adventure novel, Tasman is the product of a visit she made to the Port Arthur penal colony on the southern coast of Tasmania. Through a combination of research and imagination, she recreates the story of brutal prison life, sharing glimpses into the deprivation and hard labor faced by inmates sent there in the 1850s.

Non-fiction is another interest Paddy shares with people who work with students. Her Educating America book and materials share easy-to-use ideas to involve students as well as classroom assistants.

In her free time, Paddy writes in other genres, reads, helps in classrooms, and travels. She and her family live in western Washington, but consider the world their home base.

www.ingramcontent.com/pod-product-compliance
Lightning Source LLC
Chambersburg PA
CBHW071249300726
48975CB00002B/603